I0846748

Simon the Zealot

Simon the Zealot

A CHRISTIAN HISTORICAL NOVEL

DAVID G. FISCHER

Copyright © 2025 by David G. Fischer.

All rights reserved. No part of this publication may be reproduced, distributed, or transmitted in any form or by any means, including photocopying, recording, or other electronic or mechanical methods, without the prior written permission of the publisher, except in the case of brief quotations embodied in critical reviews and certain other noncommercial uses permitted by copyright law. For permission requests, contact David G. Fischer at fischerdg@outlook.com.

Maps and Temple Mount diagram by Rehan Waheed.

ISBN: 9-79-8-9860843-5-0 (Paperback)
ISBN: 979-8-9860843-7-4 (Hardcover with printed Dust Jacket)
ISBN: 9-79-8-9860843-4-3 (Laminated Cover)
ISBN: 9-79-8-9860843-6-7 (eBook)

Library of Congress Control Number: 2025924808

First printing edition 2025.

This book is dedicated to my beautiful wife, Laura. The love she has shown to me and our children is matchless. I can't imagine life on earth without her and look forward to being with her eternally in Heaven. I thank God every day for allowing me to meet and marry such a wonderful woman.

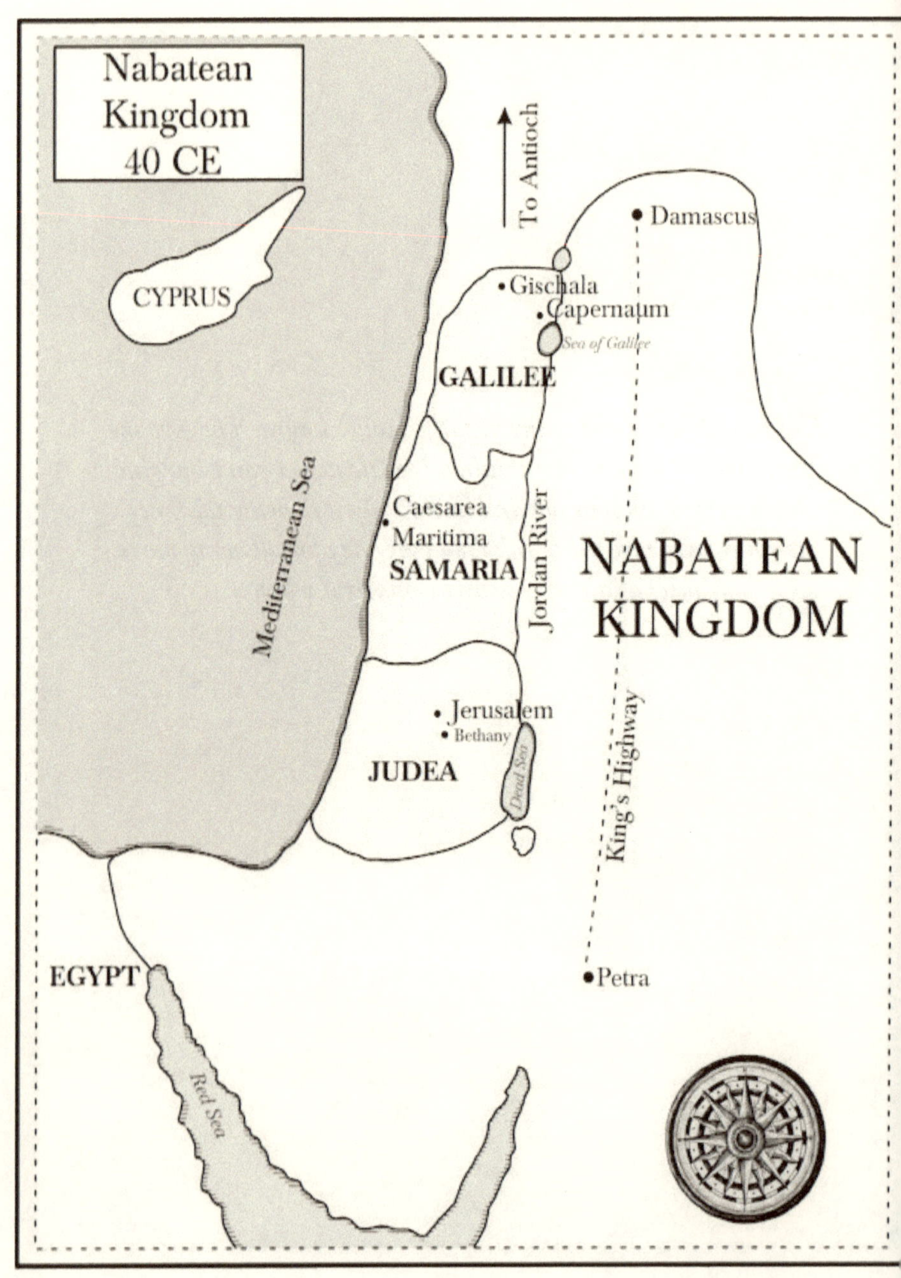

Nabatean Kingdom 40 CE
CYPRUS
To Antioch
Damascus
Gischala
Capernaum
Sea of Galilee
GALILEE
Mediterranean Sea
Caesarea Maritima
SAMARIA
Jordan River
NABATEAN KINGDOM
Jerusalem
Bethany
Dead Sea
JUDEA
King's Highway
EGYPT
Red Sea
Petra

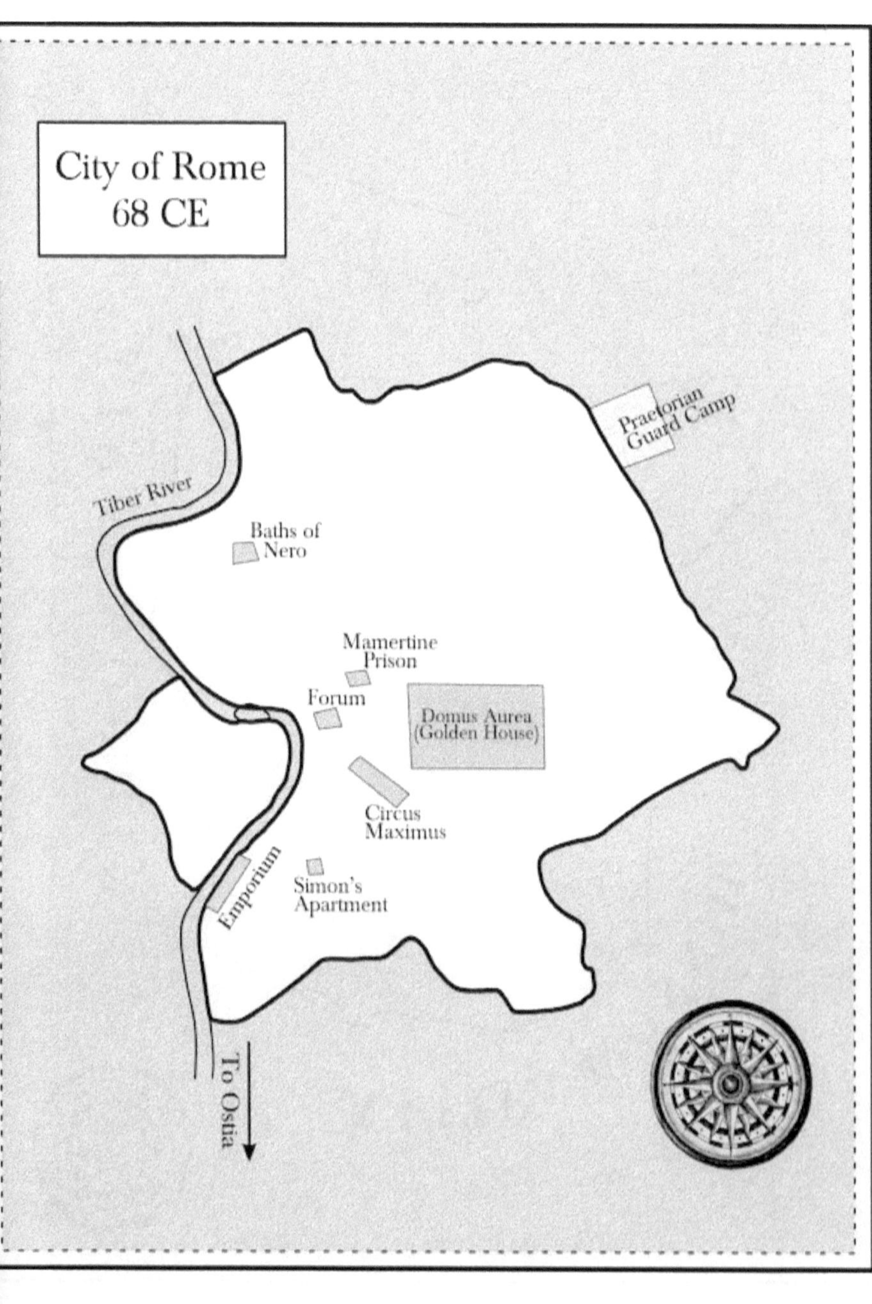

City of Rome
68 CE
Praetorian
Guard Camp
Tiber River
Baths of
Nero
Mamertine
Prison
Forum
Domus Aurea
(Golden House)
Circus
Maximus
Emporium
Simon's
Apartment
To Ostia

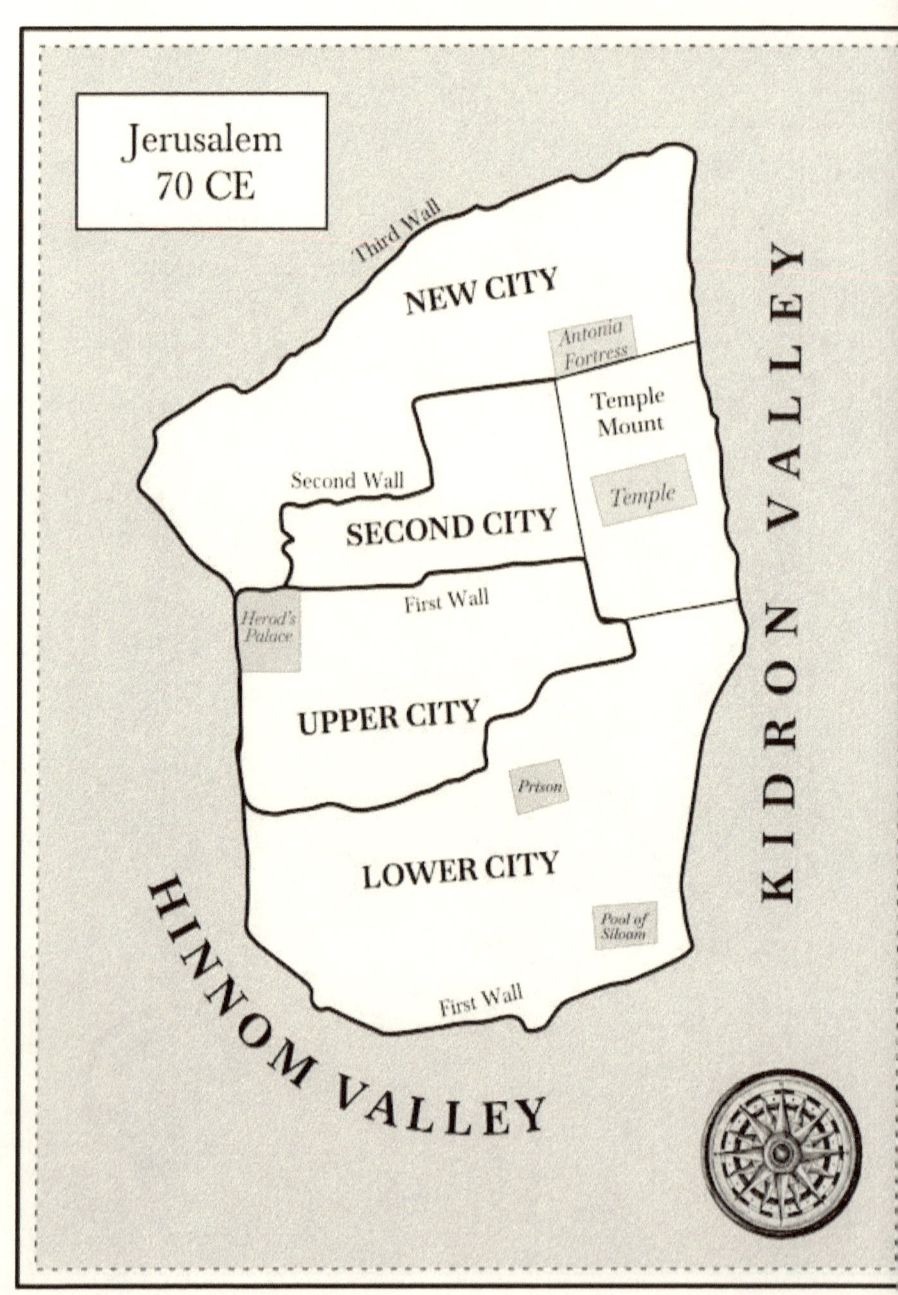

Jerusalem
70 CE
Third Wall
NEW CITY
Antonia Fortress
Temple Mount
Second Wall
SECOND CITY
Temple
First Wall
Herod's Palace
UPPER CITY
Prison
LOWER CITY
Pool of Siloam
First Wall
HINNOM VALLEY
KIDRON VALLEY

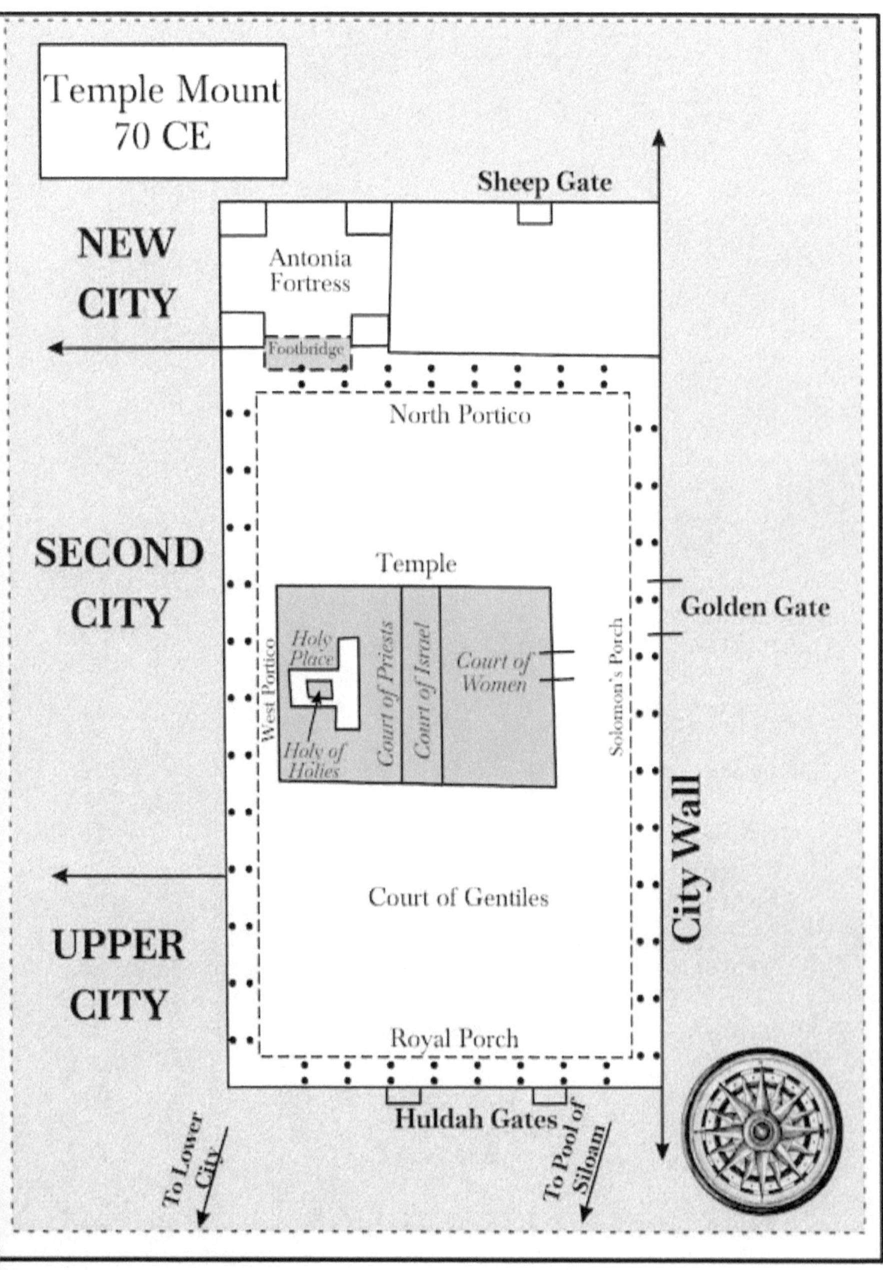

Temple Mount
70 CE
NEW CITY
SECOND CITY
UPPER CITY
Sheep Gate
Antonia Fortress
Footbridge
North Portico
Temple
West Portico
Holy Place
Holy of Holies
Court of Priests
Court of Israel
Court of Women
Solomon's Porch
Golden Gate
Court of Gentiles
City Wall
Royal Porch
Huldah Gates
To Lower City
To Pool of Siloam

CONTENTS

Introduction

Simon sobbed uncontrollably. The body of his best friend, Lazarus, lay on the floor in a pool of coagulating blood. Lacerations covered his entire body, and a gaping wound in his chest evidenced how he died. Lazarus had been severely beaten with a scourge, a whip with multiple thongs tipped with hard leather knots, prior to receiving the final death blow from a sword thrust through his chest.

Two years prior to Lazarus' execution, the Jewish leadership council known as the Sanhedrin arrested, tried, and condemned Jesus to death. After the crucified Jesus was resurrected, he instructed his followers to announce to the world that forgiveness of sins and eternal life in Heaven are freely given to those who believe in him and confess him as Lord.

The subsequent success of the Jesus movement did not sit well with the Sanhedrin. They commissioned Saul, a religious extremist who shared their views regarding the alleged dangers posed by Jesus' teachings, to extinguish the flame that Jesus had lit. Saul worked on his assignment vigorously. Showing no mercy, he imprisoned believers and forced them to recant their faith. Those who withstood Saul's threats and torture were executed.

Saul became aware of Lazarus, a scribe who was an expert in Jewish law, when Lazarus acted as defense attorney for Stephen, a leader in the Jesus movement, at his trial before the Sanhedrin. Stephen was sentenced to death, and Saul made the capture of Lazarus a priority.

After several unsuccessful attempts to track down Lazarus, Saul arrested his sisters, Mary and Martha, at their homes in nearby Bethany and jailed them in Jerusalem's public prison. Lazarus' good friend Simon, one of Jesus' twelve disciples also known as Simon the Zealot, convinced Lazarus to storm the prison with the help of several of his Zealot friends. Unfortunately, their attempt failed when Saul and his men surrounded the jail.

Saul offered safe passage to everyone other than Lazarus. Lazarus, in order to free his sisters, accepted Saul's proposal over Simon's objection. After being severely tortured, Lazarus refused to deny Jesus and was killed by one of Saul's men. Simon retrieved Lazarus' body the next day and carried it to Bethany to be buried in the family tomb.

Before escorting Mary and Martha out of the prison to

safety the prior evening, Simon promised Lazarus he would relocate the sisters to Capernaum, a city in Galilee where Jesus conducted much of his ministry. Although Simon's first impulse was to exact revenge on Saul for the murder of Lazarus, he would first need to fulfill his vow to get Mary and Martha safely away from Jerusalem.

Chapter 1

RETROSPECTIVE

Jesus chose an odd assortment of men to follow him during his three-year ministry. Most of the dozen disciples who were chosen came from humble beginnings and were not highly educated. Their prior occupations ranged from fisherman to tax collector. Arguably the most improbable selection was the full-time construction worker and part-time insurrectionist whom his fellow disciples called Simon the Zealot.

Simon was born and raised in Bethany. His father was a stonecutter who helped supply limestone blocks for many of King Herod the Great's building projects, including the Jerusalem Temple complex. Simon's father was often away from home because of his job. His mother, due to mental health issues, was incapable of providing Simon with either encouragement or discipline. As a result, Simon's early childhood lacked guidance and emotional support.

By the time Simon entered synagogue school at the age of five, he was already a bully. He matured physically more quickly than his peers, giving him an advantage in height and strength. Other boys wishing to remain on his good side joined him in aggressive behavior toward students they considered vulnerable. Intimidation of weaker classmates bolstered Simon's self-esteem which had been deflated by parental neglect.

A boy named Lazarus became one of Simon's favorite targets. They were the same age but differed in almost every other way. Lazarus was slightly built; Simon was broad shouldered and muscular. Lazarus was quiet and studious; Simon was rowdy and despised school. Lazarus was a loner; Simon enjoyed being the center of attention.

By the time he reached the age of nine, Lazarus was fed up with the steadily increasing abuse from Simon and his friends. He considered reaching out to his father, Benjamin, for help but didn't want to appear cowardly. Instead, Lazarus turned to God in prayer. A devout Jew, Benjamin taught his son to depend on God whenever he was afraid or in trouble. In this instance, Lazarus asked God to make the bullying stop.

Not long after making his request, Lazarus' prayer was answered. One day in class, on the spur of the moment, he surreptitiously gave Simon the answer to a difficult question. The rabbi, unaware of the deception, expressed his surprise and pleasure at Simon's scholarship. Although Simon understood that the accolades from his teacher were undeserved, he experienced a spike in self-esteem greater than his bullying tactics had ever provided.

Simon unexpectedly discovered that academic achievement might be more gratifying than he could have imagined. From that time forward, Simon put more effort into his studies, achieved modest success at school, and felt better about himself as a result.

The value of education was not the only lesson Simon learned that day. The kindness shown by Lazarus in spite of years of mistreatment pricked Simon's conscience. He began to view Lazarus in a different light. Simon realized that he had tormented Lazarus in order to make himself appear stronger while it was Lazarus who possessed the inner strength he was seeking.

Simon's relationships with his fellow students improved. Lazarus and the other students who had been bullied by Simon no longer feared verbal or physical abuse in or out of school. Simon made sure that no one dared to bother his new friends again.

In a short span of time, Simon had gone from shamelessly abusing those whom he considered inferior to passionately defending those whom he believed were being treated unfairly. This attitude reversal would become a guiding principle for Simon the rest of his life.

After graduation from synagogue school at age fifteen, Simon followed in his father's footsteps and began working as a stonecutter. Several years into his employment, a discussion with a fellow worker led to a radical change in the direction of Simon's life.

A Roman soldier had severely beaten a man in public for

no apparent reason other than he was Jewish. Simon agreed with his co-worker that the Roman occupation had become too oppressive and that a clean break from Rome was necessary. The fellow worker invited Simon to a meeting that he claimed would address this issue. Simon accepted the invitation and discovered that the attendees belonged to an underground political faction of Jews called the Zealots.

Zealots were passionate about achieving independence from Roman rule. Members used whatever means they could devise to sabotage the activities of Roman government officials, Roman soldiers, and Jews who collaborated with the Romans. Violence, including assassination, was not out of the question to achieve their goal.

Zealot ideology appealed to Simon's sense of fairness and concern for the welfare of his oppressed countrymen. His participation started slowly but soon developed into a committed effort that dominated his thinking and actions. After Lazarus' father was murdered by a Roman soldier over a tax dispute, Simon, with the help of his fellow Zealots, made sure that his death was avenged.

When Simon was twenty-four years old, he and his father relocated from Bethany to Capernaum in Galilee. The number of new building projects in and around Jerusalem dwindled after the death of Herod the Great. Simon's mother passed away so they no longer had family ties in Bethany. Not long after the move, a large chunk of limestone became dislodged from the quarry wall where they were working. His father's skull was crushed by the falling rock, and he died immediately.

In the months that followed, Simon experienced a growing sense of loneliness and despair. Both parents were deceased, he had no siblings, he had never married, and he was living in an unfamiliar city. Simon felt that he had nowhere to turn for comfort or advice to counter his deepening depression.

Although he had never been a pious Jew, Simon began attending Sabbath worship at a local synagogue. He hoped it would help explain why God had treated him so horribly. At one of the services, Jesus happened to be the guest speaker. Simon was so impressed with the message that he began following Jesus from synagogue to synagogue throughout Galilee.

After several weeks, Simon worked up the courage to approach Jesus and share his emotional struggles. In response, Jesus provided Simon with the comfort and hope he needed. When Jesus asked him to become one of his disciples, Simon did not hesitate to accept. His job as a stonecutter and his participation in the Zealot movement became secondary to an unwavering commitment to the man who had brought him out of despair.

For the next three years, Simon and eleven other hand-picked men followed Jesus throughout Galilee, Judea, and surrounding areas. They heard Jesus' often unorthodox viewpoints concerning many topics including the kingdom of God, loving and serving others, and keeping the Mosaic law. They personally witnessed Jesus do miraculous acts including healing the sick, feeding thousands of people, walking on water, calming a storm, and bringing two dead children back to life.

During the second year of Jesus' ministry, Simon reconnected with Lazarus, whom he hadn't seen since the death of Lazarus' father. At Simon's urging, Lazarus became acquainted with Jesus. A year later, Simon was present when Jesus raised Lazarus from the dead shortly before Jesus' own death and resurrection.

In spite of all they had seen and heard during three years of mentorship, Simon and his fellow disciples didn't fully understand who Jesus really was. They, like other Jews anxiously awaiting a Messiah, expected Jesus to use his supernatural abilities to free them from Roman rule and restore the glory days of Kings David and Solomon. Although Jesus told them he would suffer, die, and rise again, they couldn't accept that he would leave them so soon. They didn't yet understand that his mission was to free them from the consequences of sin rather than from Roman oppression.

It wasn't until fifty days after Jesus' resurrection that Simon, Lazarus, and the small community of Jesus' followers fully realized what Jesus' death and resurrection really meant. In Jerusalem during the Jewish festival of Shavuot, also known as Pentecost, the Holy Spirit was poured out on them. Unable to contain themselves, the faithful were emboldened to tell everyone who would listen that Jesus had conquered sin and death on their behalf.

The Jesus movement grew exponentially after Pentecost without significant resistance until the arrival of Saul and his band of extremist Jews. Ironically, Saul's persecution efforts drove many believers out of Jerusalem which resulted in spreading Jesus' message throughout the Roman Empire.

Believers who remained in Jerusalem risked imprisonment and even death. To Simon's dismay, one of the fatalities of the persecution was his best friend, Lazarus. In spite of Jesus' instruction to love one's enemies, Simon was determined that someday he would avenge the murder of Lazarus. Before he could accomplish that, Simon needed to fulfill his promise to Lazarus and get his sisters out of Jerusalem to safety.

Chapter 2

CONVERSION

A man of his word, Simon accompanied Mary and Martha to Capernaum, a town of about 1,500 residents located on the northwest shore of the Sea of Galilee. Two primary routes led from Jerusalem to Capernaum. Most Jews chose the longer one which took them east of the Jordan River in order to avoid Samaria, the region that stood between Judea in the south and Galilee in the north. All three regions were part of the Roman province of Judaea.

Jews and Samaritans despised each other for centuries and made every effort to avoid setting foot in the other's territory. Residents of Judea and Galilee were primarily orthodox Jews whose Temple was on Mount Zion in Jerusalem. Samaritans had Jewish and pagan pedigrees and worshipped on Mount Gerizim near the city of Shechem. Simon wanted to get Mary and Martha to safety as quickly as possible, so they travelled directly through Samaria, cutting thirty miles off the more popular 120-mile route.

After arriving in Capernaum, Simon was dismayed to discover that Saul's tentacles had already reached there. Although Saul's headquarters remained in Jerusalem, his men were identifying and arresting followers of Jesus in cities and towns throughout Galilee. Simon had not anticipated this development when making his promise to Lazarus. The original escape plan had to be revised.

Simon knew of another community of believers in the city of Damascus and decided to take the sisters there. A number of Jesus' followers fled there during the early days of Saul's rampage. Located sixty miles north of Capernaum, Damascus was outside of the province of Judaea and presumably out of the reach of Saul.

Damascus was a cosmopolitan city that embraced people of all nationalities and faiths. Simon was not overly concerned that a contingent of Jews allied with the religious leaders in Jerusalem lived there. He reasoned that the city government would not tolerate the arrest or deportation of any of its residents.

Soon after reaching Damascus, Simon found Mary and Martha a house to rent for what they hoped would be a brief stay. The sisters had ample reasons to get back to Bethany as soon as possible. Martha owned a thriving pottery business. Her employees could keep the operation going for a short time but needed her direction over a longer period. Mary and her husband, Caleb, owned and operated Bethany's only inn. Mary supervised the kitchen staff and kept the books. A prolonged absence would require hiring someone to perform her duties, shrinking an already thin profit margin.

Simon decided to remain in Damascus until the sisters had settled into their new surroundings. He was invited to stay at the home of Ananias, a God-fearing man who had founded the Damascus branch of the Way, the name that Jesus' followers adopted for their new religious movement. Ananias assured Simon that the sisters would be safe within their community, at least for the time being. Apart from harassment by local Jewish leadership, believers in Damascus lived and worshipped in relative freedom.

Several months after arriving in Damascus, the safe environment that Simon envisioned evaporated. Peter, one Simon's fellow disciples, sent a message from Jerusalem to Simon warning that the Sanhedrin had authorized Saul to expand his operations all the way to Damascus. Followers of Jesus whom Saul apprehended would be transported to Jerusalem and imprisoned. Apparently, Saul and the Sanhedrin were determined to stamp out the Jesus movement wherever it existed, even outside the borders of Judaea.

Simon wasted no time reporting the news to Ananias. "Saul is on his way here to arrest members of the Way. He left Jerusalem several days ago with a number of his men."

"I'm surprised that the Jews are risking a confrontation with the Gentile government that controls Damascus," replied Ananias.

"Saul might face some resistance when he gets here," Simon noted. "However, I don't think we can rely on the local government to stop Saul. We need to take precautions in order to avoid disaster."

"I agree completely," seconded Ananias. "When he gets here, Saul will probably meet with the leaders of the Damascus synagogue to identify believers living in the city. We need to warn our friends before Saul can get organized."

"I'm worried about Mary and Martha," admitted Simon. "I promised Lazarus that I would protect them by getting them out of Jerusalem to Capernaum. That proved to be too risky. Now it appears they aren't safe here either."

"We need to rely on God to provide direction," Ananias responded. "There is no time to waste. I'm going to invite the members of the Way to meet at my house tonight. I'd like you to be there to help explain what is happening. Please bring Mary and Martha along as well."

That evening the Damascus believers assembled at Ananias' home. After an opening prayer, Ananias started the meeting. "My friends in Christ, welcome. You all know Simon, one of the twelve who walked with Jesus during his three-year ministry. Today he received some news from Jerusalem that you all need to hear. Listen closely to what he has to say. After he is finished, we will try to answer any questions you might have."

"Fellow believers," Simon began, "as you know, our brothers and sisters in Jerusalem have experienced increasing levels of persecution ever since Stephen, one of our strongest witnesses for Jesus, was stoned to death for his faith. The instigator of this oppression is a Jewish extremist named Saul who has vowed to eliminate any trace of the Jesus movement.

"This madman has ordered the arrest, imprisonment, and execution of many believers including my good friend Lazarus, the man whom Jesus raised from the dead shortly before his own death. After Lazarus' second death, this one at the hands of Saul, I brought his sisters here to ensure their safety. You have graciously invited the three of us to live among you for which we are very grateful.

"Tonight, I come to you with an urgent warning. Saul has received authority from the Sanhedrin to travel to Damascus in order to arrest followers of Jesus. Any of us who are apprehended will be taken to Jerusalem, put in prison, and possibly killed.

"Saul and his men should arrive in Damascus soon. They will begin searching for us immediately. I suggest that any of you who are able to leave Damascus temporarily should do so. If you can't leave the city, you will need to make yourselves as inconspicuous as possible. You will also need to warn anyone who is not here today of the danger they are facing.

"I need to emphasize one other thing. If any of you are arrested, do your best to avoid cooperating with your captors. Saul will use threats and beatings to force you into exposing your friends. Be strong! Jesus predicted that his followers would be persecuted, and his prophesy is coming true. Most importantly, he promised a place in Heaven for all who remain faithful to him."

Simon paused for questions, but there were none. He continued, "I realize this is a lot to digest. There isn't much time to take safety measures, so I suggest that you act quickly. And remember, if you know of any fellow believers that aren't here tonight, please share this information with them. Lastly, remain confident that Jesus will be with us now and through eternity. God bless you all."

After the attendees had left, Simon asked Ananias what he planned to do. "I'm going to stay right here and do wherever I can to ensure the safety of my friends," Ananias promised. "As one of the leaders of the Way, I need to help maintain a united front against Saul and his men."

"You realize, of course, that you will be one of the first believers for whom Saul will look," Simon observed. "The Jews here in Damascus are aware of your leadership role. If you must remain in the city, I suggest you leave your house and keep out of sight. Saul is very persistent. When he pursues someone, he doesn't quit until he finds them. Lazarus was an unfortunate example of that."

"I appreciate your concern," Ananias replied. "I don't plan to leave Damascus, but I like your suggestion about going underground. I have a Gentile friend here who would take me in. I'm sure he would also welcome you to stay with him."

"Thank you for the offer. But I'm not concerned about myself. My purpose in coming here was to get Mary and Martha to safety," Simon explained. "That goal hasn't changed. Saul probably has no idea that the three of us are here in Damascus. I'll move in with the sisters temporarily and keep track of Saul's movements. If necessary, I will move them out of the city to a safer location. I plan to keep my promise to Lazarus."

The following day the two men sat down for the morning meal. While they discussed what might happen in the coming days, Ananias began to stare blankly into space and mumble incoherently. After a few minutes of this unusual activity, he appeared to recover.

"Are you all right, Ananias? It seemed like you were in different world for a moment."

"To be honest, I was. Jesus was speaking to me."

"What? Are you sure?"

"Yes, it was the Lord. I heard Jesus speak as clearly as I hear you now. He told me what he wants me to do. I'm ashamed to say that I had the audacity to question him."

"You aren't making any sense, Ananias. What exactly was said between you and Jesus?"

"He called me by name, and I knew immediately it was him. Jesus told me to go to the home of one of my friends named Judas who lives on Straight Street near the center of the city. He said that Saul is there expecting me. Apparently, Saul was blinded as he neared Damascus. I am supposed to put my hands on Saul, and he will be healed."

"Saul and his men must have arrived sooner than we expected. But what did you mean when you said you questioned Jesus?"

"I must have been out of my mind. I pointed out to Jesus that Saul was coming here to do harm to his followers, including me. In the back of my mind, I hoped that he might reconsider and not send me there. Despite my lack of trust, Jesus was patient with me. He explained that he has a special mission for Saul. He is going to be Jesus' messenger throughout the world, not just to Jews but also to Gentiles."

"I have no doubt that Jesus spoke to you. What are you going to do?"

"I'm leaving right now to pay a visit to Saul. Why don't you come along?"

"I'm not sure I should. After we buried Lazarus, I vowed to repay Saul for what he had done. Given the opportunity, I might be tempted to harm or even kill Saul. However, after hearing what Jesus just told you, I would be a fool to do so."

"It's your choice. But whether it is now or sometime in the future, I don't believe Jesus would allow your vow for vengeance to override his plans for Saul."

Straight Street was the primary route for travel within the city walls of Damascus. The wide street could accommodate a large volume of foot traffic, so it didn't take long for Ananias and Simon to reach their destination. The man who answered the door motioned for them to come in. He greeted Ananias with an embrace. "Hello, my friend," the man said. "I wasn't expecting your visit today. I assumed you would be going into hiding or assisting others in doing so."

Turning to Simon, he said, "My name is Judas. We met last night. I appreciate what you told us at the meeting. However, events have taken a significant turn since then. As I approached my house on the way home, I saw three men standing outside my front door. They were armed with swords, but they didn't appear to be Roman soldiers. After your warning, I thought they might be Saul's men there to arrest me. I felt the urge to turn and walk away, but for some unexplained reason I didn't."

"I know why you didn't," interjected Ananias. "Our Lord Jesus spoke to me in a vision a short time ago. He told me that Saul is here and expects me to cure his blindness."

"Your vision was accurate on both counts," Judas continued. "Two of the men were holding up a third man who was in obvious distress. His hair and clothes were disheveled, and a cloth was wrapped around his head covering his eyes. He looked to be on the verge of passing out. They informed me that his name was Saul and that he had been commissioned by the Sanhedrin in Jerusalem to carry out a special project in Damascus. Based on our meeting last night, I knew exactly what the project was.

"According to the two men, as they neared the city a bright light from the sky shined down on them, knocking Saul off his feet. While lying on the ground, Saul seemed to converse with the light, but no one could make out what he was saying. After the light disappeared, they discovered Saul had been struck blind.

"The men hoped that Saul's vision would return soon, so they set up camp outside the city, but there was no improvement. Last night Saul ordered them to bring him here. The men admitted they had no idea why he chose my house. In retrospect, we know that Jesus guided them here."

"Where is Saul now?" asked Ananias.

"He's lying down in the back bedroom," replied Judas. "He's in fairly good shape physically except for his vision, but emotionally he seems very fragile. Ever since he got here, Saul has done nothing but pray. Based on what his men said, he hasn't had anything to eat or drink since he was struck blind. He hasn't eaten since coming here either."

Judas led Ananias and Simon to the bedroom where Saul was lying. As they entered the doorway, Saul turned his head in their direction. "Who is there?" he asked in a voice marked by fear mixed with anticipation.

"My name is Ananias. I was directed in a vision by Jesus of Nazareth to meet you here. He told me that you would be expecting me."

"I was praying that you would come," said Saul more confidently. "On my way to the city, I was struck blind by a brilliant light. The voice of Jesus called me by name and asked why I was torturing him and his followers. Later I had a vision that someone named Ananias would appear and cure my blindness."

"I am that someone. Let it be as the Lord has said. You will soon see again."

Ananias removed the cloth covering Saul's eyes. He placed his hands on his head and blessed him. Saul's eyes opened slowly, and a white flaky residue fell from them. After blinking a few times, his face lit up in a broad smile.

"Praise God!" exclaimed Saul. "He has restored my sight." He glanced around the room. Assuming the man standing next to him must be Ananias, Saul sat up and clasped his hands. "Thank you for having the courage to do what Jesus directed. Coming here must have been a difficult decision. You had to be aware of how I have treated Jesus' followers throughout Judaea."

"I admit I had my doubts," replied Ananias. "But the Lord works in ways well beyond our understanding. Who am I to question the will of God?"

"I wish I had that kind of faith," observed Saul. "I'm still not sure what Jesus wants me to do other than to stop persecuting his followers."

Ananias replied, "Saul, Jesus wants you to know he has special plans for you. You have been chosen to tell the entire world about him, not just Jews but Gentiles as well. You will proclaim Jesus as Lord to everyone from common people to kings. But be forewarned that this task will be difficult and involve suffering on your part."

"I can't begin to comprehend what you just told me, but I

trust you are being truthful," responded Saul. "You restored my sight. I have no reason to doubt that you were sent here by Jesus."

Saul noticed Judas and Simon standing nearby. "Who are your friends?" he asked.

"This is Judas," Ananias replied. "He owns the house in which you are staying. He took care of you after two of your men brought you here."

"You were probably too disoriented to remember," offered Judas. "You ordered the men to return to their camp outside the city. They were told to return today to receive any further orders."

"Thank you for your hospitality, Judas." said Saul. "I would like to pay you for my stay here and for attending to my needs."

"That won't be necessary," replied Judas. "I am glad to play a part in God's plans."

Ananias continued, "This is Simon. He is one of twelve disciples who accompanied Jesus during his three-year ministry. You might remember an encounter you had with him not too long ago."

"No, I don't believe so," Saul confessed.

"You obviously don't recognize me," Simon responded, struggling to keep his emotions in check. "I was one of the men who broke into the Jerusalem prison on the night that you killed my best friend, Lazarus. The sight of his brutally beaten body still haunts me to this day."

"I recall the events of that evening," admitted Saul. "At the time I considered the outcome to be a victory for God and the Jewish faith. Now, after hearing the voice of Jesus, I am truly sorry and ashamed for what I did. I can only imagine how much you hate me right now. You could have killed me today while I was still sightless and unable to defend myself. Why didn't you?"

"To be honest," answered Simon, "if Jesus hadn't spoken to Ananias and revealed his plans for you, I would probably have considered taking your life when the opportunity arose. But it appears that you and I are called to work together toward the same goal, that is, telling the world about the love that God the Father has shown us through His Son Jesus."

"Forgive me for being skeptical, but how can I be sure that you won't change your mind about me?" questioned Saul. "What if we have a falling out sometime in the future. Will your resentment be rekindled?"

Simon replied, "For much of my life I have struggled with controlling my anger. If I or someone I love are treated unfairly, my anger can progress into hatred and even violence. Perhaps that is why I became a Zealot. I have to admit that the killing of Lazarus elevated my anger to a level I have never experienced before."

"I appreciate your candor," responded Saul. "After all the harm I've caused, I imagine you are one of many who feels that way. But I wonder how Jesus expects me to teach about love and forgiveness when the people with whom I will work, including you, can't find it in their hearts to forgive me."

"Your point is well taken," admitted Simon. "My attitude has to change. The only way I see that happening is to rely on Jesus to help me forgive. I can't do it on my own. Against all logic, Jesus urged us to love everyone, even our enemies. When asked how many times we should forgive someone, Jesus set no limits. Based on what he taught, love and forgiveness go hand in hand. One can't happen without the other."

Saul paused for a moment and then asked, "During your time with Jesus, did he always live what he taught?"

"What prompted you to ask that question?" asked Simon.

"I'm afraid that my actions against Jesus were so abhorrent he might not be willing to forgive me," Saul replied. "He could have ended my life outside Damascus just as you could have done here today, but he didn't. Ananias said that Jesus has singled me out to teach the world about him. But he also warned me that I would suffer while doing so. Am I forgiven or is Jesus prolonging my life in order to get even with me later?"

"To answer your first question," Simon responded, "in the three years he was with us, Jesus always lived a life consistent with his teachings. You can be assured that he loves you and will forgive you in spite of anything you have done."

"You certainly give me hope regarding how Jesus feels about me," Saul admitted. "But I get the feeling that you are only tolerating me to please him. You haven't said whether or not you can forgive me for what I did to your friend."

"As I said earlier, I have to depend on Jesus to give me the strength to forgive. When my anger flares up, I need to ask myself, 'Did Jesus die to save that person no matter what they have done to me?' The answer must be an emphatic 'yes.' Jesus died to redeem all sinners, including you and me. This leaves me with only one option…to forgive you as I have been forgiven. Saul, I forgive you."

"I am grateful to hear you say that," Saul replied. "I believe you are sincere. Where do we go from here?"

"I sense that you are willing to begin the task that Jesus gave you. Jesus promised that those who are baptized in his name will receive God's Spirit and be cleansed of their sins. Are you willing to be baptized?"

"Yes, I am willing. Please baptize me at once," replied Saul.

Saul, Simon, Ananias, and Judas walked to the Abana River

which flowed through the middle of the city. At a bend in the river where the current was weaker, Simon led Saul into the water and baptized him in the name of the Father, Son, and Holy Spirit. Saul emerged from the river filled with the Spirit, praising God for the love and forgiveness that He had shown him through Jesus.

"You are undeniably a new man," Simon remarked. "Your sins have been washed away, even those you might have considered unforgiveable. I accept you as a brother in Christ and reiterate my forgiveness toward you. Further, I pledge my support to work with you in fulfilling the mission we have both been assigned."

As they approached Judas' house on the way back from the river, two men were standing outside. Judas recognized them as the men who had accompanied Saul the prior evening. The two men appeared surprised to see Saul walking without assistance and approached him directly. "Sir, we've come to take you back to the camp. Your men are getting restless from lack of activity. They want to see action but need your direction to proceed."

"I am aborting our mission effective immediately," Saul answered. "We have been persecuting the followers of Jesus unjustly. There is no reason for you and the others to remain here."

"How can that be? What will we tell the Sanhedrin?" the men asked. "They are expecting us to crush the Jesus movement here in Damascus."

"Tell them that Jesus, whom they crucified, is alive and has spoken to me," responded Saul. "Tell them that Saul is now living for Jesus rather than fighting against him. My final order to you and the rest of the men is to return to Jerusalem and report to the Sanhedrin what I just told you."

The next day Ananias began notifying members of the Way that they no longer faced danger from Saul. Word spread quickly, and people who had left the city began returning to their homes. Simon moved out of Mary and Martha's rental and returned to Ananias' house. Ananias invited Saul to stay with him and Simon until he decided what to do next. The three men would be able to discuss plans for the future, relying on God's Spirit to guide their decision making.

Saul had several options to consider. He could return to Tarsus, his hometown in Asia Minor, and resume his original occupation as a tentmaker. However, that would not fulfill the mission that Jesus had given him. He could go to Jerusalem and work with Jesus' disciples. However, he would be a target of the Sanhedrin and potentially put other believers in danger. As a default position, Saul decided to stay in Damascus a while longer.

Simon offered his help. "Saul, you have been through an incredible series of events. I imagine you are still processing everything that has happened. Even though you declared your intention to live for Jesus, you know little about him. Since you have decided to stay in Damascus for now, I would be glad to share what I learned during the three years I was with Jesus."

"Everything happened so quickly that I am overwhelmed," acknowledged Saul. "I admit that my current lack of knowledge about Jesus makes it difficult to begin the task he has given me. Nevertheless, I feel confident that God has turned my life around for a reason. I gratefully accept your offer."

During the weeks that followed, Simon shared his testimony with Saul. Saul absorbed Simon's words like a sponge. As a young man, Saul had studied under the tutelage of Gamaliel, a prominent Pharisee and member of the Sanhedrin. Saul's familiarity with the writings of the prophets made it easier for him to understand what the Scriptures foretold concerning the Messiah and how Jesus fulfilled those prophesies.

Saul learned that Jesus was clearly the suffering servant of whom Isaiah spoke, that Jesus was the one whom King David acknowledged as his Lord, and that Jesus was the Redeemer that Job claimed would come. Simon's instruction helped prepare Saul for his future work. However, as Saul would find out later, there was much more that he needed to learn, some of it from Jesus himself.

Chapter 3

ESCAPE

Following Saul's orders, his men returned to Jerusalem and reported to the High Priest what had happened in Damascus. After hearing their report, Caiaphas called a special meeting of the Sanhedrin. The members were stunned by the news of Saul's defection. After all, it was Saul who had originally proposed the persecution of Jesus' followers. Prior to Saul's purge of believers, Jewish leadership and members of the Way had coexisted relatively peaceably.

The Council debated what to do next. Some members viewed Saul's apostasy with concern. They recalled his passion to preserve traditional Jewish values. Despite an unimposing physical presence, Saul had the ability to arouse that same passion in others. They worried that unless he was silenced early on, Saul would become a thorn in the side of the Jewish leaders much like Jesus had been.

Other members of the Sanhedrin felt that taking action against Saul was not necessary. They reasoned that his former role in persecuting believers would preclude Saul from a leadership role in the Way. He would never be trusted enough to play a major part in their decision making.

Following a spirited debate, the Sanhedrin decided to send a message to the Jewish leaders in Damascus warning that Saul could potentially become a problem. The message instructed them to watch Saul closely and take swift action to muzzle him if he started to pose a threat to the Jewish community there.

Meanwhile in Damascus, Saul's shared his newfound faith with everyone he met. It wasn't unusual to find him drawing large crowds on street corners throughout the city. Most dismissed him as an eccentric, but others stopped to hear what he had to say. What they heard was a personal account of his conversion and a message that God loved them enough to send the Messiah, Jesus, to save them from their sins.

Invariably, after Saul's speeches concluded, several onlookers would ask to be baptized. Both Jews and Gentiles came to faith. His fearless witness emboldened other members of the Way. As months passed, Jewish leadership in Damascus began to see the impact that Saul's efforts were having, and they began to feel threatened.

Heeding the warning given to them by the Sanhedrin, Jewish authorities met in the main synagogue in Damascus to discuss the situation. They agreed the Way had not been problematic until Saul joined their ranks. If they could get rid of him, peaceful coexistence could be restored. Some favored forcing him out of the city. Others advocated getting rid of Saul permanently. In the end it was decided that Saul would be trouble for the Jews wherever he went. His death would be the best solution.

Plans were made to kidnap Saul, take him outside the city, and kill him. Observers were assigned to monitor Saul's comings and goings to determine the best time and place to abduct him. To ensure their plan would succeed, the Jews convinced the Gentile governor of Damascus to post guards at the city gates with orders to seize Saul if he attempted to leave.

One of the appointed observers was a young man named Yosef who was secretly a follower of Jesus. As soon as he could do so safely, Yosef notified Ananias of the plot. Ananias broke the news to Saul and Simon.

"I was just informed that the Jewish leaders here in Damascus are scheming to seize Saul and kill him. Yosef, one of the men assigned to track Saul's movements, is a covert member of the Way. He informed me of their plans earlier today. I suggest that Saul leave the city immediately to ensure his safety."

"I'm not surprised," Saul replied. "A few months ago, I would have acted the same way toward anyone who followed Jesus. I'm not afraid of what they might do to me, but I need to stay alive to fulfill the mission that Jesus has given me. I agree with Ananias. It is probably best that I leave Damascus as soon as possible."

"Where would you go that is out of the reach of the Jews?" asked Simon. "They seem to have a presence everywhere."

"I might have a solution," offered Ananias. "The city of Petra might provide an answer to Saul's dilemma. Petra is the capital city of Nabatea. Nabatea is a huge kingdom that stretches all the way from our city of Damascus in the north to the Red Sea in the south. Petra is located in the southern part of the Nabatean kingdom in an isolated region of the Arabian desert. I've never been there, but I don't believe there are any synagogues in Petra. Ten male Jews are required to start a synagogue, and I have heard there are not that many Jewish residents there. Saul should be out of harm's way in Petra until it is safe for him to return here."

"I like that idea," said Simon. "But what if Jewish leadership reaches out to the Nabatean king and tries to extradite Saul to Jerusalem?"

"I don't see that as a possibility," answered Ananias. "The king of Nabatea, Aretas IV, still holds a grudge against the Jews. He has never forgiven Herod Antipas, the Jewish king who beheaded John the Baptist, for divorcing Aretas' daughter. In fact, a few years after his daughter's divorce, Aretas went to war against Antipas which ended in a Nabatean victory. I doubt that Aretas would cooperate with the Jews in any way."

The next day Saul prepared to leave Damascus for Petra. Aware that they were being watched, Ananias sent Aaron, a fellow believer, outside the city with a donkey loaded with supplies that Saul would need on his trip. Aaron would wait there until Saul joined him and then return to the city through another gate. Saul and the donkey would then follow the King's Highway all the way to Petra.

After sunset Simon, Ananias, and several other members of

the Way emerged from Ananias' house forming a human wall around Saul. Although Yosef was the only observer scheduled for duty that night, Ananias wanted to make absolutely sure that Saul's departure wouldn't be detected. As the men walked toward the east wall of the city, Yosef emerged from the darkness.

"Everything is taken care of. I am the only one on the night shift. When I file my report in the morning, I will note that there was no activity tonight. For the next few days, the other observers will not see Saul leave Ananias' house. At some point, the Jewish leaders will become suspicious and send someone to find out where he is. By then Saul will have had plenty of time to get away."

"God bless you, Yosef," remarked Saul, "I will be forever grateful for what you have done for me."

Saul and his escorts resumed their walk through the dark streets toward a home owned by a member of the Way. The house was built adjacent to the city wall which served as the back side of the residence. A second story window opening was carved through the wall from which residents could shoot arrows or throw stones to defend the city in the event of attack.

After arriving at the home, the men proceeded upstairs. A large basket made of reeds with ropes attached to its handles was lying next to the window. Saul embraced Simon and Ananias and thanked everyone for their help. He climbed into the basket and was lowered twenty feet to the ground.

A bank of clouds obscured a full moon. Saul gave thanks for the cover it provided. He waved to the men pulling the basket back through the window and walked cautiously toward the King's Highway. After reaching the road, Saul looked back at the silhouette of the city barely visible in the darkness. All was quiet. Apparently, none of the guards stationed on the walls or at the gate had seen him escape.

Initially, Saul stayed several yards off the roadway to avoid detection. Foot traffic to and from Damascus was nonexistent that evening so Saul moved onto the smoother surface of the King's Highway. After walking for several minutes, Saul heard a donkey braying and saw the outline of a man walking toward him. "Is that you Aaron?" Saul asked in a hushed tone.

"Yes, it's me. Thank God you made it out of the city safely. Did you run into any difficulty?"

"No. But without Yosef, I would probably be dead tomorrow. He warned of the death threat against me and made sure my escape would not be detected. I hope that members of the Way reward Yosef for his efforts."

"I'm certain he will get the recognition he deserves. The donkey is tied to a bush a few yards from the road. Sacks of food and other supplies are tied to its back. There is also a bag of silver coins in case you need to purchase anything. Godspeed on your journey."

"I trust that the Lord will keep me safe. God's blessings to you and the rest of the believers in Damascus. I hope to return someday to see you all again." With those parting words, Saul turned southward and began the 250-mile journey to Petra.

Chapter 4

PETRA

Saul reached his destination nearly a month after leaving Damascus. He sent word to Simon and Ananias notifying them that he had arrived safely and that his first impression of the city was favorable. Saul noted that the Nabateans spoke a version of Aramaic, the everyday language of Jews, which would enable him to share the Gospel message more easily.

As Saul became more familiar with the city, he learned that the Nabateans weren't the first settlers in Petra. The city's origins could be traced back to Esau who lived nearly 2,000 years before the birth of Jesus. Esau was the grandson of Abraham, the son of Isaac, and twin brother to Jacob. All three of Esau's relatives were considered patriarchs of the Jewish religion.

Esau was the first of the twin boys to be born to Isaac and his wife Rebekah. Even though it was only a matter of minutes before his brother Jacob was delivered, timing gave Esau the right to inherit his father's property. The birthright included the land of Canaan which God had promised to Abraham and his descendants.

As the brothers grew older, Esau showed a lack of interest in his inheritance. Famished after a day of hunting, Esau sold his birthright to his brother Jacob in exchange for a bowl of stew. Isaac was never told of the transaction between his sons. Years later on his death bed, Isaac made plans to bless Esau and make his inheritance official. Jacob, with the help of his mother, tricked his elderly and blind father into giving him the birthright by disguising himself as Esau.

After realizing his birthright was irretrievably lost, Esau threatened to kill his brother. Jacob fled 500 miles north to his mother's hometown of Haran in Mesopotamia. While in Haran, Jacob married two of his cousins, fathered twelve children, employed numerous servants, and acquired flocks of sheep as well as herds of cattle and donkeys.

Twenty years after fleeing from Canaan, Jacob returned to the land of his birthright. To his relief, Esau did not seek revenge for Jacob's earlier trickery. However, the relation-ship between the brothers remained strained. For a period of time, the two clans attempted to occupy the same territory, but Canaan could not support the number of animals that both brothers had accumulated. Esau reluctantly relocated his household to a desert region south of Canaan while Jacob and his family remained in the fertile land inherited from his father.

The land in which Esau settled was called Edom. The name Edom derived from the red hue of the mountains that dotted the region. Its borders extended from the southernmost tip of the Dead Sea to the northern tip of the Gulf of Aqaba. Although much of the area was barren and uninhabitable, a number of towns and villages sprang up in Edom to facilitate commerce along the major trade routes that crisscrossed the region.

During the centuries that followed, animosity between descendants of Esau and Jacob grew. When Moses and the Israelites requested safe passage through Edom on their way back to Canaan after 400 years of bondage in Egypt, the Edomites denied the request.

Much later, King David conquered Edom and subjugated its people to Jewish rule until King Jehoram, the fifth successor to David's throne, failed to put down an Edomite rebellion. Edom once again became a free country.

Three hundred years after Edom regained its independence, Babylon invaded Judah. The Babylonians destroyed Jerusalem and took the majority of the Jewish population into captivity. The Edomites openly celebrated the defeat of the Jews, who never forgave this affront.

The Edomites were later driven out of their country by the Nabateans, a semi-nomadic tribe from northern Arabia. The displaced Edomites settled in Idumea, a region in southern Judea. The Judean government forced the Edomites to convert to Judaism. Ironically, the descendants of Esau were coerced into becoming Jews, the descendants of his brother Jacob.

Prior to driving out the Edomites, the Nabateans lived as nomads, moving their flocks and herds across the Arabian desert from one grazing spot to another. After Edom was conquered, the country was renamed Nabatea. Soon thereafter, the lifestyle of the Nabateans changed dramatically.

International trade grew rapidly after Greeks and Romans brought much of the known world under common rule. Incense, primarily frankincense and myrrh, was in high demand and was transported by camel caravan from southern Arabia along trade routes that crossed through Nabatea to the port of Gaza in Idumea. From Gaza the cargo was carried by ship to cities along the coast of the Mediterranean Sea.

Merchants crossing the barren desert needed to secure water and food for themselves and their camels and were willing to pay handsomely to do so. Before being conquered, the Edomites provided these services in their towns and villages. The Nabateans recognized the potential for acquiring great wealth and abandoned their nomadic ways, settling in former Edomite communities along the trade routes.

An example of this cultural transformation took place in the former Edomite village of Selah. The Nabateans transformed this insignificant settlement into a majestic capital city of 20,000 residents which they renamed Petra, meaning "the rock."

Although located on a major trade route, Petra was not a logical choice to become the commercial and political center of the Nabatean kingdom. Annual rainfall was less than two inches which normally would have rendered the area uninhabitable. However, the Nabateans were successful in making Petra an oasis in a desolate land.

Nabatean engineers laid miles of ceramic pipes to channel water from a nearby mountain to the city. Dams and reservoirs were constructed to store water and control flooding during the brief winter rainy season. Water was diverted to huge underground cisterns dug out of rock in the surrounding desert to provide water for flocks and herds outside the city. The cisterns were carefully concealed from outsiders.

By the time Saul settled in Petra, the Nabatean kingdom and its capital city were at the peak of their prosperity. Petra appeared to present a tremendous opportunity for Saul to share his newfound faith in Jesus with a people who had never heard the message of God's saving grace. However, as Saul would soon discover, the messenger of good news is not always well received.

Chapter 5

VISIT

Months after Saul fled Damascus, the Sanhedrin called off its purge of believers after failing to find a satisfactory replacement for Saul. An informal truce with the Way was established all the way to Damascus. Followers of Jesus could once again worship without fear of imprisonment.

Simon took advantage of this development to escort Mary and Martha back to Bethany, fulfilling the promise he made to Lazarus. After the sisters were safely home, Simon resumed working with Peter, John, and the other disciples in Jerusalem. The original disciples, now known as Apostles, were recognized as the doctrinal and administrative authorities of the new Jesus movement which began to spread throughout the world, just as Jesus had commanded.

Simon and Saul exchanged correspondence regularly. Simon informed Saul that the persecution he had spearheaded was no longer in effect and invited him to relocate to Jerusalem with the caveat that his defection might still be fresh in the minds of the Jewish leaders.

Saul declined Simon's invitation, stating that he was excited at the prospect of witnessing to the residents of Petra. Saul expressed confidence that the Nabateans would hear the message and be filled with the Holy Spirit just as he had been in Damascus.

As months passed, Simon noticed a subtle change in Saul's letters. His initial optimism seemed to diminish over time. Saul had experienced positive results during the short time he witnessed in Damascus. Simon speculated that Petra presented a more difficult challenge.

The two cities differed from each other in many ways. Damascus was in close proximity to other thriving cities and towns. The weather was mild, and a river flowed through the middle of the city making it a desirable location in which to live. The population of Damascus was diverse and included a mixture of Jews, Syrians, Egyptians, and Greeks as well as Nabateans.

Petra was located in the middle of a barren desert and isolated from any major population centers. Merchants transporting goods through Petra did not usually live there, so most of the city's permanent residents were Nabatean.

In Damascus, Saul's converts had primarily been Jews who had heard something about Jesus. Some had seen Jesus perform miracles or heard him teach. By virtue of their Jewish heritage, many of the Jewish converts were looking forward to the coming Messiah. Making the connection between Jesus and the Messiah was not overly complicated.

In Petra, Saul's audience was composed almost exclusively of Nabateans who worshipped a pantheon of home-grown gods as well as several Greek and Roman deities. Saul arrived in Petra during a period of kingdom-wide peace and prosperity that, in the opinion of its citizens, was largely due to assistance from their gods. Nabateans had little incentive to abandon their familiar array of deities for a single god, especially one of Jewish origin.

After months of growing concern about Saul's well-being, Simon decided that it was time to pay him an unannounced visit. A novice missionary like Saul living in a pagan city with no support from fellow believers might become discouraged enough to abandon his calling. Simon hoped to find out what Saul was experiencing in Petra and to encourage him to continue the mission that Jesus had assigned.

Simon's 150-mile journey from Jerusalem to Petra followed a popular trade route. The first half ran directly south along the western side of the Dead Sea. The second half turned southeast through a desolate stretch of desert almost entirely devoid of vegetation. As Simon made his way through the barren wasteland, single rock formations appeared, jutting up from the sand like huge monuments. The solitary outcroppings later merged into a series of mountain ranges separated by narrow canyons.

After several days of travel, Simon sensed that he was nearing Petra. The road he had been following led into a narrow canyon pathway, the walls of which rose hundreds of feet straight up from its floor. A man-made arch spanned the entrance. The foot traffic coming his way picked up considerably.

The canyon floor was smooth, consisting of sand and rock pebbles compressed by countless footsteps over hundreds of years. Simon, a stonecutter by trade, noted that the walls were sandstone. He marveled at the swirling patterns and beautiful colors of the rock face which appeared to be carved by an ancient river.

The pathway meandered through the canyon, thirty feet at its widest and ten feet at its narrowest. The vertical walls ranged from 200 to 600 feet high. Simon glanced upward and saw blue sky in the slit between the sides of the rock face above. He gave thanks for the shade which sheltered him from the brutal desert sun.

After walking for half an hour, Simon finally reached the end of the pathway and emerged into a huge open-air plaza encircled by an extension of the canyon's sandstone cliffs. At the far side of the plaza, the facade of a Greek or Roman temple had been carved into the face of the cliff. It looked to Simon like an enormous two-dimensional sculpture set in a rock picture frame.

Simon estimated the façade's dimensions to be about eighty feet wide and nearly twice as tall. It stretched upward for two stories, the first of which was topped by an ornate canopy supported by six Corinthian columns. The second story consisted of two alcoves skirted by six smaller columns. The architecture reminded Simon of Herod's palace in Jerusalem except that Herod's palace was a free-standing building while the Petra facade was a rock carving on a sandstone cliff.

Simon decided to take a closer look. He crossed the plaza,

carefully sidestepping the people, donkeys, and camels gathered there. A series of stone stairs brought him to a wide porch which led to two tall thick wooden doors leading into what appeared to be a man-made cave dug into the sandstone rock.

The cave turned out to be a large room about forty feet square capped by a thirty-foot ceiling. Tables and couches were placed around the room where men sat reading from papyrus scrolls illuminated by oil lamps. The only natural light in the room came from the open front doors. A number of men were going in and out of several smaller adjacent rooms, apparently depositing or retrieving scrolls.

Simon realized that he was in a library. He had heard about large libraries in major cities throughout the Roman Empire including Alexandria in Egypt and Ephesus in Asia Minor. He didn't expect to see such an impressive center of learning in a remote location like Petra.

Simon had little difficulty locating Saul since most Nabateans spoke Aramaic. After making several inquiries, Simon was directed to one of the many pagan temples in the main part of the city. There he found Saul standing outside the entrance.

As Simon approached, Saul spotted his friend and ran to embrace him. "Simon, I can't believe you are here. I'm so glad to see you. It's only been about nine months, but it seems like a lifetime since I last saw you in Damascus. Tell me, what brings you to Petra?"

"Actually, you are the reason I am here. I've been worried about you. The tone of your letters has changed over time. You seemed so confident soon after you arrived, but lately you seem to be doubting yourself. I feared you were becoming discouraged so I came to see if I could help in some way."

"I appreciate your concern. However, I could have saved you a trip if you had shared your concerns. I remain totally committed to the mission that Jesus assigned me. It hasn't been easy to accept rejection here in Petra, especially after the success I had in Damascus. Most people here think I am delusional. My hope is that I am planting a few seeds that the Holy Spirit can nourish."

"It's interesting that you mention planting seeds. That is exactly what Jesus taught in one of his parables. He likened sowing seed to spreading the message of God's kingdom. Not all seed will fall on fertile soil, but the seeds that do will produce an abundant harvest. Even if we don't see immediate results, we can be assured that the Holy Spirit will nourish that seed and cause it to grow."

"I appreciate your words of encouragement. Now that you are here, I hope you will stay for a while. I'm living in a rented apartment near here. It isn't fancy, but there is space for both of us. I was able to secure a part-time job with a local tent maker. My work schedule is flexible which gives me time to witness for Jesus."

"I didn't plan a lengthy stay. However, I will accept your invitation only if you allow me to pay for half the rent while I am here. If I decide to stay longer, I should be able to find some work as a stonecutter. It appears that Petra is literally carved out of stone."

"Yes, the entire city is encircled by steep sandstone cliffs. Temples, tombs, and even homes are either carved into the cliffsides or constructed of sandstone blocks. Water is transported in canals from nearby mountains and stored in reservoirs dug

into the stone. When the Greek army tried to attack Petra several hundred years ago, the topography of the city helped the
Nabateans defeat them. But for now, let's get you cleaned up
and rested after your journey. You will have plenty of time to
learn more about Petra."

Chapter 6

REVELATION

The next day at the morning meal, Simon initiated the conversation. "I was glad to hear that you remain upbeat about your work here. Tell me, what has been going on since we last saw each other?"

"After leaving Damascus, I was brimming with confidence," answered Saul. "Jesus had selected me to tell the world about him. I had initial success in Damascus, so I was confident that with Jesus' help I would be able to fulfill the mission here in Petra. It didn't take long for reality to set in.

"When I arrived, there were no members of the Way in Petra. A handful of Jews live here, but there are too few of them to start a synagogue. My message was foreign to the Nabateans who had their own gods. As time passed, I began to question my decision to come to Petra."

"So, I did interpret your letters correctly. But now you claim to be optimistic. What has changed?"

"In the past I've always faced challenges head on, believing that I was the one in control. Then Jesus humbled me, first with blindness and more recently with the inability to make the Nabateans believers in him. I realized that in order to fulfill what he wants me to do, I needed to place my future in his hands. He didn't fail me."

"What do you mean by that?"

"A month ago, I was sitting on my bed deep in prayer when I went into a dreamlike state that seemed too real to be a dream. I was looking into a light brighter than the sun. Squinting into the glare, I saw what appeared to be the silhouette of a man standing in front of me. A powerful but soothing voice spoke, 'Saul, I have heard your prayers. Today you will learn everything you need to fulfill the mission I have given to you.' I recognized the voice of Jesus, the same voice that spoke to me on the road to Damascus."

"What happened then?"

"Jesus asked me if I believed in him, and I answered yes. He asked me to explain what I believed. I had to admit that my understanding of who he was and what he had done was limited. Only a few months earlier my life had been turned upside down. At that time, I was told that I would be Jesus' messenger to the Gentiles. I was baptized and assured of forgiveness. You shared some of your experiences as a disciple. That was the extent of what I knew. I acknowledged that my belief system was still evolving."

"You probably sold yourself short. But knowing Jesus as I do, I'm sure he was patient with you."

"Yes, he understood that only a short time had passed since I learned the truth about him. He promised to reveal what I needed to know and believe in order to witness on his behalf. He said the Holy Spirit would use my words to bring countless numbers of non-believers spanning multiple generations from countries across the world to faith."

"I'm intrigued. What happened next?"

"Jesus kept his promise. I'm still trying to digest everything he shared with me. I'll do my best to give you a synopsis of what I consider to be the most important topics he covered. You have probably heard much of what I am about to tell you since you were so close to Jesus. But as a novice believer, everything he said to me was eye-opening.

"The first topic Jesus addressed was the nature of God. As a devout Jew, I always took pride in worshipping the one true invisible God that Abraham, Isaac, and Jacob worshipped. Throughout Jewish scripture beginning with the Torah, God made it clear that there is only one God and it is Him.

"Jesus confirmed that there is only one God, but he added a wrinkle that I would never have imagined without his guidance. Jesus revealed that God has existed from eternity as three distinct and co-equal Persons who remain unified as one true God. The three Persons are the Father, His Son Jesus, and the Spirit of God whom he also referred to as the Holy Spirit. The Father created a perfect world, Jesus became a man and died to save a sinful world, and the Holy Spirit brings sinners to saving faith in Jesus.

"Jesus described the nature of God as "one in three and

three in one." He emphasized that this should not be confused with "one who does three different things" or "three who act in concert but remain separate" which are ways to explain God rationally but incorrectly.

"I admitted that I didn't understand how "one" and "three" could be used to describe the same God. Jesus assured me that this was a mystery beyond human understanding and had to be accepted by faith and not by reason. However, knowing about the nature of God would be essential to my ability to teach the truth about Him.

"The next topic Jesus covered was God's involvement in creation of the universe. He gave me a brief glimpse of how it happened. At a word from God the Father, all of the stars and planets burst out of a single point of nothingness and took their places in the skies. The world in which we live became the focus of God's attention. He equipped the earth with everything necessary for life and created all manner of living creatures. Finally, God made a man and woman in His image to supervise His creation. Everything was perfect including the relationship between God and the humans He made. I was in awe of what God had done.

"The next topic was not as uplifting as the first two. Jesus showed me a series of images of how sin originated. I saw Satan being expelled from Heaven prior to the creation of the world because he desired to be equal to God. I witnessed the moment when Satan, disguised as a snake, convinced Eve to eat the forbidden fruit and give some to her husband in order to be like God. From that time on, humans were doomed to lives filled with pain and sorrow. Life would end in death followed by an eternity of punishment. I was astonished to see that blind ambition, in this case an irrational desire to emulate God, was the root cause of every sin that followed.

"Continuing with the same topic, Jesus showed me more images of sin and its consequences. I saw the murder of Abel by his brother Cain. I saw the flood that destroyed all mankind other than Noah and his family. I saw generation after generation of Israelites and Jews defeated by their enemies and forced into exile because they worshipped other gods. He showed me many more instances too numerous to mention.

"At that point I asked if God knew in advance that sin would spoil His perfect creation. Jesus replied that God is all-knowing. My next question was why, with this knowledge, did God create the world in the first place.

"Jesus replied that the love of God is beyond understanding but compared it to a husband and wife deciding to have children. They know in advance that there will be pain in childbirth and difficulties in raising a child, yet they still choose to produce offspring who are theirs to love, to teach, and to carry on the family name.

"To further answer my question, Jesus added that although God knew humans would sin, He also knew in advance that they could be brought back to Him. Bringing mankind back into perfect communion with God was the mission the Father assigned to His Son. Jesus willingly became the sinless sacrifice required to make sinners blameless in the sight of God. This was the only way that sinners could live in God's perfect presence after they die.

"The last topic Jesus addressed was the successful completion of the mission he had been assigned. He explained the need for him to leave the glory of Heaven and come to earth as both God and man. He had to be God to remain sinless and become a man in order to die.

"Jesus showed me snippets of his life on earth from his birth in a stable in Bethlehem, to his ministry in Galilee and Judea, to his suffering and death on a cross, to his resurrection from the grave. Throughout his life, Jesus was tempted by Satan but refused to sin. In the end, Satan was defeated when Jesus died and rose again. This fulfilled his mission on earth and allowed Jesus to return to Heaven to prepare a place where all believers will join him in everlasting glory."

"That is quite a history lesson with a bit of the future added in," remarked Simon. "What else did Jesus reveal to you?"

"Jesus put a great deal of emphasis on how to get to Heaven. It was certainly a different approach than I had been taught as a young Jew. He told me that living with God forever in Heaven is not dependent on anything sinners can do on their own. Keeping the Mosaic Law and offering animal sacrifices in the Temple are no longer required since he was the complete and final sacrifice necessary to forgive sins. He said that efforts to offset past sins by doing good are doomed to failure and attempts to avoid sinning in the future will be futile.

"Jesus made it clear to me that the only way for sinful people to become acceptable to a perfect God is through him. The shedding of his blood on the cross freed sinners from the otherwise disastrous consequences of their sins. Jesus assured me that everyone who believes these truths is forgiven completely and unconditionally. That will be my message to those who God allows me to reach.

"Jesus also said that in spite of the forgiveness we have been granted, God still desires that sinners live a life of obedience.

Once a person becomes a true believer, he or she is expected to obey God out of gratitude for being forgiven. Motivation to do the will of God should result from thankfulness rather than fear of punishment or desire for reward."

"Jesus certainly provided you with a roadmap for sinners to enter Heaven. How did you feel after hearing what Jesus told you?"

"I felt the weight of the world lifted from my shoulders. When I was baptized in Damascus, you assured me that my sins were forgiven. But I still worried that I needed to do something more to make amends for my role in persecuting believers.

"Jesus revealed that all my past, present, and future sins were paid for. Nothing I do on my own can make me blameless in the eyes of God. Jesus already accomplished all that is necessary. This realization fills me with joy, and nothing short of death can keep me from sharing the good news with the entire world."

"Saul, I was greatly moved by your account. Jesus has provided you with insights that our church leaders, including me, have failed to fully grasp. Most importantly, Jesus has revealed to you that believing in him is the only path to forgiveness and eternal life with God in Heaven."

"I'm glad that you believe that Jesus spoke to me. I am a new believer and we haven't known each other for a long time, so I wouldn't have blamed you for doubting what I just told you. But I know what I saw and heard, and I know it was Jesus who revealed it to me."

"Well said, Saul. I have one more question that I need to ask. You said that this encounter with Jesus happened about a month ago. We have corresponded at least once since then. Why didn't you bring this up earlier?"

"I could have written you right after it happened. However, I didn't want to tell you about the revelation until we could meet in person so you had the opportunity to ask questions. I was planning to come to Jerusalem to see you if you hadn't come here first."

"What you heard from Jesus is truly life changing. I'm relieved that even though your progress here might seem slow, Jesus has provided you with the encouragement to move forward. What you learned from Jesus will keep you motivated wherever you go."

"Yes, Simon, I am blessed. Jesus has given me a running start, but it is only the beginning of the race. I look forward to witnessing wherever he leads me. Whatever happens, I know that God is in control and that His Spirit will guide me in the right direction."

Chapter 7

ARETAS

For the next few weeks, Simon accompanied Saul as he moved about the city. Simon saw that Saul's passion for witnessing remained strong. However, after almost a year in Petra Saul had failed to form personal relationships with his Nabatean audience. Simon understood that the best way to establish credibility with prospective converts is to get to know them personally and show that you sincerely care about them. Saul would need to find a way to develop relationships with the city's Nabatean residents. God would soon provide a solution.

Petra was a city prone to earthquakes. Several fault lines ran through the area and minor tremors were so common that residents ignored them. One afternoon, as Simon and Saul were witnessing near one of the free-standing pagan temples in the center of the city, the earth began to shake violently. Panic set in as the sandstone blocks that formed the four walls of the temple began to crumble causing the wooden roof to collapse.

Many of the worshippers inside were able to escape to safety, but a number of others were not so fortunate. One casualty was a temple priest who was fleeing out of the entrance just as it imploded. His legs were pinned under a large piece of timber, and he was screaming for help. Without hesitation, Simon and Saul ran to the man, lifted the wooden beam off his legs, and carried him to a safer location.

The man cried out in pain as Simon lifted the robe gently from his right leg. A fractured bone was protruding through his skin, and blood was seeping from the wound. He replaced the robe so the man wouldn't see it. "Try to stay calm," Simon advised. "We are here to help you."

The man recognized Saul. "Aren't you the one who is perverting our people with false claims regarding a foreign god?" he asked. "Why are you helping a Nabatean priest?"

Saul replied, "We are followers of the only true God who loves everyone He created, even those who don't know Him yet."

"Tell me, how bad is my leg?" the man pleaded. "The pain was unbearable a moment ago, but now I can't feel anything."

"You are seriously injured," answered Simon. "Your leg is shattered, and you are losing blood."

"Is there anything you can do for me?" asked the priest. "I'm afraid I am about to die."

"There is something that can be done," answered Simon. "But it won't be because of us. I can call on the name of Jesus, the one of whom Saul and I testify. He can give us the ability to heal you."

"I'm not sure I have a choice," the priest said. "I could pray to my gods, but I've never seen them actually heal someone. If your God can do so, then prove it to me."

Simon reached down and placed his hand on the man's forehead. "In the name of Jesus who has saved us by his suffering and death, let this man's leg be made whole again. Open his heart to believe in you."

The priest looked up at them in amazement. "I can feel my leg again, and there isn't any pain." He sat up and lifted his robe. The leg that had been crushed was just as it had been before the earthquake.

"It appears your God has listened to your prayer," the priest continued. "I can't thank you and your Jesus enough. But I implore you, don't stop now. There must be others inside the temple who need help."

As he spoke, an aftershock hit the city. It wasn't as strong as the first quake but strong enough to dislodge more blocks from the weakened walls. Simon, Saul, and the priest made their way into the rubble to help victims still trapped inside.

"You are commanded to appear before King Aretas. You and your friend need to come with us right now." A Nabatean army officer along with several of his men were standing at the door of Saul's rented apartment.

Seeing that he had no choice in the matter, Saul went back into the apartment to get Simon. "What is this about?" asked Simon as they walked out the door. "He wouldn't tell me," replied Saul. "But a prayer for our safety would be in order."

The soldiers led the two men through the city to the palace of King Aretas IV. Like most other free-standing structures in Petra, it was built with sandstone blocks carved out of the cliffs surrounding the city. A high wall encompassed the palace grounds and one gate led into it. Once they passed through the gate, the contrast between the mostly barren landscape of the city and the lush grass, trees, and plants within the walls of the palace was like emerging from dark to light. Water from the surrounding mountains was transported to the palace by a series of aqueducts that also supplied water to the rest of the city.

Simon and Saul were led into the palace and ushered into a large room. At the opposite side of the room King Aretas sat on his throne, a scepter in his right hand. The king summoned the two men to him.

"I've heard some amazing things about you," the King declared. "One of our priests testified that you miraculously healed his broken leg during the earthquake. He and other witnesses saw you heal additional victims who had been injured. I was told that you gave credit to one of your gods. Tell me about him."

"Your majesty," responded Simon, "we worship only one God. He created the earth and the sky and all living creatures. When God did so, everything was perfect just as He is. But the man and woman He created, the ancestors of all mankind, disobeyed Him. As a result of their disobedience, death came into the world, and all people were doomed to eternal punishment after they die.

"However, God still loved the humans He created. He sent His Son named Jesus to earth to become a man. Jesus suffered and died on behalf of everyone who has ever lived or will live. In other words, although he was sinless, he endured the punishment for sin that all mankind deserved. After three days in the grave, God raised Jesus from the dead to show that He has power over death. Now everyone who believes in Jesus will also be resurrected after death and live with God forever."

"That is an extraordinary account," Aretas stated. "How do you know all of this happened?"

"I know this because I followed Jesus for three years as one of his disciples," Simon replied. "I saw him perform more miracles than I could count. I heard him declare that he was the Son of God sent to save the world. Many of us saw him crucified on a Roman cross. Hundreds of us saw him after he was raised from the dead. The risen Jesus spoke to us and ate with us. Finally, I and other disciples watched him ascend into the sky. He told us he would return one day to take us to be with him forever."

"Your God is not much different than the gods that Nabateans worship," stated the King. "Our gods can appear in human form when they have a reason to do so. They care enough about us to make us one of the great kingdoms of the world. Years ago, we were able to defeat the powerful Greek army when it tried to take over our city. Now we are a dynasty that stretches all the way from Damascus in the north to the Red Sea to the south. Our gods have helped make us a wealthy and prosperous nation."

"Your majesty," interjected Saul. "Unlike my friend Simon, I did not have the opportunity to follow Jesus when he was on earth. In fact, I despised him so much that I persecuted those who believed in him. It wasn't until Jesus spoke to me directly from the sky that I realized he is my Lord and Savior. I became a believer, and since then I have tried to convince others to believe in him as well. I know that Jesus is the only way that anyone can be saved from eternal punishment after they die."

"That is an interesting story that some might consider plausible," replied the King. "But I know, based on our success as a world power, that Nabateans don't need any gods other than those of our fathers. However, it appears that you and your Jesus have an extraordinary ability to heal.

"The reason I brought you here today is that my grandson was born deaf. Consequently, he cannot speak intelligibly. He is now twelve years old. Over the years he has been treated by our finest physicians, but they have not been able to help him. Our priests have offered sacrifices on his behalf, but our gods have not yet answered their prayers. When I heard about the healing you did after the earthquake, I brought you here to see if you might be able to cure his deafness. I will pay you any sum of money if you can do so."

"Your majesty, I know that Jesus can heal your grandson," stated Simon. "However, Saul and I would not desire or accept any reward, monetary or otherwise. We only hope that after you see for yourself that Jesus has the power to heal, you will allow us to freely share our belief in Jesus with your fellow Nabateans."

"You have my word," replied the King. "I'll send for my grandson, Aeneas, and his mother immediately. In the meantime, tell me more about this Jesus in whom you believe so strongly."

A few minutes later, the boy and his mother appeared and were summoned to the throne. "Phasaelis, my dear daughter, these men are from Judea and have been staying in Petra for a time," explained Aretas. "I brought them to the palace because they restored several seriously injured people to health after the recent earthquake. I questioned them a little while ago, and they seem confident that they can cure Aeneas with the help of their God named Jesus."

"Father, I appreciate your thoughtfulness," replied Phasaelis. "But you and I both know that we have done everything possible to help my son. Our gods are the most powerful in the world and they haven't responded to our prayers. Our physicians are the most advanced anywhere and they cannot help him. Why would two foreigners be able to cure Aeneas?"

"Your majesty, with your permission I would like to answer your daughter's question," Simon offered. "You both complained that your gods have not listened to your prayers. Our God is not like that. He always hears our prayers. Jesus told us that whatever we ask God in his name will be given to us. While he was on earth, Jesus performed miracles that no mere human could do. He healed dozens of men and women suffering from all sorts of ailments including deafness. He also walked on water, calmed a storm, turned water into wine, and fed thousands of people with only a few pieces of bread and a handful of fish. Jesus also brought several people back from the dead. One of them was a close friend of mine named Lazarus. After accomplishing all of these things, Jesus gave up his life so that sinful mankind could live with him forever in a place of total joy and happiness called Heaven.

"At Jesus' direction, Saul and I and hundreds of other believers are telling the world about him just as we are sharing it with you today. Jesus has given us the power to perform miracles so that people will believe in him. If you permit us, we will show you the power of Jesus by healing your son. Perhaps you and your entire household will become believers as well."

"That is a very bold claim," observed Phasaelis. "You are not the first to promise a cure, but you are the first to give credit to your God and not yourself. That gives me hope that the impossible might become possible."

"Does that mean you will allow Jesus to heal your son?" asked Saul.

Phasaelis looked up at her father who nodded his consent. "Yes," she said, "I want you to open up his ears."

Simon stood facing the boy and placed his hands on each ear. He prayed, "Father in Heaven, you brought us here to bear witness to Your power over all things. We are in the presence of a powerful king who rules over a mighty nation. We ask that You show him that You are the only true God, and that You have control over all things. Please give this boy the gift of hearing. In the name of Jesus, we ask it."

Simon removed his hands from Aeneas' ears. His mother, who was standing directly behind the boy, spoke his name. He turned in the direction of the first sound he ever heard and saw that it came from his mother. Aeneas hugged his mother tightly. After seeing his grandson cured, King Aretas called out in a loud voice, "May the God of Simon and Saul be praised!"

"This is truly a miracle," exclaimed Phasaelis, tears flowing down her cheeks. "How can I thank you?"

"As you said earlier, the impossible did become possible,"

exclaimed Simon. "Jesus healed your son, not us. All we did was ask him for help and believed that he would."

King Aretas called one of his courtiers to the throne. "I want you to publish a decree and distribute it throughout the kingdom. I declare that from this time forward, the God of Simon and Saul shall be worshipped in every Nabatean temple from this day forth. He will have equal standing with Dushara, the sun god; Al-Quam, god of the moon; and Al-Uzza, the goddess of stars."

"Did I hear you say you worship three gods?" asked Saul.

"We have many other gods, but these three are our supreme beings," answered Aretas.

"That is very interesting," Saul responded. "We worship only one God, but He exists as three persons we call the Father, Son, and Holy Spirit. It is a mystery that only God can understand. The Father is the person who created the world and everything in it. Jesus is the Son of the Father who came to earth to save sinners. The Holy Spirit is the one who brings people to faith in God. They are three co-equal persons who exist as one God."

"Perhaps my decree should be modified to declare that the 'three in one' god shall be worshipped by all Nabateans," suggested Aretas.

"Allowing us to tell your countrymen about our God is all we ask," Simon stated. "Perhaps one day you will recognize that our God is the only true God."

From that day on, Simon and Saul were treated as celebrities in Petra. Simon stayed with Saul for another month before returning to Jerusalem. During that time, a number of Nabateans came to faith. Saul remained in Petra teaching and performing miracles, all the while giving glory to God for any success he might have.

Chapter 8

JERUSALEM

After Saul lived and worked in Petra for nearly three years, God prompted him to move on from there. A small but faithful congregation of Nabatean believers had been established. Saul believed that the body of believers would grow in his absence. He promised to correspond with them regularly to address any concerns or questions they might have.

Saul notified Simon of his plans. He would first return to Damascus. After spending a few months with Ananias and the other believers, he would travel to Jerusalem to visit Simon and get acquainted with the other Apostles.

Simon alerted the church leaders of Saul's plans. Peter and

James, the brother of Jesus, agreed to a meeting but expressed their concerns. Even though Simon had given them glowing reports about Saul, it was difficult to erase the memories of his involvement in the persecution of believers.

Sensing their uncertainty, Simon asked his friend Barnabas to vouch for Saul. Barnabas, a native of Cyprus who became a respected member of the Way, happened to be in Damascus shortly after Saul's conversion. Barnabas told Peter and James how impressed he was with Saul's passionate witness for Jesus and encouraged them to warmly welcome Saul into Jerusalem's community of believers.

Saul arrived in Jerusalem the day before the scheduled meeting and stayed the night in Simon's home. During the evening meal, Simon informed Saul of the apprehension that Peter and James expressed. Saul offered a prayer that God would help the Apostles understand and embrace the mission that Jesus had assigned him.

The meeting was attended by Saul, Simon, and most of the other Apostles. Several of them had already left for the mission field. Shortly after the meeting, Simon and Saul returned home and shared their thoughts about the outcome. Saul wondered whether or not they believed his account of the revelations he received in Petra. Simon assured Saul that those at the meeting considered Saul's conversion to be genuine and believed that his passion for witnessing was sincere.

The next morning, Peter invited Saul to stay at his house for a few days so they could become better acquainted. His visit with Peter lasted two weeks. During that time, Peter introduced Saul to other members of the Way who warmly welcomed him into the fellowship.

As he had done in Damascus and Petra, Saul witnessed boldly for Jesus in Jerusalem. Enough time had passed since parting ways with the Sanhedrin that Saul was able to teach in public without incident. The Holy Spirit worked through Saul and brought many non-believers to faith.

However, not everyone received Saul's message with an open mind. A group of Hellenists arrived in Jerusalem to celebrate a religious festival called Sukkot. Hellenists were Jews who had relocated to Greece and adopted the Greek language and culture but still followed the requirements of the Mosaic law. One of the requirements of the law was to observe three pilgrimage festivals every year in person at the Temple in Jerusalem. For Jews living outside Jerusalem, this often meant traveling long distances.

One of the three pilgrimage festivals was Sukkot, also known as the Feast of Booths. Originally established at the time of Moses, Sukkot memorialized the wanderings of the Israelites in the wilderness and gave thanks to God for the autumn harvest.

The other two pilgrim festivals requiring attendance in Jerusalem were Passover and Shavuot. Passover commemorated the liberation of the Israelites from Egypt. Shavuot, also known as the Feast of Weeks or Pentecost, was held seven weeks after Passover and celebrated the giving of the Mosaic law at Mount Sinai and the beginning of the spring wheat harvest.

Five days before the beginning of Sukkot, another Jewish holiday which didn't require a pilgrimage was observed. Yom Kippur, known as the Day of Atonement, was an annual day of fasting during which Temple priests offered sacrifices for the sins of the entire nation. Some of the Hellenists arrived in Jerusalem a week before Sukkot in order to observe Yom Kippur.

At the time of Moses, Yom Kippur was commemorated by

sprinkling the blood of a goat on the altar in the Tabernacle. After the sacrifice, the High Priest laid his hands on the head of a second goat and confessed to God all of the sins the Israelites had committed that year. In this manner the sins of the people were transferred onto the second goat, referred to as the "scapegoat." The scapegoat was led out of the Israelite camp into the desert never to return, symbolizing that the sins of the people had been forgiven and forgotten by God.

By the time of Saul's visit to Jerusalem, Yom Kippur was observed in much the same way. However, the second goat was no longer led out into the desert to die. Instead, the scapegoat was taken from the Temple to a cliff outside the city and thrown to its death in the valley below.

On the day of Yom Kippur, Saul, along with Simon and several other Apostles stood preaching under Solomon's Portico on the Temple grounds. Saul proclaimed that sacrifices of goats or any other animals were no longer required because their sins had been paid for by Jesus. He proclaimed that Jesus was the final perfect sacrifice that Jewish prophets had foretold.

Several Hellenist Jews stopped to listen. After hearing Saul profess Jesus as the Messiah, they accused him of being a traitor to the Jewish religion. Saul remained calm and tried to reason with them, appealing to them through the Scriptures that Jesus was the Son of God who came to save the world from sin.

The more Saul spoke, the more vocal the Greek Jews became. Seeing that Saul could not be intimidated, the Hellenists left Solomon's Portico and entered the Temple to present their sacrificial animals to the priests.

Five days after Yom Kippur, the first of seven days of Sukkot began. By then the number of Hellenists in Jerusalem had grown much larger. Saul continued to preach boldly on the Temple grounds despite being persistently interrupted. Saul offered to debate the Hellenist Jews knowing that Greeks enjoyed intellectual sparring. They refused, and their opposition to Saul's teaching intensified.

Heated exchanges continued for several days until one evening Simon answered a knock on his door. The man standing there introduced himself as Alexander, a Hellenist. "I understand that Saul is staying here with you. I have come to visit in secret because I believe what you both are saying about Jesus is true," he stated. "I need to warn Saul that some of my fellow Hellenists are planning to kill him on the last day of Sukkot. I know he has done nothing to deserve death. In fact, he deserves thanks for revealing what Jesus has done."

"Alexander, I am grateful for your concern," interjected Saul who overheard the conversation from the next room. "I am even more thankful that the Holy Spirit has led you to believe in Jesus."

After Alexander left, Simon suggested that they tell Peter and James about the plot. Once the four men got together, they all agreed that using physical violence in order to stop the Hellenists was not an option. Apart from being badly outnumbered, Jesus would not want his followers to resort to bloodshed.

Simon suggested taking Saul somewhere outside Jerusalem until the Hellenist Jews returned home, perhaps in nearby Bethany where Simon was born and raised.

Saul proposed another solution, "This might be a good time for me to visit my family in Tarsus. I haven't seen my parents for years. I can work in my father's tentmaking shop while witnessing to the people there. In God's time I can return to

Jerusalem or go wherever else He sends me."

"We would miss you here," said James. "You have contributed greatly to everyone's understanding of God's love for us in Christ. But if you feel the urge to return home, we pray God's blessing on you."

Simon added, "You will need to leave right away. The Hellenists could move their plans up a day or two. It would be best for you to leave tonight after dark. I will accompany you to Caesarea Maritima where you can find a ship that is bound for Tarsus. No one except the four of us will know where you have gone."

"Secretly escaping from cities after dark is getting to be a habit I'd like to break," joked Saul. "I appreciate your help and most of all your friendship."

"Be sure to keep in touch," said Peter. "We want to know how things are going in Tarsus. Simon and the rest of us will keep you informed of events here in Jerusalem."

Chapter 9

ANTIOCH

After Saul left for Tarsus, animosity between Jews and the Way lessened. The church used this opportunity to take the Gospel message to communities outside of Jerusalem. God used the Apostle Peter to lay the groundwork for this effort.

In a dream while visiting the seaside town of Joppa, Peter was told to eat food considered unclean according to Mosaic law. When Peter refused, he was told that what was formerly deemed unclean was now clean. The significance of the dream became clear when he was invited to the home of a Roman centurion in Caesarea Maritima. Peter accepted the invitation and shared the good news about Jesus with the centurion's family and friends.

They were all baptized and visibly received the Holy Spirit.

Peter reported his experience to other leaders in the church. Most were overjoyed that Gentiles had heard the message of salvation through Jesus. However, a few criticized Peter for associating with uncircumcised Gentiles. After learning that the Holy Spirit had filled the Gentiles with the same faith to the same degree as Jewish converts, the naysayers adopted Peter's point of view.

At Peter's prompting, leadership of the Way in Jerusalem decided to send Barnabas, the man who had earlier vouched for Saul, to Antioch in Syria. Antioch, located 300 miles north of Jerusalem, was one of the largest and most important cities in the Roman Empire. Founded during the reign of Alexander the Great, Antioch became a center of commerce due to its location on the major trade route from Asia Minor in the north to Egypt in the south.

During the persecution of Jesus' followers by Saul, many of them fled Jerusalem and settled in Antioch. When Barnabas arrived, he discovered a faithful group of fellow believers as well as an untapped mission field. He encouraged Antioch believers to reach out to the Gentile majority in their community. As a result, the church in Antioch grew appreciably. It occurred to Barnabas that Antioch would be an ideal environment for Saul, who had been designated by Jesus to reach out to the Gentiles, to witness.

Barnabas wrote to Simon asking where Saul had gone after leaving Jerusalem years earlier. Simon, Peter, and James had not disclosed his location out of concern for Saul's safety. Barnabas made it clear to Simon that Antioch presented a golden opportunity for Saul to accomplish what Jesus asked him to do. Simon responded that Saul was living at his parent's home in Tarsus working as a tentmaker and evangelist. Simon notified Saul to expect a visitor from Antioch.

Barnabas wasted no time making the 90-mile trip from Antioch to Tarsus. Tarsus was the capital city of Cilicia, a Roman province in the southeast corner of Asia Minor on the Mediterranean Sea. Tarsus, like Antioch, was an important center of commerce and culture. Saul was born there thirty-seven years earlier to Jewish parents. Because Tarsus was considered a "free city" by Rome, Saul was granted Roman citizenship at birth.

Barnabas stayed in Tarsus with Saul for two days. During that time, they discussed the mission opportunities God had presented to the church in Antioch. The men prayed together, asking God for direction in accordance with His will. After much soul searching, Saul agreed to accompany Barnabas to Antioch.

The journey to Antioch was emotional for both men. Barnabas was ecstatic that he would have a solid partner to help spread the Good News. Saul looked forward to starting a new chapter in fulfilling the mission Jesus had assigned him. Saul felt comfortable with Barnabas and believed the two of them would work well together. The only downside for Saul was saying goodbye to his family and the community of believers in Tarsus.

After settling into his new home, Saul wrote to Simon expressing his excitement over witnessing for Christ in Antioch. People from all over the world travelled through the city in order to trade their goods, and many remained there permanently. Consequently, the population was racially and culturally diverse with Greeks, Romans, Jews, Arabs, and Egyptians living in relative peace and prosperity. It was an ideal environment to teach and baptize people of all nations.

During the year following Saul's arrival, the church in

Antioch grew from several hundred believers to nearly a thousand. Residents of Antioch initially regarded the believers as a fringe group of Jews but soon recognized that members of the Way were a distinct religious body. To distinguish them from the Jews, people living in Antioch began calling believers "Christians" meaning "belonging to Christ." The name caught on quickly and became a badge of honor for followers of Jesus throughout the Roman Empire.

Chapter 10

PERSECUTION

While things were going well for the congregation in Antioch, the same could not be said for the church in Jerusalem. Persecution of Jesus' followers had historically been initiated and carried out by the Jewish Sanhedrin. That was about to change.

Herod Agrippa I was the grandson of Herod the Great and nephew of Herod Antipas. Antipas was the king who beheaded John the Baptist. Because of his social and political connections with Roman Emperors Caligula and Claudius, Agrippa was named king over the province of Judaea which included the regions of Judea, Samaria, and Galilee. He was also given jurisdiction over several other nearby regions.

Agrippa was a Jew by birth. Although he spent most of his youth in Rome, Agrippa was familiar with Jewish customs and traditions. Whether out of sincere religious conviction or an attempt to curry favor with his Jewish subjects, Agrippa strictly followed Mosaic laws, regularly worshipped in the Jerusalem Temple, brought sacrificial offerings to the priests, and observed Jewish festivals. However, his display of Jewishness was not enough to win over the general population. The citizenry wanted lower taxes and removal of Roman troops, both of which were out of Agrippa's control and not in his best interests.

Unable to win the support of the masses, Agrippa decided to ingratiate himself with the Sanhedrin. He knew that the Sanhedrin had sentenced Jesus to death a decade earlier and over the following years tried to eliminate any trace of his existence by persecuting his followers. The attempt failed, and the Sanhedrin grudgingly coexisted with the Jesus movement. Agrippa decide to pick up where the Sanhedrin had left off.

Agrippa's first targets were the apostles James and John, sons of a Galilean fisherman named Zebedee. Agrippa learned that the brothers were two of the three disciples that Jesus considered his closest confidants. Peter was the other.

The brothers shared a modest home in the Lower City southwest of the Temple. After Jesus was crucified, Mary, Jesus' mother, lived with John and his brother until her death several years later.

Agrippa posted observers near their home to track their daily movements. The observers noted that after the evening meal, James and John would usually walk a mile or two together through the city streets and then return home. One night as they walked, the brothers were surrounded by a group of men they didn't recognize.

"Come with us," one of the men ordered. "You are both under arrest."

"What have we done?" asked John incredulously. "You must have us confused with someone else."

"You have been ordered to appear before King Agrippa in the morning," the men said brusquely. "You will be held in prison until your trial."

"Of what have we been accused?" asked James.

"You have been charged with subverting the Jewish religion by promoting the teachings of a convicted criminal who was crucified for calling himself the Son of God," they replied.

"You are correct that we are followers of Jesus who was crucified and who is the Son of God, but he was not a criminal," stated John. "We have been allowed to worship him without interference for years. Why are charges being brought against us at this time?"

"I am not in a position to question the king, and neither are you," said the men. "Save your questions for tomorrow when you stand trial."

James and John were taken to the Jerusalem prison, the same place where Simon's friend Lazarus was killed. They spent the night in prayer, asking God to keep them safe and submitting themselves to His will. The next morning the brothers were escorted to Agrippa's palace, known as Herod's Palace, located in the Upper City.

The palace was built by Herod the Great, Agrippa's grandfather. It was an enormous structure built mostly of marble, second in grandeur only to the Temple. Two main buildings with accommodations for several hundred guests were separated by a courtyard filled with gardens, ponds, and trees.

Agrippa was sitting on his throne in a massive room used to conduct judicial functions. The brothers were ordered to stand in front of him. "I've heard quite a bit about you from my friends in the Sanhedrin," Agrippa began.

"Your majesty, the members of the Sanhedrin do not consider us friends," remarked James. "If they have accused us of any crimes, I hope you give us a chance to defend ourselves."

"You are correct in your assessment of how they feel about you," noted Agrippa. "Ever since your rabbi, Jesus, began teaching contrary to what Jewish scriptures teach, the Sanhedrin considered him a heretic. They had him crucified, but you and his other followers persisted in perpetuating his memory. The Sanhedrin's attempts to quiet you have failed so far, but they remain determined to do so. I consider myself a pious Jew and am inclined to side with my fellow Jews. However, as you requested, I am willing to give you a chance to defend yourselves before I pronounce judgement."

"Your majesty, you say that you are a pious Jew," responded John. "Then you must be familiar with the term Messiah which means 'anointed one.' Jewish prophets including Isaiah, Jeremiah, Ezekiel, Zechariah, Micah and even King David pointed to the coming of the Messiah with great anticipation. The good news is that he has already come, and his name is Jesus."

Agrippa countered, "Those same prophets said the Messiah would make the Jewish nation great again. If Jesus had been the

Messiah, he would have freed the Jews from Roman rule, and I wouldn't be here talking to you today."

"Unfortunately, the Jews have a misunderstanding of what the Messiah was sent to do," John stated. "Instead of restoring a kingdom on earth, Jesus made it possible for those who believe in him to be part of his kingdom in Heaven. I understand that you offer regular sacrifices at the Temple. One of those is a sin offering of an unblemished lamb. What if I told you that you don't have to make those sacrifices anymore?

"Christians believe that Jesus, the sinless Son of God, became the complete and final sacrifice for the sins of the entire world when he shed his blood on the cross. He died not only for past sins, he also paid for every sin that mankind will commit in the future. That is why Temple sacrifices are no longer necessary.

"Three days after he died and was buried, Jesus was raised from the dead by his Father. The perfect relationship between God and man that existed in the Garden of Eden has been restored. Those who believe in Jesus as Lord are forgiven and will be resurrected to live in Heaven with him forever. Those who reject Jesus as their Savior will be resurrected to suffer forever in Hell."

"That is a powerful statement," remarked Agrippa. "Unfortunately, you failed to convince me that Jesus was anyone other than an imposter who brainwashed his followers into believing he was the Messiah. As a devout Jew, my relationship with God depends on my obedience to Him as found in the Torah. It is not dependent on allegiance to a dead man.

"After hearing your defense, I have decided what action to take. One of you will remain in prison, and one of you will be released. The one who is released will return to your friends and warn them if they continue to teach about Jesus, the imprisoned brother will face the consequences."

"Your majesty," replied James, "I will stay in prison, and my brother can go free. He will communicate your message, but I am sure that they will refuse to stop teaching about our Lord and Savior. The same ultimatum was given to us in the past. Now, many years later, we are facing the same threat. We do not fear what you or anyone else can do to us because, in either life or death, Jesus is with us."

"Then so be it," said Agrippa. "I will release your brother. He is ordered to return here in two days with an answer to my demand. If his answer is not satisfactory, you will be punished accordingly."

That evening, John called together the Apostles and other leaders of the church. He told them what Agrippa had said and asked for their opinion. To a man, they agreed that they would never stop witnessing for Jesus. They recalled how the crowds reacted to Jesus as he rode triumphantly into Jerusalem a week before his crucifixion. When the Pharisees asked him to quiet the people, Jesus replied that if those praising him were silenced, even the stones would cry out.

The next morning, a day before Herod's deadline, John returned to Agrippa's palace. When asked for his answer to Agrippa's demand, John stated that no one, not even an emperor, could silence Jesus' followers. John asked to see his brother, but Agrippa refused stating that he would see him again soon enough.

That afternoon, John answered a knock at his door. No one was there, but two cloth bags, one much larger than the other, lay outside the entrance. John picked up the smaller bag and looked inside. It was the severed head of his brother James. He didn't need to open the other bag to find out what it contained.

Agrippa sent word to the Sanhedrin that he had executed one of Jesus' favorite disciples. In response, the chief priest, Josephus ben Camydus, and several other members of the Sanhedrin made a personal visit to the palace to praise his efforts. Agrippa was ecstatic. His actions produced the result he hoped they would.

Four weeks after James was executed, Saul and Barnabas arrived in Jerusalem from Antioch. Their arrival coincided with the week of Passover, but they were not there to celebrate the Jewish festival. The two men were bringing food and supplies to the Christians in Jerusalem. A severe famine had impacted the region, and believers in Antioch responded in a spirit of generosity and love. However, the recent murder of James made it clear that famine was not the only threat facing Jerusalem believers.

Simon invited Saul and Barnabas to stay with him while they were in the city. One afternoon, Simon left home to purchase food in the marketplace while Saul and Barnabas remained behind.

Suddenly, the front door flung open and Simon burst into the room. "Peter was arrested by Herod Agrippa's soldiers a few hours ago," he exclaimed. "I heard about it from one of the vendors while I was shopping. Word is spreading quickly throughout Jerusalem."

"I knew it was only a matter of time before Agrippa would

target other Apostles," Saul affirmed. "Although there has been an informal truce between Christians and Jews for nearly a decade, hatred of Jewish leadership toward Christians has been simmering and is now coming to a boil. I'm sure that Agrippa's actions are an effort to get in the good graces of the Sanhedrin. Regrettably, what is happening now is reminiscent of how I persecuted Jesus' followers years ago."

"What happened to James was tragic," sighed Barnabas. "I hope that Peter doesn't experience the same fate. Where have they taken him?"

"He is being held in the same prison that housed James," answered Simon. "I'm afraid Agrippa also plans to execute Peter. I agree with Saul that he is probably trying to curry favor with the Sanhedrin. Agrippa will probably wait to kill Peter until Passover is over to avoid desecrating the Jewish holy week. Maybe we have time to do something to free him. Let's start with prayer."

The night before Peter was to be tried, a large number of Christians met at the home of John Mark's mother. Simon, Saul, and Barnabas were in attendance. Her spacious home served as a safe house during Saul's persecution of believers and now played the same role during Agrippa's purge of church leaders. All prayed together for Peter's safe release, asking that God's will be done.

The solemnity of the moment was interrupted by a loud knock at the front door. The sound of prayers gave way to silence. Fear of discovery by Agrippa's soldiers permeated the air. One of the servant girls named Rhoda, oblivious to potential danger, approached the door and asked, "Who is there?"

"It is me, Peter," a man's voice replied. "Please let me in."

Rhoda recognized the voice as Peter's. But instead of unlocking the door, she ran back into the room where everyone had been praying and shouted, "It's Peter. I heard him outside the door. What should I do?"

"It can't be Peter," someone said. "He's in chains. Agrippa would not have let him out of prison the night before his trial. You must be hallucinating."

"No, I'm not," argued Rhoda. "I heard him with my own ears."

Frustrated that the group doubted her, the servant girl returned to the door and cautiously opened it. Her intuition was confirmed. Rhoda hugged Peter warmly and led him to the prayer group. "Now do you believe me?" she exclaimed. A collective gasp could be heard as Peter stood before them.

Simon spoke up, "How did you get out of that hell hole?"

"It was a miracle," Peter answered. "I was sleeping on the floor of my cell chained between two guards. Outside the cell another guard was keeping watch. Suddenly, an angel poked me in the side and woke me up. My shackles fell away, and the angel told me to get up and follow him. I thought I was dreaming.

"The cell door opened seemingly on its own. We walked past the guards as if they were in a trance. On our way out of the prison we encountered several other prison employees, but they didn't even glance our way as if the angel and I were invisible. The large iron gate that led out of the prison opened, and we walked out into the street. Before I could react, the angel disappeared. I came directly here to let you know that God had freed me."

"Praise the Lord!" exclaimed the group in unison. They embraced Peter and thanked God for delivering him from a probable death sentence. Despite their initial elation, everyone knew that Agrippa would not take Peter's escape lightly. He would use every means at his disposal to recapture him.

Peter had the same mindset as the others. "I should leave Jerusalem for a while, at least until Agrippa calms down," he said. "I didn't expect to get a fair trial, but given what happened to James, I would probably not receive a trial at all."

"Why don't you stay with one of Lazarus' sisters in Bethany?" Simon suggested. "You are familiar with the area and could easily hide outside the town if Agrippa's men searched for you there. Mary still operates the inn with her husband and Martha still owns a pottery shop. Either of them would be happy to house you for a time. You know them well, and they are both very fond of you."

"That's an excellent idea, Simon," Peter responded. "I will leave for Bethany immediately. As soon as Agrippa realizes that I have escaped, his troops will be looking long and hard for me."

"I'll go with you," offered Simon. "Two travelers might attract less attention than one. Agrippa's men will be looking for a lone fugitive."

The next morning a twenty-man cohort of Agrippa's soldiers arrived at the prison to accompany Peter to Agrippa's palace to stand trial. When the prison warden sent for Peter, his assistant returned saying that he found the guards asleep and the prisoner missing from his cell.

The captain of Agrippa's troops was outraged and ordered the warden to bring the guards to him for questioning. None of them could recall anything that happened the previous night, and none of them were quick witted enough to invent a story that might exonerate them. Their fate was sealed. The guards were executed on the spot.

The captain gave orders to his soldiers to find Peter and return him to the prison. An intensive city-wide search turned up nothing. Agrippa was notified of the situation and loudly voiced his displeasure. He had publicized Peter's upcoming trial, expecting to get more accolades from the Sanhedrin. Many of the top Jewish leaders were expected to be at the proceedings as witnesses for the prosecution. Embarrassed to admit the truth, Agrippa left word with the High Priest that the trial was postponed so he could quell an unexpected uprising in Caesarea.

Peter remained hiding in Bethany for two months until Agrippa died of a severe stomach ailment. Many Christians viewed Agrippa's untimely death as an act of God. Instead of appointing a new king, Rome decided to govern Judea directly through Roman procurators. Absent the ego and temperament of Agrippa, the persecution of believers ended abruptly. Peter returned to Jerusalem, and the church came out of hiding to openly proclaim the Gospel.

Chapter 11

ROME

Enabled by the Holy Spirit, most of the Apostles left Jerusalem to share the Gospel in other countries in obedience to Jesus' command to teach all nations. Judas Thaddeus, later known as Jude, went to Persia to preach. Thomas, the disciple who initially doubted Jesus' resurrection, travelled to India. Nathaniel, whom Jesus saw under a fig tree, went to Armenia along with Matthias, the disciple who replaced Judas Iscariot. Andrew, Peter's brother, ministered in Greece. Matthew, the tax collector, relocated to Ethiopia.

During this period, the Christian church in Rome petitioned the church in Jerusalem to provide apostolic leadership in order to sustain and grow the community of believers there. After prayerful consideration and discussions among church leaders, it was decided to send Simon to Rome. He accepted the assignment willingly and immediately began preparations for the journey. The church in Rome was notified that their request had been approved, and the Apostle Simon was sent on his way.

The sea voyage to Italy took a little over three months. It was uneventful with the exception of several stretches of rough seas that are common in the Mediterranean. The ship was loaded with cargo bound directly from Caesarea Maritima to Rome so there was no need to load or unload at various ports along the way. Most of the cargo consisted of jars of olive oil, a product in huge demand in Rome. Olive oil was essential for cooking, fuel for lamps, an ingredient for perfumes, and as a lubricant. Other items on the ship included grain, spices, wine, timber, and marble.

Simon arrived at the port city of Ostia on the west coast of central Italy. Ostia was located at the mouth of the Tiber River about twenty-five miles southwest of Rome. It was the largest seaside port in Italy with over 50,000 residents. Ostia's strategic location made it a hub of commerce as well as a buffer against invaders who might otherwise use the river to attack Rome.

The ship on which Simon sailed to Italy was an ocean-going vessel too large to sail upriver to Rome. As a result, the cargo bound for Rome was unloaded onto barges in Ostia and floated the remainder of the way. Simon paid a small fee and boarded one of the barges.

The leisurely trip up the river provided Simon with a view

of the verdant countryside that flanked the river, a stark contrast to the desert landscape of Judea. The smooth movement of the barge was a pleasant alternative to the sea voyage he had just experienced. Simon's thoughts turned to the church in Rome. Would he find a community of believers living in peace or would he find a church dealing with internal strife and external persecution?

As soon as the barge docked in Rome, Simon went in search of Andronicus and his wife Junia. Andronicus owned a clothing boutique near the Circus Maximus. His shop made garments of all kinds from simple tunics to elaborate togas and stolas. Andronicus and Junia were Jews who migrated to Rome hoping to establish a profitable business there.

Simon became acquainted with the couple years earlier when they traveled from Rome to Jerusalem to observe Passover. Instead of returning home immediately, Andronicus and Junia decided to stay in Jerusalem for seven more weeks to observe Shavuot, also known as Pentecost. Passover and Pentecost were two of the three festivals along with Sukkot that the Law of Moses required Jews to observe annually in Jerusalem.

It was on the day of Pentecost that Andronicus and Julia learned that a man named Jesus had been crucified during Passover and rose from the dead three days later. They heard a man named Peter announce to a huge crowd that Jesus was the Messiah of whom the prophets had testified. The couple were baptized that day along with three thousand others who came to faith after receiving the Holy Spirit.

Before they returned to Rome, Andronicus and Junia wanted to learn everything they could about Jesus so they could tell their friends and relatives about him. The Apostles, including

Simon, were more than pleased to teach them. Subsequently, the husband and wife became two of the original founders of the Christian movement in Rome. In spite of resistance from orthodox Jews, during the years that followed they steadfastly continued to witness for Christ.

It didn't take long for Simon to locate Andronicus' house. "Who is there?" asked Junia responding to the knock at the door.

"It is me, Simon. I just arrived from Jerusalem."

Junia swung the door open and jumped into Simon's arms. "I'm so glad to see you. Andronicus and I owe you and the other Apostles our very souls. I often think of Peter's message on that Pentecost years ago. It's been much too long since we've seen you."

Simon hugged Junia tightly. "I am so happy to see you again. Those days seem like a lifetime away. They were exciting times. But as you know, you owe your souls to the grace of God in Christ. We were just the messengers."

"Andronicus is still at work but should be home shortly. While I make you something to eat, I can fill you in on some of the things happening here in Rome. I was overjoyed when we heard you were coming."

"I appreciate your hospitality. I haven't had anything to eat since I left Ostia."

"When Andronicus and I left you and the other Apostles in Jerusalem and returned to Rome, we were accompanied by about a hundred other Jewish pilgrims who had also been baptized and came to faith. Now there are thousands of followers scattered throughout the city. We are hoping that you can help us become more organized. As we've grown, it is more difficult to avoid false doctrine as well as to efficiently administer aid to our fellow believers in need."

At that moment, Andronicus walked through the front door. His face broke out into a huge smile as he embraced Simon. "If we had known when you were arriving, we would have been there to greet you when you landed in Italy. But since you came by ship, it was impossible to contact each other."

"By the grace of God, I made it safely to Ostia and took a barge the rest of the way. Now that I'm here, I want to assist the church in Rome in any way I can. I'm eager to share Jesus' message of love and forgiveness. I hope to be a source of comfort and strength to all of you."

Three years after reaching Rome, Simon lay in bed reflecting on events that had taken place since his arrival. During this period, the Roman government and its citizens were largely indifferent to the Christian movement. Similar to the residents of Antioch, Romans initially viewed Christianity as an adjunct to the Jewish religion. This allowed the church to grow relatively unimpeded except for opposition by Jews who viewed Jesus and his followers as threats to their orthodoxy.

In the city of one million residents, there were now about 2,500 Christians who worshipped regularly in believers' homes. They read the scriptures, sang hymns, prayed, and partook of the meal that Jesus instituted the night before he was crucified. New converts were baptized and assimilated into the church. Christians supported each other in difficult times. Those who were depressed, anxious, sick, or dying were uplifted by their brothers and sisters in faith.

Throughout his stay in Rome, the community of believers

had taken good care of Simon. He was allowed to live rent free in an apartment building owned by a wealthy fellow Christian. During his travels throughout the city, Simon was regularly invited to share meals with member families. Clothing and other essentials were supplied through member contributions. Virtually all of Simon's material needs were provided free of charge, which allowed him to devote his full time to church matters.

Simon worked hard to earn the benefits he received. He addressed several critical issues to help the church move forward, one of which related to administration. As the church spread throughout the metropolitan area, groups of Christians became isolated from each other. As a result, variations in teachings and practices sprang up.

This might not have presented a problem for an established church, but for a religious movement that was still in its developmental stage, the danger of veering from Christ's teachings was real. Simon saw that centralized leadership was needed. He helped establish a leadership group representing each of the city's geographical districts to coordinate the church's administrative and doctrinal efforts on a citywide basis.

Another issue Simon addressed involved expanding the scope of the mission. The first believers in Rome were Jews who had come to faith during Pentecost. After returning home, they shared with their Jewish friends what they had seen and heard in Jerusalem. From those humble beginnings, the Holy Spirit grew the movement to include other Jews who believed that Jesus was the promised Messiah. Although most Jews in Rome considered Christians as heretics to traditional Judaism, a foothold was established in the city.

Simon reminded the believers in Rome that Jesus wanted

the message of salvation taught to all nations. This encompassed the vast majority of the city's population. Simon encouraged believers to mirror the efforts of his friend Saul, now called Paul, and his companion, Barnabas. Word had reached Rome of their successful missionary efforts to the Gentiles in Asia Minor and Greece.

Simon cautioned that outreach to the Gentiles would not be easy. He used Paul's initial experiences in Petra as an example. Like the Nabateans, Romans believed in a plethora of gods. Few Romans, if any, had a background in Jewish history which pointed to a coming Messiah. The concept of sinning against God's commandments was foreign to them. They were content with their own gods whom they believed had brought them prosperity and world domination.

Simon made it clear to his fellow Christians that witnessing to any non-believer, particularly a Gentile, requires developing a personal caring relationship prior to sharing the Gospel. Creating a relationship based on trust gives credibility to the messenger and the message. The Holy Spirit would accomplish the rest.

In spite of the hurdles that had to be overcome, Simon recognized the tremendous potential that Rome represented for the Christian movement. Rome, its tentacles reaching into nearly every corner of the world, was a potential springboard to spread the Gospel to all nations, just as Jesus had commanded.

Chapter 12

ABIGAIL

During the third year of his stay in Rome, Simon turned forty-two years old. He had never been married or seriously considered it. Looking back, he realized that having a family of his own had not been a priority.

As a boy, Simon was the school bully more interested in intimidating weaker classmates than trying to impress girls. Later he worked with his father as a stonecutter and traveled where work was available. He became a member of the Zealots, an organization that sometimes resorted to violence. Simon was chosen to be one of the Jesus' disciples and travelled with him for three years. After Jesus' return to Heaven, Simon's main priority became spreading the Gospel message even during periods of persecution. None of these lifestyle choices were conducive to having a wife and raising a family.

One evening a month after his forty-second birthday, Simon's priorities shifted dramatically. A worship service had been scheduled in the home of Priscilla and Aquila, a Christian married couple who owned a tentmaking business located near the Circus Maximus. They were Jews who had become believers through the witnessing efforts of Andronicus and Junia.

While waiting for the service to begin, the most beautiful woman Simon had ever seen walked through the door. Her smile immediately brightened the room. After briefly surveying her surroundings, the woman took a seat at the back of the gathering which now numbered a dozen or more believers. Simon had not seen her at any church functions before, and he suspected that this might be her first time attending Christian worship. In any case, he was inexplicably drawn to her.

"Hello, my name is Simon." he said, trying to remain calm while his heart raced wildly. "I don't believe I've had the pleasure of meeting you. Are you new to this group?"

"Yes, I am," she answered timidly, "A friend told me that Christians are people who love and support each other. Those are qualities that appeal to me, so I decided to see for myself. My name is Abigail. I'm the maidservant of Poppaea Sabina, the wife of Rufrius Crispinus. Rufrius is in charge of the Praetorian Guard, the bodyguards who protect Emperor Claudius."

"I'm glad you came tonight. We welcome everyone to join us as we share the good news concerning Jesus, our Lord and Savior. I see that you came here alone. Do you have any other family in the city? We would welcome them to join us as well."

"My family history is a bit complicated. Although I have lived in Rome most of my life, I was born and raised in Jerusalem. When I was ten years old, my uncle led an insurrection attempting to free Jews from Roman rule. The rebellion failed, and many of those involved were imprisoned, including my uncle. Unfortunately, my father was implicated even though he had nothing to do with the uprising. As a result, my parents and I were arrested and shipped to Rome as slaves."

"That's interesting. I was a member of the Zealots, an organization that would have been sympathetic to what your uncle was doing. I might have known your uncle. What was his name?"

"Jesus Barabbas. Later I heard that he was jailed in Jerusalem for a long time and later released by the Roman governor. I believe the governor's name was Pilate. I don't know what happened to my uncle Barabbas after that."

Simon was dumbfounded for a moment. "You are the niece of Barabbas? I didn't know him personally, but I know of him. I was taken aback just now because I realized he played a significant role in the crucifixion of Jesus. Your uncle Barabbas was released by Pontius Pilate as part of God's plan to redeem us from sin."

"After what you just said, I don't know if my uncle is someone I should be proud or ashamed of, but I would like to learn more."

"I don't know anything about Barabbas after his release, but I would be glad to share more about his interaction with Jesus."

"Maybe we can discuss that at a later time. I believe I was telling you about my family history. After we arrived here, I was separated from my mother and father. Rufrius Crispinus, a wealthy young man, purchased me at a slave auction. I performed household tasks and was treated well, perhaps because of my young age.

"I thought my master would never marry, but when he was twenty-nine, he married Poppaea Sabina. She was only fourteen years old at the time. I was appointed to be Poppaea's maidservant. I was twenty by then, and I think she thought of me as an older sister. We became friends in spite of the difference in social status. As a result, Poppaea emancipated me from slavery. I am now a free Roman citizen because of her."

Their conversation was interrupted by the start of the worship service. The order of service incorporated some traditional Jewish synagogue elements including a scripture reading with commentary, prayers, and singing of psalms. Elements added by Christians included the sharing of the Lord's Supper and collection of contributions to help the needy.

"That was probably a lot to take in at one time," Simon commented after the service concluded. "You said you were only ten years old when you were taken from Jerusalem. I don't suppose you recognize much of what went on here tonight."

"Actually, it was not that long ago. The worship service brought back pleasant memories of my family in the synagogue. I especially recall worshipping one God, a far cry from the plethora of gods the Romans venerate. I must admit, however, that I have no familiarity with Jesus. The friend I spoke of earlier tried to explain Jesus to me, but I couldn't grasp what she meant. Perhaps you could help me with that."

"I would be glad to. But it is getting late, and I'm sure you need to get home."

"Poppaea allows me time off one day a week. I chose today in order to come here. I'm glad that I did, and I look forward to meeting more Christians. It appears my friend gave me some good advice."

"if it isn't too presumptuous on my part, may I escort you home? It's not safe for young ladies to walk alone at night. On the way, we can talk more about Jesus."

"I would like that."

After returning to his apartment, Simon reflected on what had happened that night. He realized that he had not wanted the evening to end. No woman had ever affected him like Abigail did. He couldn't wait to see her again.

After a relatively brief courtship, Simon and Abigail were married the following spring. The engagement didn't follow Jewish tradition, but not by choice. Since Abigail had no idea where her parents were after the family was separated, Simon could not ask her father for permission to marry his daughter. Simon and her father could not sign a *ketubah*, a marriage contract binding him to her during the engagement period. The wedding ceremony was, on the other hand, typically Jewish. Consummation of the marriage was followed by a five-day celebration of eating, drinking, and dancing attended by many of the Christians living in Rome.

Marriage agreed with Simon, and he was able to continue his work for the church in Rome more effectively than before. Abigail was equally happy with married life but had to make several adjustments to her work life. Ever since being purchased as a slave, she had lived in servant quarters on the Crispinus property. Later, as Poppaea's maidservant, Abigail was on call day or night to meet her mistress's needs. That would have to change.

Soon after she and Simon were engaged, Abigail approached Poppaea and announced their wedding plans. Poppaea offered her congratulations, but Abigail could tell that she was troubled and asked what was wrong.

"I'm concerned you might leave your employment here," Poppaea admitted. "I depend on you for so much and, even more importantly, I consider you my friend. Although I have given you your freedom and you are legally able to go elsewhere, I hope you would consider staying."

"I appreciate your kind words and the kindness that you have shown me over the years. I, too, consider you to be my friend," Abigail replied. "However, you must understand that I need to be with my husband. Living here and constantly being at your bidding will not allow me to be a wife and, if God wills, a mother. I would love to stay in your employ if there is some way to make it work for both of us."

Poppaea paused a moment and then responded, "There might be a solution to satisfy us both. I admit I have been spoiled. By living at my residence, you have been at my beck and call every hour of the day and night. What if you were to arrive here each morning at dawn and leave each evening at dusk? I will pay you a fair wage for your time. You can take time off with prior notification. If I don't need your services for a time, you would not be required to be here at all. Does that type of arrangement sound agreeable to you?"

"Yes, you are being very generous," replied Abigail. "I would like to discuss this with my fiancé before committing, but I believe he will support my desire to remain in service to you."

"I will discuss this with my husband as well," said Poppaea.

"Rufrius should have no problem with the change since you work directly for me. Besides, he would no longer have to bear the cost of feeding and housing you."

Soon after Simon and Abigail were married, the religious landscape in Rome changed dramatically. Ever since the first believers returned to Rome, orthodox Jews actively opposed Christians and their message. The animosity grew in the years that followed as the Christian movement expanded. Ultimately, riots and violent confrontations with Christians instigated by the Jews erupted in the city.

The Roman government practiced tolerance with religious groups throughout the Empire as long as Roman gods were not denigrated. However, Rome would not tolerate disruption of the peace and calm it had so carefully cultivated. Emperor Claudius had enough of the troublesome Jews. His solution was to banish them from Rome.

Unfortunately, Christians of Jewish ancestry were considered by Claudius to be Jews and therefore subject to exile. Since the majority of Christians in Rome were Jewish converts, the number of Christians remaining in the city declined dramatically. Many stalwart believers, including Andronicus and Junia as well as Priscilla and Aquila, were forced to leave their homes and businesses for an indefinite period, perhaps never to return.

The edict presented a dilemma for Simon and Abigail. Abigail became a Roman citizen when Poppaea emancipated her from slavery. Consequently, she was not subject to banishment even though she had been born Jewish. Simon, on the other hand, was required to leave Rome. The newlyweds could remain together only by relocating outside of Rome.

The couple went to God in prayer, asking for a way for Simon to remain in the city. God heard their prayer, and they developed a strategy that looked promising. The first step was to convince Poppaea and her husband, Rufrius, that Jewish Christians were victims and not instigators of the religious unrest plaguing Rome. The second step was to convince Rufrius to make a personal appeal to Emperor Claudius on Simon's behalf.

Miraculously, Simon was granted an exemption from the edict. In addition, Poppaea appeared close to adopting Christianity in her life. Despite having no prior exposure to the Gospel, she appeared to grasp the concept of sin, the importance of forgiveness, and the need for someone other than herself to make payment for her sins. She also seemed to agree with the possibility of resurrection of the dead.

Although she didn't abandon her belief in Roman gods, Poppaea declared that she considered Christianity a legitimate religion. A seed had been planted that, with the help of the Holy Spirit, might mature in the future.

After Simon was cleared to remain in Rome, he reasoned that his leadership role in the Christian community would change. Christians of Jewish ancestry had been banished, and Gentile Christians were left to carry on the work of the church. Although there was no longer opposition from orthodox Jews, evangelism efforts needed to be focused on individuals who worshipped Roman gods and had no familiarity with concepts such as a Messiah. In addition, the Roman government frowned on activities that would cause its citizens to abandon the official religion of Rome.

Simon was confident that Gentiles who had already become Christians would stay faithful. However, he was concerned that church growth might stagnate. To his surprise, the number of non-believers coming to faith each month was greater than before the edict. Gentile Christians, who had often been considered second class by their Jewish Christian counterparts, were now the drivers of church governance and growth, and they made the most of the opportunity.

The exile of Jews from Rome lasted five years until Claudius died, and the edict was repealed by his successor, Emperor Nero. At the start of their exile, Priscilla and Aquila relocated their tent making business from Rome to Corinth. Two years later, they met the Apostle Paul in Corinth during his second missionary journey. When he moved on, they traveled with him to Ephesus in Asia Minor where they established another business. The couple returned to Rome as soon as the edict was lifted. Not surprisingly, many of the other Jewish Christians who left Rome, including Andronicus and Junia, either delayed their return or never went back.

The banished Christians who returned to Rome found the church they left nearly unrecognizable. Most members were now Gentile converts. To Simon's credit, none of the changes were doctrinal. As leader of the church during the five-year exile, he made sure that Gentile Christians in Rome continued in the true faith.

Changes that returning Jewish Christians discovered were mainly cultural. Before the exile, Jewish believers retained many of the traditions and practices of Judaism. They clung to Mosaic laws such as circumcision and prohibition against eating certain foods. During the exile, Gentile Christians felt free to remain uncircumcised and eat and drink whatever they desired.

The culture clash caused increasing division within the church in Rome. The Christian community that had once been united by their common faith was separating into factions based on divergent practices. Simon understood the gravity of the situation and sought guidance from Jerusalem.

A few months after making his inquiry, Simon received a letter from James, the brother of Jesus and the recognized leader of the Christian movement. James informed Simon that five years earlier a leadership council had convened in Jerusalem to address this matter. The council concluded that all Christians, particularly Gentiles, were no longer bound by the majority of Mosaic Law including circumcision and dietary restrictions. However, the council did retain bans on eating blood, meat containing blood, and meat from strangled animals as well as prohibitions against idol worship and sexual immorality. The council's decision was transmitted to all of the Chrisitan churches throughout the Roman Empire.

Simon wondered why the church in Rome had not received notification years earlier. He concluded that the news might have been delivered but overlooked during the turmoil created by Claudius' edict. Nevertheless, Simon could now share official guidelines with the church in Rome that would hopefully unify Jewish believers and Gentile believers again.

Despite Simon's efforts, contentiousness between the two Christian factions was not fully resolved. Word of the problems reached beyond the borders of Italy. The Apostle Paul, who was in Corinth near the end of his third missionary trip, sent a letter to the church in Rome. Although the letter focused mainly on the Gospel, it also admonished the believers in Rome for judging each other, particularly regarding what they ate or didn't eat. Paul also expressed his desire to visit Rome sometime in the future.

Paul's letter was respectfully received by the congregation in Rome, but most were not familiar with Paul. In order to give the contents of the letter additional credibility, Simon provided the congregation with a first-hand account of Paul's conversion and subsequent ministry.

With Abigail's blessing, Simon decided not to wait to see his friend. Within days of receiving Paul's letter, he arranged to sail to Corinth hoping that Paul would still be there. When Simon arrived, he found Paul accompanied by several companions including Timothy and Luke. Paul was surprised at the unexpected visit and overjoyed to see his friend.

"Simon, it's great to be together again. I believe the last time we saw each other was in Jerusalem when I was leaving for Tarsus after receiving a death threat. So many things have happened in my life since then. I'm sure you can say the same."

"I'm overjoyed to see you too. Who would have thought that the Christian movement would have grown so quickly and spread so widely? It is amazing how the Holy Spirit has helped make disciples throughout the world."

"God has been more than good, but you and I know there is much more to do."

"By the way, before I forget, Priscilla and Aquila send you their best. They returned to Rome as soon as Emperor Claudius' ban was lifted. I understand that during your second missionary trip you worked with them here in Corinth making tents."

"That's correct. Greet them in my name. They probably told you that when I left Corinth, they traveled to Ephesus with me. I continued on to Jerusalem to report on my missionary journey and get some rest. They stayed there spreading the Gospel. I'm glad to hear they made it back to Rome. They have been a blessing to everyone who worked with them."

"How long have you been in Corinth this time?"

"I've been here almost three months. I retraced my steps and visited the many churches that were planted during my last trip. They are all prospering."

"What are your plans from here?"

"I originally planned on sailing from Corinth back to Judea, possibly visiting a few churches located in coastal cities on the way. But Timothy and I found out that some Jewish trouble-makers in the area have made plans to damage the ship, hoping to end our lives. We've decided to change our plans and head north by land to Troas and then secure a ship to take us home from there."

"You said in your letter that you wanted to visit Rome. Why don't you come back with me now? I can provide housing for you and your companions and introduce you to all the Christians there. I especially want you to meet my wife, Abigail."

"Did I hear you correctly? Are you really married? I thought you would be single forever. You always had so many things going on in your life, and you never expressed any interest in settling down."

"I have to admit, Abigail took me by surprise. Now I can't imagine living without her. God richly blessed me by allowing me to be her husband. I'd suggest that you find a woman to marry, but I know that you are wed to your commitment to Jesus. I remember the day in Damascus when Ananias told you that Jesus chose you to be his messenger to the Gentiles. You are certainly fulfilling that commitment."

"Thanks for your vote of confidence, Simon. God has much more work for me to do. With regard to marriage, I don't believe any woman would put up with my travels. With regard to your invitation to visit Rome, I would honestly like to do so. However, for the second time in my missionary journeys, God has pointed me in a direction that He wants me to go and not where I was planning to go.

"The first time it happened, I was on my way to northern Asia Minor when a vision redirected me eastward to Macedonia and southward to Achaia. In retrospect, I understand that God was sending me to establish churches in cities such as Phillipi, Thessalonica, and Corinth. During my latest journey I found them to be thriving, proving that God always knows what is best for us.

"Recently the Lord directed me to return to Jerusalem. I trust he has a plan for me there. If it is his will, he will bring me to Rome someday, but not right now."

"I understand. I admire your complete trust in the Lord, something I strive for but often fall short of. I wish you Godspeed in your journey. Stay safe and visit us in Rome at some point."

"God's blessings to you as well. Give my congratulations to

your lovely bride on her selection of a good man of faith. Keep the church in Rome faithful to our Lord and Savior. I hope to see you again soon."

When Simon returned to Rome from Corinth, he found Abigail in a panic. He sat her down and asked what was wrong. Through tears, she attempted to explain. "While you were gone, Poppaea told me that she is divorcing her husband. She didn't give a reason, but I can tell she has made up her mind."

"She just had a baby a few months ago. Maybe it is stress from being a new mother. Are you sure that her decision is final?"

"Yes, she has already moved out of the house. Rufrius didn't try to stop her."

Poppaea had been married for fourteen years. Although the marriage hadn't always been smooth, it became even more strained when Rufrius, six years into their marriage, was removed from his command of the Praetorian Guard by Emperor Claudius' wife, Agrippina. At that point, the lavish lifestyle Poppaea had enjoyed ground to a halt. Poppaea missed the prestige of being the wife of a husband who reported directly to the emperor. For the next eight years after Rufrius' demotion, disappointment with her husband grew. Now that she had a child, Poppaea needed to ensure that she and her son maintained a favorable position in Roman society.

It was not unusual for a wife in Rome to initiate a divorce. Roman culture allowed either party in the marriage to divorce without claiming fault by the other. Because adultery could be punished under the law, no cause divorce became the preferred solution for problem marriages. For disgruntled husbands and wives, obtaining a divorce in Rome was as uncomplicated as getting married.

Simon understood why Abigail was so upset. She had worked for Poppaea for over a decade and was genuinely concerned for her mistress. She didn't want to see Poppaea hurt and hoped to continue the relationship they had built over the years.

There was no guarantee that Poppaea could afford to employ Abigail after the divorce. Roman law generally allowed the divorced woman to reclaim the entire dowry paid by her family. The amount of the dowry was established prior to the marriage, paid at the time of the marriage, and used during the marriage to set up the newly married couple's household. Since Poppaea was born into a prominent wealthy family, her dowry was substantial. However, Poppaea had no skills that would produce a steady income stream after the reclaimed dowry was depleted.

Another of Abigail's concerns was the fate of the child after the divorce. If Poppaea were to lose custody, a significant portion of Abigail's current duties would be eliminated making ongoing employment with Poppaea less likely. In that case, Rufrius would need childcare, but Abigail had no interest in working for Poppaea's soon-to-be ex-husband.

Six months after Poppaea's divorce, Poppaea married Marcus Salvius Otho. As a result, Abigail was able to remain as Poppaea's maidservant. However, the new marriage raised questions. Abigail expressed her feelings to Simon. "I'm having difficulty understanding why Poppaea would marry Otho. He is a mid-level politician with little social status. In addition, he has been called effeminate. He sometimes wears a wig and makeup, and I have observed him spending an inordinate amount of time on his appearance. Am I missing something? How could he appeal to a woman like Poppaea?"

"I believe there might be more to it," Simon replied. "We both know that your mistress is driven by a desire to elevate herself in Roman society. I've heard that Otho is more than an obscure politician. He is a close advisor and good friend of Emperor Nero. Poppaea might be using him as a ploy to get closer to power. There is no one more powerful on earth than Nero."

"Simon, do you remember when we discussed Poppaea's marriage to Marcus Otho?"

"I do remember. A month ago, you wondered why she had married him. How are they doing so far?"

"It appears you were correct when you suggested the marriage might be a scheme to raise her social status and that Otho might not be the final step toward her ultimate goal. Today while her husband was away, I answered a knock at the door and was shocked to see Nero standing there. His guards were ordered to remain outside.

"Poppaea greeted him as if she were expecting his visit. She took him into the house and told me they were not to be disturbed. After Nero left, Poppaea made me promise that I wouldn't tell anyone, including Otho, that Nero had been there. However, I couldn't keep this news from you. It appears they are having an affair."

"That is incredible. I was under the impression that she wanted to be close to power, but this looks like she wants to own it. What are you going to do?"

"I'm going to continue to serve Poppaea and her son as I have in the past. Her dealings with Otho and Nero are no business of mine unless she is in danger of being hurt by either of them. Then I will do all I can to protect her."

Chapter 13

NERO

Neither Simon nor Abigail knew much about Emperor Nero prior to his interest in Poppaea. Since he might have an impact on their lives in the future, they decided to look into his background. What they discovered was a self-absorbed young man whose success was largely a product of his mother's ambition.

Nero's biological father died when Nero was three. Eight years later his mother, Agrippina, married Emperor Claudius becoming his fourth wife. The marriage was performed without fanfare because Agrippina's father was Claudius' brother, making her the Emperor's niece and blood relative. Under Roman law, this was considered incest. It took legislative action by the Roman Senate to allow marriage between uncles and nieces.

To ensure her son's future prospects, Agrippina persuaded Claudius to adopt Nero and make him his sole heir even though he had a biological son, Britannicus, by a prior marriage. To further ensure that her son would become emperor, Agrippina arranged a betrothal ceremony between Nero and Octavia, Claudius' biological daughter and therefore Nero's stepsister, legal because it didn't involve blood relatives. Agrippina also removed those whom she perceived to be sympathetic to Britannicus from positions of influence.

By the time Claudius died, the road was paved for Nero to succeed him. He was only sixteen years old at the time. Power was transferred without opposition, just as Agrippina had planned. A year later, Britannicus died at the age of thirteen, allegedly poisoned on orders from his stepbrother, Nero.

"Today something happened that could harm Poppaea or even cost her life," Abigail announced to Simon. "Nero's mother, Agrippina, discovered the affair between Poppaea and Nero. While Otho was away from home, Agrippina paid a visit to Poppaea, and I overheard their conversation. Apparently, Agrippina wants Nero to remain married to Octavia. She threatened to tell Otho about the affair and punish Poppaea if she didn't break off the relationship with her son."

"That is serious. How did Poppaea react to the threat?"

"From what I could tell, Agrippina's visit frightened her quite a bit. Poppaea understands the influence that Agrippina has on Nero. She knows that Agrippina was responsible for his rise to power and that he continues to defer to her judgement in most matters. As soon as Agrippina left the house, Poppaea penned a letter and sealed it. She ordered one of the servants to deliver the letter directly to the Emperor. I can only imagine what she wrote."

"If Nero thought he was keeping the affair a secret, he knows better by now," Simon observed. "More importantly, he realizes that Agrippina will do anything, including harming Poppaea, to stop the affair. Depending on how much he values his relationship with Poppaea, this might be a turning point in his life, an opportunity to free himself from the shackles of his controlling mother."

It took less than a year for Simon's theory to prove accurate. Nero's affair with Poppaea continued as did Agrippina's opposition to it. Finally, Nero had enough and plotted to kill his mother. Because of Agrippina's popularity with the people of Rome, her death needed to appear natural or accidental.

Nero's first two attempts to kill his mother failed miserably. Poisoning was the first method he tried because it would leave no evidence. Unbeknownst to Nero, Agrippina took precautions against such an occurrence by regularly ingesting small amounts of the most common poisons which created immunity to them. A second attempt involved collapsing the ceiling in Agrippina's bedroom while she was sleeping. Somehow, she escaped with only minor injuries.

Oblivious to her son's subterfuge, Agrippina agreed with her son's suggestion to spend a few days outside of Rome where each of them had a private villa on opposite sides of a lake. One evening, Nero hosted a dinner at his villa in honor of his mother.

During the dinner, Nero's men intentionally disabled the boat that Agrippina had taken across the lake. He blamed the damage on random vandalism and offered a boat from his fleet for her crew to take her home. Nero sent a second vessel to follow Agrippina's boat under the pretense that his men would bring back the boat she borrowed.

In the middle of the lake, Agrippina's boat split in two and sank at a rapid pace. It had been deliberately sabotaged by Nero's men. Agrippina and her maidservant fell overboard. The maidservant, not a swimmer, called out for help as she bobbed up and down in the water. Nero's oarsmen in the second boat rowed in the darkness toward the terrified voice. Believing that the floundering woman was Agrippina, they clubbed the maid-servant until she disappeared below the surface.

The next day Nero received a message from his mother informing him that she had survived the accident. Agrippina had been a strong swimmer since childhood. Despite suffering minor injuries during the incident, she was able to navigate her way back to her villa. Nero, shocked by his mother's seeming invincibility, decided it was time to forego any further pretense. He ordered several of his guards to cross the lake to Agrippina's villa. There they beat and stabbed her to death. To hide the truth from the public, Nero claimed that his mother had died in an accident on the lake and the body was not recovered.

After Agrippina was eliminated, no one remained to inter-fere with Nero's extramarital affair except his wife, Octavia, and Poppaea's husband, Marcus Otho. Otho was easy to deal with. He was assigned to the governorship of the province of Lusitania on the western coast of Spain. Before Otho left Rome, Nero coerced him into divorcing Poppaea. Otho still loved his wife but was helpless against the power of the Emperor.

Nero, since the day he married, held Octavia in low regard. Although she was well liked by both Rome's high society and regular citizenry, Nero decided to divorce her. The decision was made easier by the fact that Poppaea was pregnant with his baby, and Octavia had not been able to produce a son to continue his bloodline. Wasting no time, Nero married his pregnant mistress only twelve days after his divorce was final.

With both Otho and Octavia out of the picture, Nero's personal life should have improved dramatically. This was not the case. Their newborn daughter died three months after birth. To make matters worse, the public continued to support Octavia after the divorce to the extent of demanding that Nero remarry her.

Not long after losing her child, Poppaea turned her grief and anger toward Nero's ex-wife. Poppaea convinced Nero to banish Octavia to southwest Italy. This stirred up the populace even more. To avoid a potential uprising, Nero created false charges against Octavia, accusing her of adultery while they were married. He sent soldiers to kill her, ordering them to leave no evidence that might implicate him. Before disposing of the body, the soldiers cut off Octavia's head and brought it back to Poppaea. Out of sight, out of mind; the public soon forgot about Octavia.

Through all the intrigue swirling around her mistress, Abigail continued to work for Poppaea. Abigail shared everything that happened with Simon, and they agreed to remain quiet about it.

Chapter 14

TRIAL

Unexpectedly, Simon received a letter from Paul stating that he was on his way to Rome. In the letter, Paul explained that he had been arrested and jailed in Jerusalem after returning from his third missionary trip. The charges against Paul, which falsely accused him of bringing a Gentile into the Temple, had been brought by Jewish leaders attempting to silence him.

The Roman army stepped in to stop the near riot that ensued. While held in the Roman garrison, Paul revealed he was a Roman citizen. In order to protect him from death threats made by the Jews, Paul was transferred to Caesarea Maritima to be tried by the Roman governor, Felix. After two years of house arrest and the appointment of a new governor named Festus, Paul appealed his case to Emperor Nero, a right he had as a Roman citizen.

Paul's letter reminded Simon of their earlier discussion in Corinth. Simon had invited Paul to visit Rome, but God had different plans for him at the time. Now his friend was on his way, not as Simon's houseguest but as a prisoner awaiting trial before Nero. Simon vowed to do everything he could to make Paul as comfortable as possible and hopefully get the bogus charges dropped.

"He's here," exclaimed the messenger.

"Who is here?" asked Simon.

"Paul is here. His ship landed in Puteoli a few days ago. He and the centurion guarding him are resting there before they make the trip up the coast to Rome."

"That's wonderful. I've been waiting for a long time for this moment. We need to let everyone know so we can greet him properly."

The next day a crowd of over one hundred Christians made their way down the road from Rome in the direction of Puteoli, an Italian port city southeast of Ostia. Halfway between Rome and Puteoli, they saw Paul coming toward them. As the crowd approached, the centurion guarding Paul drew his sword and prepared to defend himself and maintain custody of his prisoner.

Simon, who led the procession, went forward and addressed the soldier, "Put your sword away. We are not here to free Paul, we are here to welcome him." Simon walked around the centurion and wrapped his arms around his friend and fellow Apostle.

"You should have come to Rome with me when I invited you the first time," Simon joked. "It would have been much more pleasant for both of us."

"Hello again, my friend," said Paul. "As I told you in Corinth, God had plans for me. Even though I was under house arrest in Caesarea for two years, it was a productive time. I was able to witness to a king and two governors as well as the soldiers who guarded me. Gentiles came from all over the region to hear the message I preached. You know as well as I do that God's plans are much better than ours."

"In any case, I am overjoyed to see you again," remarked Simon. "Look at all the believers that are here to welcome you. Your reputation as a man of God precedes you. Over the years I have shared with them the story of your conversion and of God's plan for you to be a messenger to the Gentiles. I'm hopeful you will be able to continue your mission in Rome."

Simon's words were prophetic. The centurion assigned to Paul was very lenient. He allowed Paul to rent a house in the city and receive visitors on a daily basis. Paul took full advantage of his privileged house arrest.

Utilizing the strategy employed during his three missionary journeys, Paul initially reached out to the Jews in the area. He invited Jewish leaders to meet with him, explaining that the charges against him were false and that he had done nothing to offend the Jews in Jerusalem. Now that he was in Rome, Paul wished to share news of the Messiah with them.

The Jewish leaders stated they had heard nothing about the incident to which Paul was referring. In fact, they knew nothing about Paul at all. Further, they acknowledged their animosity toward followers of Jesus. In their opinion, Christian teachings were a threat to the Jewish faith. Despite this, they expressed willingness to return to hear what Paul had to say.

The Jewish leaders never came back. Shortly after meeting with Paul, they received a letter from the Sanhedrin in Jerusalem requesting that they serve as character witnesses against Paul. The Sanhedrin claimed Paul had started riots everywhere he went and that he profaned the Temple in Jerusalem. The letter stated that since the Sanhedrin had been unable to silence Paul, it was now up to the Jews in Rome to complete the job. A rabbi named Asher, ruler of the largest synagogue in Rome, was appointed to lead the effort.

For the next two years, Paul met with anyone who was willing to listen to the message of salvation through Jesus Christ. Both Jews and Gentiles expressed interest in hearing about the unique religion that professed a God who loved them enough to die for them. The Holy Spirit led many of them to faith. The converts, in turn, proclaimed the message to their relatives and friends. Simon rejoiced in the growth of the church which had been enhanced by Paul's efforts.

During his visits with Paul, Simon informed him of developments regarding the upcoming trial. Abigail regularly quizzed Poppaea about Paul's status. Poppaea, who had earlier helped Simon remain in Rome during Claudius' ban of Jews, was willing to provide information to Abigail based on their long-term relationship.

Abigail reported that delays in Nero's court were not unusual. The backlog of cases was large because Nero expressed little interest in court proceedings. Additionally, trials involving crimes taking place in Rome took precedence over those committed in other parts of the Empire.

After nearly two years of house arrest, Abigail finally had solid news for Paul. The good news was that the trial had been scheduled to take place within a few weeks. The bad news was that Paul would be transferred to Mamertine Prison prior to the trial.

The centurion who accompanied Paul to Rome and supervised his confinement was ordered to return to Jerusalem. During the two years guarding Paul, he had become a Christian and a close friend of Paul. Their parting was filled with tears and prayers.

Conditions were abysmal in the Mamertine Prison. The facility was the oldest prison in Rome, built in the center of the ancient city over 600 years earlier. Originally constructed to house common criminals, the prison was now reserved for enemies of the state accused of serious crimes against Rome.

The prison had two levels. The ground floor, called the Carcer, was the shape of a large rectangle and accessible from the street. Cells housing prisoners lined three of the four walls. The middle of the room was reserved for guards who administered the prison. The ground floor cells were used to hold prisoners whose trials were pending.

The other level was directly below the first. This underground dungeon, called the Tullianum, had a floor that was circular in shape and approximately twenty feet in diameter. Stone walls rose from the floor to form a twelve-foot-high dome. A trapdoor capped the domed ceiling and served as the only access between the two levels. The Tullianum was designated for convicted enemies of the state who were awaiting execution.

The only light reaching the Tullianum came through a small iron grating in the trapdoor. Guards lowered the convicts into the dungeon by ropes. Food and water were lowered to the prisoners on an irregular basis and a slop bucket served to transfer prisoners' waste back up. The space was damp all year long, and the temperature was dictated by the season, unbearably hot in the summer and freezing cold in the winter. Absence of air circulation allowed no relief from the stench.

When Paul arrived at Mamertine, he was placed in a cell at ground level. Another prisoner in his cell told Paul that security was considerably tighter than usual after his arrival. Several additional guards were assigned both inside and outside the facility. Enhanced security had been requested by Jewish leaders who contended that Christians sympathetic to Paul might attempt to free him. The Captain of the Guard was not willing to risk losing a prisoner since that would mean losing his own life. To the dismay of Simon and Abigail, no visitors were allowed to enter the prison or to drop off items of food or other necessities. No written correspondence was allowed to go in or out.

The morning of his trial, Paul was escorted by the Captain of the Guard and a number of his soldiers to Nero's palace. Once inside, Paul was struck by the opulence of the palace. The hallways were elegant beyond belief. Mosaic murals lined the walls and the ceiling. Gold overlaid most surfaces that the murals didn't cover. Columns of marble framed the doorways leading to various chambers along the way. The floors were of multicolored porcelain tile cut in various shapes with gemstones placed in the grouting.

After walking a considerable distance, the Captain and his prisoner reached an immense wooden door with images of Roman deities carved into it. Two soldiers from the Praetorian Guard were standing at attention in front of the entrance. "We are here at the order of the Emperor," said the Captain. "He asked that my prisoner, Paul from Judaea, be brought here for trial. Please announce that we are here."

One of the guards opened the door narrowly and disappeared to the other side. After a few minutes he reemerged, opened the massive door, and motioned for the Captain and his prisoner to enter. Paul, restrained in wrist and ankle shackles, shuffled into the most grandiose room he had ever seen.

The ceiling was domed and painted blue and white to resemble a beautiful cloudy sky. Sunlight filtered into the room through windows high up on the walls. Full length statues honoring emperors and senators of Rome lined the sides of the room. Beautiful paintings hung everywhere. The white marble floor sparkled in the light, partially covered by a huge purple rug ringed with gold tassels.

Across the room opposite the door, Nero sat on his judgement seat. The large throne was covered with gold and precious gems. It sat on a marble platform which elevated the Emperor above anyone else in the room. Nero wore a white silk tunic under a purple toga bordered with gold embroidery. On either side of the platform were half a dozen Praetorian Guards in full armor with spears and swords at the ready. A man whom Paul recognized as Asher, ruler of the Jewish synagogue, stood a respectful distance from Nero's right side.

Nero motioned for the men to come forward. The Captain of the Guard led Paul to a position several feet in front of the throne and saluted. They stood in silence until Nero spoke. "You have been accused by Governors Felix and Festus of disrupting the peace established by Rome in the city of Jerusalem. They claim that you instigated riots which had to be quelled by Roman soldiers at the risk of their lives. This is considered a crime against the state and should have been adjudicated locally. However, under your right as a Roman citizen, you appealed to be tried before the Emperor.

"In addition to this charge, it has recently been brought to my attention that you are recruiting citizens of Rome to join your Christian cult while under house arrest. Your accuser's name is Asher, a Jewish synagogue leader here in Rome. Although we tolerate the coexistence of other religions throughout the Empire, it is considered a crime to encourage Romans to abandon the gods they worship.

"Further, Asher says that you are teaching that a man named Jesus was crucified but allegedly came back from the dead and is planning to become a king. Although I don't believe any of this, gullible people might. In that case, I might have an insurrection on my hands. Now that you are aware of the charges, what do you have to say in your defense?"

"My name is Paul, your Excellency. Thank you for providing an explanation of the charges against me and the opportunity to make a defense. First of all, please allow me to address the initial charge stemming from events in Jerusalem. I was worshipping at the Temple when number of Jews falsely accused me of defiling the Temple. They said I had brought a Gentile into the Temple which is punishable by death. Nothing could be further from the truth.

"The accusation sparked a rumor that spread throughout the Temple grounds. A crowd formed and threatened to kill me. Thanks to quick action by the Roman soldiers on duty, I was taken to the Antonia Fortress until the matter could be sorted out. In the meantime, a planned attempt to kill me was exposed.

"After finding out that I was a Roman citizen, the Captain transported me to Caesarea Maritima to be tried before Governor Felix. Believing that I was innocent but unwilling to offend my Jewish accusers, Felix kept me under house arrest for two years. Festus succeeded him and decided to appease the Jews by moving the trial back to Jerusalem. I knew that I would be killed either in Jerusalem or on the way there, so I appealed my case to you, mighty Nero."

"If what you say is true," observed Nero, "your trial today is the result of an unfortunate combination of religion and politics. However, the man to my right, your accuser whose name is Asher, has corresponded with Jewish leadership in Jerusalem, and they tell a much different version of those events."

Paul countered, "Other than eyewitnesses who were present during my arrest, my best defense witnesses would be Felix and Festus. They both told me on separate occasions that I would have been found innocent were it not for pressure from the Jews."

"I'm afraid they aren't available to assist in your defense," Nero revealed. "I removed Felix from office due to financial corruption. He died shortly thereafter. Festus was actually a reasonably good governor, but he died a few months ago. Therefore, I have only your word for what happened and what the governors thought about your case.

"Fortunately for you, I'm tired of dealing with past crimes that involve a foreign religion. They have no impact on me today. Let's move on to the charges that Asher has brought regarding your conduct here in Rome. What do you have to say about that?"

"Your Excellency," responded Paul, "with regard to his first charge, my accuser incorrectly stated that I am encouraging Romans to abandon their gods. I am under house arrest and can only receive visitors as allowed. If anyone chooses to seek me out and ask questions about what I believe, I share my views with them. They have the opportunity to share their beliefs with me. That should not be a crime any more than my discussion with you.

"Regarding the second charge that Christians want to make Jesus a king, he is already a king. But His kingship is not a threat to you or to Rome because it is not a kingdom established here on earth. Rather, Jesus rules in Heaven, a place similar to what Romans call the Elysian Fields.

"Christians believe that after we die, our bodies will be resurrected and join Jesus in his Heavenly kingdom eternally. Jesus confirmed this by rising from the dead and returning to Heaven to prepare a place for us. Hundreds of people saw his resurrected body with their own eyes. His closest followers saw him ascend into Heaven. He spoke to me from Heaven, so I am a living witness to his kingship."

"What you said is difficult to comprehend," said Nero with a puzzled look on his face. "From what I just heard, life after death appears to be the primary goal for you Christians. What about your time here on earth? Don't you want to enjoy life to the fullest? That's my goal. I do whatever I want to do whenever I want to do it. I've accumulated enormous wealth and power and want to enjoy it while I can. Nothing that might happen after I die could be as pleasurable as what I am experiencing now."

"With all due respect, your Excellency, Christians believe we are here on earth to serve the one true God, not for self-gratification. The reason we put God first and us second is because of what He has done for us. He has saved us from the punishment that our sins deserve by sending his Son Jesus to be sacrificed on our behalf."

"Once again you are speaking in terms I don't understand," admitted Nero. "You need to explain more clearly what you are talking about."

"Thank you for your patience, your Excellency. In order to comprehend what Jesus did for us, one needs to understand the concept of sin. When God created the first man and woman, they were made in His image. That is, they were perfect in every way. Their relationship with God was perfect as well.

"However, at one point they disobeyed a direct command that God gave them. We call such disobedience against God a sin. If someone disobeyed your direct order, you might call it disloyalty or treason. Once the first man and woman sinned, they were no longer perfect and the relationship they had with Him was ruined. They could no longer stand before a perfect God without fear.

"As a result of their sin, the man and woman were punished. For the rest of their lives on earth, they would experience pain and sorrow and work hard to make a living. Even worse, they were doomed to die someday. Their bodies will be resurrected and tormented eternally in Hell, a place similar to what the Greeks call Hades and Romans call Infernum. All people since then, including you and I, have inherited that imperfection and will suffer the same fate."

"Stop there a moment," ordered Nero, still puzzled. "Initially, you said that Christians will go to Heaven after they die. Now you are telling me that all people are sinners, including Christians, and will be punished in Hell after they die. Which is it? You need to get your story straight. You're wasting my time with your contradictory nonsense."

"Your Excellency, this is where Jesus enters the picture. In spite of their sinful condition, God still loved the humans He created. God provided the first man and woman and all future generations of mankind a way to become acceptable to Him in spite of their sinfulness. But it couldn't happen through their own efforts. It required intervention by God Himself. It required God to become a man. That man was Jesus.

"A virgin by the name of Mary conceived a son, not by a human father but by a miraculous act of the Spirit of God. Her son was named Jesus which means 'God saves.' He was both God and man at the same time. Because he was God, Jesus was sinless. Because he was a man, he could die. That combination allowed Jesus to be the perfect sacrifice for the sins of all people including yours, Excellency. The punishment we deserve for our sins, whether past, present, or future, was endured by Jesus when he suffered and died on a cross in Jerusalem.

"After three days in the grave, God raised His Son Jesus from the dead as proof of his victory over sin and death. Because of what Jesus did, everyone who believes in him as their Lord and Savior is no longer condemned to eternal punishment in Hell. Instead, those who believe in Jesus will rise from the dead and live forever with God in Heaven."

Nero sat silent for a few moments, thinking about what Paul just said. "If what you say is true, Jesus has provided the world not only with forgiveness but also with a license to sin. If believing in him guarantees me a place in Heaven, why would I stop sinning as long as I believe? If you are saying that I can do anything I want without any consequences, perhaps I could be persuaded to believe in this Jesus."

"Excellency, in order to answer that, please allow me to ask you a question. If a man's life were saved by the actions of another man, would he mistreat the man who saved him?"

Nero paused for a moment. "I think not. The man who was saved would owe the other man a great debt, one that could never be repaid."

"You have answered well. That is exactly why a person who truly believes that Jesus saved him by suffering and dying to pay for his sins would do everything within his power to stop sinning. You used the words 'owe a great debt.' God loved you and me so much that He sacrificed His Son for us. That is a debt we could never repay. If we truly believe that Jesus died for us, we can't help being grateful. Out of thankfulness we will be sorry for our sins and attempt to do better in the future.

"On the other hand, if we continue to sin deliberately after knowing what Jesus did for us, as you suggest, we are in effect slapping Him in the face instead of thanking Him. Such behavior would indicate that Jesus' sacrifice isn't meaningful to us. Knowing and believing are two different things. Our actions will show whether we simply know or really believe what Jesus has done for us."

"After listening to what you just said, "replied Nero, "I have no chance of becoming a Christian. I've ordered people murdered including my mother and my first wife. I've taken another man's wife for my mistress and then married her. These actions would easily qualify for what you call sin.

"However, I am not sorry for anything I have done. Given the chance, I would do it all over again. I will continue to do whatever I want without compromise and without regret. Why would I give up my current lifestyle based on your unfounded and foolish beliefs? I'm enjoying myself right now. I'm not concerned about what might happen after I die."

"Your Excellency, I might not be able to convince you to become a believer today. But a seed has been planted in your heart that will hopefully grow and flourish. When you are on your death bed wondering what will happen next, you might look back to our conversation and remember what Jesus has done for you. Even at that late date, you can confess your sins and believe that Jesus paid for all of them no matter how terrible they were. Life with God forever in Heaven would still be available to you."

"I think I've heard enough from you. Normally, I would pass judgement today. However, you have brought up issues that I would like to explore. Captain, take this man back to prison. I will announce my verdict after I've had a chance to deliberate further."

After Paul was led out of the room, Nero turned to Asher and said, "Contrary to your accusations, I don't see this man Paul starting a rebellion against Rome. Christians appear to be more concerned with the afterlife than living today or tomorrow. At this point I don't consider him a criminal or a threat to the state. In fact, I pity him for being so misguided by the fraudster he calls Jesus."

"Your Excellency, I realize that you have complete authority in this matter. But you have a chance to do away with a man who has been a thorn in the side of Jews throughout your Empire. If you don't perceive him as a threat to Rome at this point, perhaps there is something I can offer to persuade you to change your mind."

Nero's sensed an opportunity to enrich himself and responded, "When Felix was Governor of Judea and Samaria, he held Paul prisoner for several years. He was hoping that the Christians would pay to have him released. Is that what you had in mind when you used the word 'persuade'?"

"Most revered Emperor, in your infinite wisdom you have managed to read my mind. I believe that I can make it worth your while to reach a verdict that will please Jews in Rome and Jerusalem. Ironically, Jewish authorities in Jerusalem paid one of Jesus' followers to betray him, ensuring his crucifixion. Thirty years later, we Jews have a chance to accomplish something similar by rewarding you for eliminating one of Jesus' most dedicated followers."

"So be it. All we have left to do is determine the amount of persuasion you are willing to pay. I must admit that lining my pockets is more appealing than providing justice to a deranged religious fanatic."

"I can't believe you won't do this for me," exclaimed Poppaea with tears in her eyes. "You said you loved me more than anything else. Besides, you are compromising your principles in return for an insignificant sum of money."

"Poppaea, you know I love you more than life itself," replied Nero. "But this man Paul is delusional along with his Christian friends. He believes in a single God who became a man and came to life after he died. Even more bizarre, Paul is counting on a life after death in a place called Heaven at the expense of enjoying his life on earth. I'd wager he would prefer to die over remaining alive. By sentencing him to death, I would be doing him a favor."

"You are making a big mistake," Poppaea reiterated. "Before you and I knew each other, I asked Emperor Claudius to exclude my maidservant's husband from the edict banishing Jews from Rome. He was a Christian, but Romans considered Christians of Jewish origin to be Jews at that time. When the two of them came to me for help, they shared their Christian beliefs. They convinced me that the Jews were to blame for conflicts with Christians and not the other way around. In my opinion, nothing has changed.

"I admit that Christian teachings are difficult to understand and accept. However, there is logic to their belief that a person's existence goes beyond death. I would like to think that we will exist after death and that it will be better than what we are experiencing now.

"Don't worry, dear husband. I haven't become a Christian. I still worship the gods of Rome. However, I respect the way Christian's lives are dedicated to their God. Unlike the impersonal gods we believe in, their God appears to be loving and caring. He demands obedience but is quick to forgive. Even if what they believe isn't true, they have hope for the future. Isn't there some way to resolve this without putting an innocent man to death?"

Nero thought for a moment and replied, "There might be a solution that would satisfy both the Christians and Jews. Instead of finding Paul innocent or guilty, I could release him on the condition that he leaves Rome immediately. Further, he could never return to Jerusalem where this whole matter started. Would that make you happy, my dear Poppaea?"

Simon and Abigail couldn't believe their eyes when they saw Paul standing in the doorway. "Is it really you, Paul?" exclaimed Abigail as she ran to hug him.

"We were just praying for your release," said Simon. "Was this another miraculous escape like Peter's experience in Jerusalem? Tell us what happened. Have you been set free or are Nero's soldiers looking for you right now?"

Paul smiled at Simon's reference to Peter's escape from prison. "My story isn't as dramatic as Peter's, but he and I both owe our freedom to God's grace and the prayers of our Christian friends. I am as surprised as you are to be talking to you right now. I was asleep in my cell when the Captain of the Guard opened the door and motioned for me to come out.

"I assumed that I would be lowered into the Tullianum to await my execution. Instead, he said I was free to go. He informed me that Nero ordered my release conditional on my immediate departure from Rome. He also required that I never return to Jerusalem. I imagine these conditions were prompted by the Jews."

"What are you going to do?" asked Simon.

"I need to report back to the prison today to sign my release papers. If I violate the conditions I will be subject to immediate execution," Paul replied. "There is a ship waiting in Ostia that will take me to Spain. The Captain of the Guard will escort me to Ostia to ensure my departure. Ironically, I've wanted to travel to Spain for a long time. It has the potential to be a fruitful mission field."

"It seems odd that Nero didn't ban you from Rome permanently as he did with Jerusalem," Simon observed. "Any idea why?"

"I'm not sure, but I don't think he regards me as a threat to Rome," Paul responded. "However, if I ever decide to come back here, I would likely be risking my life given Jewish animosity toward me."

"We owe a debt of gratitude to Poppaea," noted Abigail. "I made her aware of Paul's situation when he arrived in Rome two years ago. She agreed to let me know anything she heard about his pending trial. She is the one who informed me of Paul's upcoming trial date. Thankfully, she convinced her husband to release Paul. God is good to those who love and believe in Him."

Several months after Paul's release, the Apostle Peter arrived unexpectedly in Rome from Jerusalem. He had written to Simon that he planned to visit, but the letter was lost in a shipwreck off the coast of Crete. After Peter's arrival, Simon informed him that Paul had recently gone to Spain and might not return any time soon. Peter was disappointed but not discouraged by the news and committed himself to helping Simon in any way he could. Simon gave thanks that another Apostle was available to assist in administration of the church in Rome.

Chapter 15

FIRE

It was a hot dry evening in the middle of July. From their apartment on the second floor of a seven-story building in the Aventinus region in southwest Rome, Simon and Abigail awoke to the smell of smoke. Simon rose from the bed and went to the window. What he saw made the hair on his arms stand up.

Only half a mile northeast of their apartment a wall of fire thirty feet high engulfed the Circus Maximus, an enormous stadium dedicated to chariot racing and other entertainment events. The oblong track was over 2,000 feet long and nearly 400 feet wide. The bleachers that surrounded the track could accommodate 150,000 spectators. Under and near the bleachers were dozens of shops where retailers and manufacturers peddled their merchandise.

Although the primary wind direction was away from the apartment, updrafts from the fire blew embers high into the air that swirled in every direction. Simon could see small fires igniting near his apartment. He rushed into the adjoining room where Peter was fast asleep. Peter was staying with Simon and Abigail until he could find a place of his own.

"Peter, wake up," Simon urged. "We need to get out of here quickly." Peter sat up, disoriented at first but wide awake in a matter of seconds.

"What's happening?" Peter asked.

"We need to get out of here. Rome is on fire," replied Simon. "I've never seen anything like it before. The wind is whipping the flames through the entire city. I'm not even sure which direction we need to go."

The three of them hurriedly dressed and ran down the stairs of the apartment taking nothing except the clothes on their backs. As they stepped out of the door to the street, their lungs filled with thick acrid smoke. The street was filled with people running in panic from the flames now spreading quickly from the Circus Maximus. Simon, Abigail, and Peter joined the surging crowd, having no idea where they might end up.

After running through winding streets that snaked through several residential areas, they emerged into an open space lined with commercial buildings. Simon saw that they were near the Emporium, the port where barges docked after making their way up the Tiber River from Ostia. The Emporium had been Simon's first stop in Rome.

Adjacent to the Emporium was the Horrea Galbae, a

complex of warehouses that stored virtually anything sold or manufactured in Rome, from jars of olive oil to grain to marble slabs. Wealthy Romans also used the smaller storage buildings to secure personal items such as silver, gold, artwork, and jewelry. Between the warehouses and the river were shops where retailers and wholesalers sold or auctioned their goods.

That evening the commercial space along the river wasn't filled with merchants. Instead, it was overrun by people desperate to save their lives. The main section of the fire continued to spread northeast driven by the wind, but smaller fires ignited in the opposite direction which threatened the Horrea Galbae and the Emporium.

Simon wondered if the fire had destroyed the wood and plaster apartments where they lived. In any case, it was evident that thousands of residents would be homeless by the time the fire was under control. The three of them paused to pray for the safety of Christians who might be in danger throughout the city.

Those fleeing to the Emporium realized that their current location posed a significant risk to their safety. If the wind shifted in their direction or a stray spark floated into the area, it wouldn't take long before the warehouses and their contents would burst into flames. Some of the materials stored there were extremely flammable and could explode if exposed to extreme heat.

Two escape options became clear. The first was to head south along the east bank of the Tiber River which led out of the city into uninhabited land filled with trees and brush. However, that area could prove as flammable as the Emporium.

The second option was to cross the Tiber to reach the west side of the river. The nearest bridge was nearly a mile north but getting there would require going directly toward the fire. The only feasible ways to cross the river were by boat or by swimming.

Fortunately, several barges had docked and unloaded at the port earlier in the day. The captains and their crews planned to sleep on their vessels that evening and return to Ostia in the morning. In desperation, people on the dock began climbing onto the barges demanding to be taken to the other side. After their vessels were packed to the point of sinking, the barge captains had no choice but to shove off from the dock.

That night hundreds of passengers were ferried across the river. After emptying their passengers on the far side, the barges turned around and returned to the Emporium. This process continued all night and into the morning until everyone on the east side of the river had been transported to the opposite bank.

Simon, Abigail, and Peter boarded one of the barges as the morning sun began to shine dimly through the hazy air. Smoke from the fire had burned their lungs all night, forcing them to breathe through moistened cloths held over their faces. By the grace of God, the wind continued to blow away from them, and the fire hadn't reached the Emporium. For the first time since he viewed the fire, Simon felt confident that the three of them would be safe.

As the barge crossed the 300-foot-wide expanse of water, they saw that the Circus Maximus had been leveled. Flames were now visible in the middle of the city and appeared to be moving toward the Esquiline Hill on Rome's east side. After reaching the west side of the river, they thanked God for His protection. They again prayed for the safety of their fellow Christians and all those who continued to face danger.

Six days later the fire appeared to have burned itself out. However, despite efforts to cool the smoldering ashes, the fire reignited and flames spread out of control for another three days. By the time it was over, Rome had been nearly destroyed.

Ten of the fourteen regions in the city had been totally or largely decimated. Four regions were relatively unscathed by the fire, including the one in which Simon and Abigail lived. Their apartment was not damaged, but a thick layer of ash had settled throughout the building.

Soon after the fire was extinguished, Christians banded together to help those in need. Believers reached out to house, feed, and clothe neighbors who had lost their homes whether or not they were Christians. Worship services that had been conducted in homes across the city were now combined in larger facilities in regions that did not sustain damage. Simon viewed this as a blessing, a way for church members in different locations to connect with each other. However, neither he nor Peter could imagine the adverse impact the fire would later have on the Christian community.

Chapter 16

DEFAMATION

Nero was twenty-six years old when most of Rome was destroyed by what residents of the city named the Great Fire. He had been emperor for ten years. During the first five years of his reign, Nero was popular among the citizenry. Young Nero was advised by several wise and experienced counselors including Seneca, the famous philosopher, and Burrus, the commander of the Praetorian Guard. These advisors essentially ruled the Empire during this period.

With the help of his advisors, Nero initiated laws that endeared him to both the patricians who comprised the upper class of society and the plebeians who made up the lower class of farmers, craftsmen, and soldiers. Under their guidance, Nero improved relations between himself and the Senate. He eliminated capital punishment, lowered taxes, and required court trials to be held in public rather than in secret. Nero banned gladiator entertainment and replaced it with artistic and athletic competitions in which he sometimes participated. During these early years, his shortcomings were overlooked by the public as imperfections of an immature young man.

By the end of his first five years as emperor, Nero's behavior had changed dramatically. He took sole control of decision making by dismissing his advisors and having his mother killed. Absent guidance from responsible adults, his relatively innocent vices evolved into a hedonistic lifestyle filled with excessive drinking, partying, and sensual pleasures. The popularity he had enjoyed during the first five years of his reign turned into near universal disfavor during the second five. His self-indulgence and depravity were clear to everyone but himself.

Nero became extremely paranoid. Anyone suspected of being disloyal was in danger of being murdered, including members of the Senate. He became obsessed with his public image as his popularity appeared to drop considerably. Ironically, Nero didn't realize that much of the loss of popularity was due to his performance in plays, reading and writing poetry, and playing his lyre, all of which he did ostentatiously in public. Such activities were considered beneath the dignity of anyone wealthy or in authority and were deemed appalling when done by an emperor.

To his credit, after the fire Nero was initially proactive in helping those impacted by it. Soon after the fire was extinguished, Nero allowed the homeless to use government buildings and even his own palace for temporary housing. He ordered the government to subsidize the price of grain and corn which made food more affordable for the masses.

Over the three years following the fire, Nero focused on improving the appearance and safety of Rome. He converted a haphazardly constructed city into an extravagant showplace. Narrow winding streets were turned into wide straight thoroughfares. Commercial and government buildings that had been constructed of wood were rebuilt using stone block. Multistory apartment buildings of questionable construction were replaced by solidly built structures which were limited to only two stories.

Nero made other changes that directly benefited the residents. A fire department was established, and open spaces were created complete with walkways, grass, trees, and ponds. Swampy areas that had promoted disease were filled in with rubble removed from the fire. Nero also restored the Circus Maximus allowing chariot races and other entertainment events to resume.

The improvement most appreciated by the public at large was a new bath complex in northwest Rome. The complex, called the Thermae Neronis, was the second public bath built in Rome. It provided huge heated and unheated pools of water in which to relax or swim. Water for the pools came from a nearby aqueduct. The heated pools were warmed by wood-fueled furnaces through which water was piped. The complex itself was massive and beautiful. Marble and stone columns supported roofs that covered gymnasium and exercise areas. A large courtyard featured grass and plants and fountains. Best of all, it was free and open to the public.

All of these improvements came with a large price tag. However, because most of the changes benefited the citizenry, Nero faced little initial criticism. Unfortunately for him, Nero didn't stop there. While rebuilding and beautifying Rome, Nero started a construction project that would contribute to his fall from power and ultimately to his death.

From his youth, Nero considered himself to be an accomplished actor, poet, and musician. Unlike previous emperors who had been government officials or generals, the arts were more important to Nero than politics or the military. Prior to the Great Fire, Nero decided that he deserved a grand palace to showcase his self-avowed appreciation of creativity and culture. The fire that burned nearly seventy percent of Rome laid bare a huge amount of land in the middle of the city which gave him an opportunity to build a residence worthy of an emperor like himself.

Nero began construction on a palace that would have no equal in the Empire. He called it the Domus Aurea or Golden House. As the name suggests, the palace and its grounds were opulent. The entire complex covered 250 acres in the center of Rome, northwest of Circus Maximus and adjacent to the Forum. The site was so expansive that it connected three of the seven Hills of Rome.

In order to build this grand edifice, Nero hired the best architects, engineers, and artists from both Italy and Greece. He made sure that every detail had his stamp of approval. Nero, who became more decadent as he grew older, built the palace with lascivious entertainment and debauchery in mind.

Hundreds of rooms were available for party guests who could eat and drink to excess and spend the night with high class prostitutes provided by Nero.

No expense was spared to furnish the palace. Beautiful frescoes adorned the walls of the rooms and hallways. Stucco ceilings were inlaid with mosaics and precious stones. Gold leaf was used on many surfaces throughout much of the interior, befitting the name Golden House.

A 120-foot statue of Nero stood in a large vestibule at the street entrance of the palace. The statue was so large it could be seen miles away. One of the many dining rooms featured a domed ceiling that revolved. Slaves cranked a mechanism that turned the dome which was painted in the likeness of the sky. Rose petals and perfume showered down from the ceiling on the diners below.

The palace grounds were as spectacular as the Golden House itself. Nero and his guests could stand on a huge columned terrace and view a gigantic man-made lake. They could stroll through vast gardens filled with trees and flowers. Beautiful fountains and ponds dotted the landscape. Exotic animals imported from around the Empire roamed the grounds.

Blinded by arrogance, Nero didn't consider the effect that this colossal extravagance would have on public opinion. Wealthy patricians had opposed Nero for a long time, recognizing that he was a danger to the political, cultural, and economic condition of the Roman Empire. However, the lower and middle class plebeians who benefited from Nero's largesse after the fire tended to be less critical of Nero in spite of his moral shortcomings.

Construction of the Golden House was a game changer.

No one in Rome, rich or poor, could justify appropriating a significant portion of their city's most valuable land to satisfy the whims of a self-indulgent emperor.

The Golden House also had an effect on the pocketbooks of Rome's citizens. Nero's extensive rebuilding of the city consumed most of the funds in Rome's treasury while construction of the Golden House depleted it. In order to raise funds to complete his palace project, Nero increased taxes not only in the city of Rome but across the entire Roman Empire as well.

Nero's sagging popularity made him a target for conspiracy theories. Critics spread rumors that Nero was responsible for the Great Fire or, at a minimum, that he took joy in the destruction of Rome. Before the fire, Nero had publicly criticized the city's architecture and the condition of his former palace. By creating a refurbished Rome with the Golden House as the centerpiece, Nero created a rational basis for these rumors. His complicity in starting the Great Fire, whether legitimate or not, became reality in the eyes of many Roman citizens.

Nero was in deep trouble, and he knew it. He needed something or someone to deflect suspicion from himself. The answer became clear to him one day as he walked through the hallways of his palace. Nero overheard one of his servants talking to a fellow worker, telling him about Jesus.

Nero hadn't paid attention to Christians since Poppaea advocated for Paul's release from prison. However, the servant's comments jogged his memory of the discussion he had with Paul during his trial. Nero had not understood what Paul said so he completely disregarded it. He decided to find out more about Jesus and his followers.

The next day Nero arranged a meeting with Asher, the synagogue ruler who had disparaged Paul during his trial. "I want you to tell me more about the Christians, particularly about the man they call Jesus," demanded Nero.

"Your Excellency," replied Asher cautiously, fearing that Nero might be considering becoming a Christian, "before I answer, may I ask why you want to know about Jesus?"

"Although it is none of your business, I will tell you anyway," Nero replied condescendingly, "I overheard one of my servants talking about Jesus and it made me recall some of what Paul said about him. I thought you might have more insight than uneducated domestic help."

"Thank you for indulging my curiosity, your Excellency," said Asher. "I'm glad that you came to me for guidance on this matter. There are several thousand Christians here in Rome. The name Christian describes followers of a man named Jesus, also known as the Christ. It is a religious sect that believes that Jesus will deliver the Jews from Roman rule and make himself a king. While alive, he assembled a band of followers who were going to help him accomplish his plan.

"Jewish leaders in Jerusalem discovered this insurrection plot and brought Jesus before the Roman governor, Pontius Pilate, to be tried for treason. He was found guilty and crucified, but his followers stole his body from the grave and claimed that he rose from the dead. Through deception and lies, his disciples have convinced gullible people, Jews and Romans alike, that this resurrection story is true. They expect Jesus to appear again to defeat Rome and declare himself king. They intend to carry out a rebellion even if Jesus doesn't reappear soon."

"Your portrayal of Jesus and his followers is interesting," commented Nero. "We both heard Paul's defense at his trial. His version of Jesus is nothing like yours."

"Can you blame him for lying?" asked Asher. "He was fighting for his life at the time. Why would he tell the truth about his treasonous plans if it would condemn him to death?

Nero thought for a moment. "If what you say is correct, do these Christians currently pose a threat to Rome?"

"Your Excellency, I would consider them a threat to Rome as well as a perversion of my Jewish heritage," replied Asher. "In addition to fomenting a rebellion, they discourage your citizens from worshipping any of the Roman gods. And to show how disgusting they really are, Christians engage in cannibalism during a secret rite in which they actually eat flesh and drink blood."

"If I wanted to meet with the top Christian leaders here in Rome to hear their side of the story, who would they be?" asked Nero.

"Your Excellency," replied Asher, "A man named Simon has been in Rome since Claudius was emperor. Recently, another man named Peter arrived to assist Simon. They were two of Jesus' closest followers and traveled with Him for three years until his death. In my opinion, the reason they came to Rome was to convince both Jews and Romans to abandon their respective religions and become Christians. With enough followers, they could overthrow the government. I would consider the two of them to be the ringleaders of this dangerous sect."

"I have one more question," said Nero. "Do you think it is possible that these Christians had anything to do with starting the Great Fire?"

"I wouldn't doubt it," replied Asher. "I know that a majority of them lived south of the Circus Maximus as well as across the Tiber River west of the Emporium. Out of the fourteen regions in Rome, those were two of the four regions not impacted by the flames.

"I heard rumors that Christians were predicting a fire would take place in Rome, but no one took them seriously. It might be more than coincidence that Peter arrived in Rome shortly before the Great Fire started. I don't have any direct proof that Simon or Peter or any other Christians were involved, but the circumstances appear incriminating."

"That is all I need to know," said Nero, abruptly ending the conversation. "Thank you for providing exactly what I needed. You are dismissed."

Nero never attempted to meet with Simon or Peter to hear their side of the story. Soon after his meeting with Asher, Nero launched a public relations campaign. Using the misinformation he had received from Asher, supplemented with his own manufactured falsehoods, Nero intended to shift the focus of rumors concerning the Great Fire from himself to the Christians.

Nero discovered that shifting the blame was relatively easy. Ever since followers of Jesus established a presence in Rome, they were viewed with suspicion. Many Romans thought of Christians as overbearing. Like Jews, Christians tolerated worship of only one God and refused to participate in sacrifices to Roman deities or worship of the emperor. They didn't hesitate to impose their beliefs on anyone they met. It took little effort to convince Romans that Christians were enemies of the Empire, capable of burning down their city.

As the smear campaign gained momentum, Nero ordered his soldiers to arrest Simon and Peter. He intended to force confessions out of them whether they were guilty or not. He would then parade them in front of the public as the masterminds of a Christian insurrection.

Poppaea learned of Nero's plan and warned Abigail that her husband was in danger. Simon and Peter were moved to a safe house north of Rome. When Nero learned that they couldn't be found, he flew into a rage.

After failing to make Simon and Peter the primary scapegoats for the fire, Nero decided to pin blame on the entire Christian population of Rome. By then about 5,000 Christians, including women and children, were living in the city. Nero ordered his soldiers to begin rounding up Christian men, particularly those identified as leaders of the church.

Dozens of Christians were arrested daily and brought to the Mamertine Prison. Normally this would have caused overcrowding of the facility. However, it was not an issue since Christians were not afforded a trial. After their arrival at Mamertine, believers were beaten until they confessed to be involved in setting the fire and coerced into compromising the identities of other Christians.

Whether they cooperated with the prison officials or not, all of the men arrested were declared guilty of conspiring to start the fire. After being removed from Mamertine, they were executed in public. Those who were not Roman citizens were often crucified. Some were tied to trees or poles, doused with flammable liquid, and set on fire. Others were wrapped in the skins of wild animals and killed by dogs that tore them apart.

After six months of carnage, Nero escalated his efforts. He began targeting Christian women as well as men. Wives were forced to confess that their husbands were involved in starting the fire. Women who complied were released, and women who refused were executed.

Nero's abuse of women was more than Poppaea could tolerate. She decided to confront her husband and beg him to end the slaughter. She had reason to think Nero would agree to her request. Poppaea was six months pregnant. She and Nero were enjoying life together and looked forward to producing a new heir to the throne. In her estimation, he would want to please her in any way possible.

Shortly after Simon went into hiding, Poppaea suggested that Abigail move into her residence. Nero's original palace had not been damaged in the fire, and the Golden House was still under construction. A spacious suite was available near Poppaea's bedroom so Abigail would not have to commute from her apartment every day or live alone in Simon's absence. She also granted Abigail time off to visit her husband if it didn't interfere with Poppaea's schedule.

Abigail accepted Poppaea's invitation. Nero and Poppaea lived in separate quarters within the palace so Abigail's presence would not create any issues for the Emperor or his staff. Further, Nero had no idea that Abigail was the wife of one of the men he tried to implicate for setting the Great Fire.

One evening Nero appeared unannounced at Poppaea's

bedroom door. He was clearly intoxicated, and the gleam in his eye indicated why he was there. Poppaea sensed an opportunity to make her case for ending the Christian persecution.

"Darling, I didn't expect to see you tonight, but I'm glad you are gracing me with your presence," she said invitingly. "I was hoping we could make love before my pregnancy advanced much further."

"You are beautiful, my love, even more so while you are carrying the next emperor in your womb."

"Before we go to bed, would you mind if I asked you for a favor?"

"Of course not. Everything I have is yours. What do you desire?"

"Do you remember when I asked you to show mercy to Paul, the Christian who had been accused of treason by the Jews? We both knew he was innocent of the charges. Now you are persecuting the entire population of Christians for a crime that both of us know wasn't done by them. I understand that you need to deflect the false rumors that you were responsible for the fire, but destroying the lives of innocent people can't be your only alternative.

"The Christian community has been decimated. You have convinced the populace of Rome that the Christians, and not you, were responsible. Do you need to continue this killing? Isn't it time to bring this carnage to a halt? I implore you to show mercy on innocent Christians like you did for Paul."

Nero stood facing his wife, a frown forming over his lips. He swayed forward from the effects of the wine he had been drinking but caught himself before falling headlong to the floor. "How dare you question my motives and my character?" he shouted almost incoherently.

Without warning, Nero cocked his arm and with a clenched fist swung wildly at his wife. Without time to defend herself or dodge the blow, Poppaea's face absorbed the full force of his fist. She fell limply to the floor landing on her side, her nose bleeding profusely.

Poppaea remained conscious, moaning and clutching her belly. But Nero's rage, fueled by an excess of liquor and Poppaea's apparent disloyalty, erased any empathy he might have for his wife and unborn child. Nero shifted his weight to his left foot and, with every ounce of his strength, slammed the other foot into her midsection.

Without a hint of remorse, Nero turned to leave. To his surprise, a woman was standing in the open doorway. She ran past Nero and knelt next to Poppaea's motionless body. The woman checked for signs of life and, finding none, looked up at the stunned Emperor. "I think she is dead," she said quietly. Nero, suddenly sober, stormed out of the room.

Moments earlier, Abigail left her quarters and went to Poppaea's bedroom to ask if she needed anything before retiring for the night. She opened the door to see Nero punch his wife in the face and kick her prostrate body in the abdomen. Abigail could have turned and run away before Nero saw her but love for her mistress was stronger than the urge to flee.

After Nero left the room, Abigail remained with Poppaea trying to revive her without success. Seeing her efforts were futile, she turned her attention to the unborn baby but couldn't detect a heartbeat or any movement in the womb. Blood was flowing through Poppaea's gown in the area where the baby would have emerged. The rest of the evening, Abigail sat on the floor weeping, cradling Poppaea's head on her lap.

The next morning several of Nero's male servants entered Poppaea's bedroom to remove her body. "You need to come with us," said one of the servants to Abigail. "The Emperor wants to talk to you."

Abigail stood in front of Nero's throne, the same spot where Paul had been tried two years earlier. The Emperor ordered his attendants out of the room and began questioning her. "Last night you showed your affection for my wife when you saw her lying on the floor. Unfortunately, she had slipped and fallen on the marble surface and hit her head on the edge of the bed. I was leaving to get help when you appeared at the door. When I saw you had the situation under control I returned to my quarters. Is that what you saw happen?"

Abigail realized that Nero was trying to find out what she had seen. His back was to the door when he assaulted Poppaea, and he didn't notice Abigail open the door. He hoped she didn't see any of the blows that he inflicted on his wife. If she agreed to his version of events, Abigail would avoid his wrath and perhaps save her life.

"Your Excellency," Abigail replied, her voice trembling, "I want you to know that I loved your wife like a sister. I have served as her maidservant since she was fourteen years old. We became very close over the years. I can't lie. I saw you strike her with your fist. I saw you drive your foot into her pregnant belly while she lay on the floor, her face bleeding and bruised. It is a sight that I will never forget, and in good conscience I cannot deny it happened."

"I'm sorry to hear that. It appears that you are not willing to change your version of the story to agree with mine. Is that the case?"

"If I were to lie about what happened, I would be disobeying the will of my God."

"You must be a Christian. Poppaea always had a soft spot for Christians. I don't know why. You have all been deceived by a treasonous villain who advocated the downfall of Rome."

"With all due respect, Jesus was neither treasonous nor a villain," Abigail countered. "He is the Son of God who died for our sins, rose from the dead, and is preparing a place for us to be with him forever in Heaven. That is what Christians believe."

"I can see that you are not afraid of me," sneered Nero. "As I told Poppaea when she pleaded with me to release one of your leaders named Paul, Christians appear to prefer death to life here on earth."

"You are correct," affirmed Abigail. "I am not afraid of what you can do to me even if it means dying. God will take me to be with Him after I die because Jesus's suffering and death have made me acceptable to Him."

"I am inclined to grant your death wish," Nero stated. "I can't afford any more scandals during my reign. Since you refuse to be silent about what happened last night, I have no choice but to have you executed. Is there anyone that you want me to inform of your death? Because of your loyalty to Poppaea, I will tell them you died in a terrible accident, and your body could not be recovered."

"I won't disclose the names of any of my relatives or friends. You have tortured and killed enough Christians already," Abigail replied defiantly.

Nero ordered his guards to take Abigail to the Mamertine Prison to be executed that day. Her body was buried in an unmarked grave outside the city.

Chapter 17

SEARCH

"I'm starting to worry," Simon admitted to Peter. "Abigail was supposed to be here today. She hasn't missed any of our scheduled visits since you and I moved to the safe house."

"I wouldn't be too concerned. Isn't she living at the Emperor's palace? Doesn't Nero's wife treat her like a sister? I can't think of a more favorable situation for a Christian during this period of persecution."

"You're probably right. But until I see her again, I am going to double my prayers for her safety."

Later that evening, two men knocked at the front door. Simon recognized them as Benjamin and Joseph, the men who usually escorted Abigail to the safe house when she was given time off to visit him. She was not with them.

"Where is Abigail?" asked Simon with a tone of urgency in his voice.

"We aren't sure," replied Benjamin. "When we went to the palace this morning to bring her here, she didn't meet us outside the main entrance as she usually does. We waited there for hours asking anyone leaving the palace if they had seen her. Later that morning, we saw soldiers leading a woman out into the street. She looked a bit like Abigail, but we couldn't be sure because they were shielding her from our view."

"I had a strange feeling that the woman might be Abigail," Joseph admitted. "I left Benjamin at the palace and followed the guards. They took the woman into the Mamertine Prison and came out without her. I tried to get into the prison to ask who the woman was, but I was ordered to leave the area and not ask any questions."

"After Joseph returned, we stayed at the palace entrance a while longer," added Benjamin. "No one we talked to knew Abigail, but one of the servants told us a rumor was spreading that the Emperor's wife, Poppaea, might have been involved in an accident of some sort. He couldn't provide any details. No one else we questioned knew anything about the rumor. If something had happened to Poppaea, we assumed that Abigail would be by her side which would explain why she didn't meet us as planned."

"We knew you would be worried," explained Joseph, "So we came here tonight to let you know what we found out, as incomplete as it was. We will return to the city immediately and try to find out more. If Poppaea is injured, Nero will make a public announcement soon. That should give us an idea of where Abigail is."

"Thank you for coming here today and for all the effort you made to find my wife," said Simon. "What you told me is very concerning. I'm going back with you. I need to find out if Abigail needs my help. My personal safety is secondary at this point."

"I'd like to go along with you," said Peter. "I'm also very concerned about Abigail."

"We need you to stay here for now," Simon countered. "One of us needs to be in a position to lead the Christian church here in Rome."

Simon's first stop in the city after parting ways with Benjamin and Joseph was the apartment that he and Abigail shared. Hopefully, she was there or left some indication of where she had gone. A quick scan of the apartment revealed nothing out of the ordinary. Everything was in place. Dust had accumulated on the furniture indicating that she had not been home for some time, understandable because Abigail was living full-time at the palace.

The couple had several Christian friends who lived in the same complex. Simon paid them a visit in the hope that they had news about Abigail. None of them had seen her recently. Since they hadn't seen Simon for a while either, they assumed he and Abigail were traveling together.

As Simon was leaving, a non-Christian neighbor walked by in the hallway. "Have you heard?" the neighbor asked. "Nero just announced that his wife Poppaea is dead. She had a miscarriage, and the doctors were unable to save either her or the baby. They discovered it was a boy who would likely have been the next emperor. Nero is reported to be overcome with grief and has asked that Romans throughout the Empire observe a week of mourning."

Simon now understood why Abigail had not met him at the safe house. She must have been assisting the doctors while they treated Poppaea. She was probably helping to organize Poppaea's belongings for distribution to the family. Simon reasoned it would only be a brief time until she returned to their apartment.

"Have you heard anything more about the funeral arrangements?" Simon asked. "When and where will it take place? Will the public be able to view the ceremony?"

"A procession through the city is planned for next week. I understand it will take longer to prepare the body. Instead of cremation, which is normal for royalty, she is going to be mummified. Nero has always been an admirer of the Egyptians and their view of the afterlife. I also heard that the Senate is planning to deify her which is also rather unusual."

"Do you think Nero is going overboard in memorializing his wife?"

"I will deny saying this if questioned, but many Romans, including me, have been skeptical of anything Nero has said or done regarding the Great Fire. He couldn't have built his Golden House if most of Rome hadn't burned down. His persecution of Christians for starting the fire is suspect. Although I'm sad about what happened to Poppaea and her child, I imagine her death will generate a great deal of sympathy for Nero and deflect some of the speculation about his involvement in the fire."

"Regardless of whether or not the sorrow over his wife's death is genuine, my wife worked for Poppaea at the palace. I haven't been able to locate her, and I need to find out where she is and make sure she is safe. I'm afraid Nero might blame her for not taking proper care of Poppaea."

"Your fears are justified. I hate to say it, but anyone who serves Nero is at risk of incurring his wrath. He is hot-tempered when he doesn't get his way and inflexible when people don't agree with him."

For the next several days, Simon searched for Abigail. She did not return home even though her duties at the palace should have been over. He inquired at the palace and visited Mamertine Prison. No one claimed to have known or seen her. It seemed improbable that Abigail, a person who held a highly visible job at the palace, could disappear without a trace. However, no news could be considered good news in this instance. As long as he had breath, Simon was determined to exhaust any and all resources to find his wife.

One morning before beginning his daily search, Simon answered a knock at his door. A short, nondescript woman stood there holding a piece of paper that had been folded and sealed. "Are you Simon, Abigail's husband?" she asked.

"Yes, I am," he answered. "What is your name? Do you have any news about my wife?"

The woman handed Simon the paper. "My name is not important. I'm probably in trouble for being here. I worked in the palace with Abigail. Several nights ago, she asked me to deliver this to you. I have no idea what it says, but I could tell she was distraught at the time. After learning of Poppaea's death, I can understand why."

"Have you seen Abigail since then? I've been searching for her for the last few days with no success. No one in the palace will admit to even knowing her."

"That is why I was reluctant to come here. I haven't seen her since she handed me this paper. Soon after I left Abigail, rumors began to spread that something had happened to Poppaea. Later I heard that Nero met with your wife privately. After the meeting she was escorted out of the palace. That afternoon we were told that Poppaea had died after a miscarriage, but no details were given, and nothing was said about Abigail. I wouldn't be surprised if Nero is trying to hide information about Poppaea and Abigail."

"That might explain why I haven't had any success locating her. Perhaps she is being held somewhere against her will. I appreciate your bravery in coming today. I won't let anyone know that you were here. Not knowing your name is probably a good idea."

Simon invited the woman in, but she declined. "I need to get back to the palace. I don't believe anyone followed me here, but Nero has eyes all over Rome. I hope you find Abigail soon and that she is safe and well.

Stunned by what had just happened, Simon retreated into his apartment and unsealed the folded document which read:

My Dearest Husband,

I am writing to you from Poppaea's bedroom after witnessing something so heinous that I will have a difficult time describing it without weeping. As I do every evening, I went to Poppaea's room to see if she needed anything before retiring for the night.

I opened her door only to see Nero hit his wife in the face with a closed fist. She collapsed on the floor, bleeding and moaning. Nero stepped forward and kicked her in the stomach. He turned to leave and was startled to see me at the door.

I ran to Poppaea's side and found that she was not breathing. After I told him she was dead, he exited into the hallway. The smell of liquor on his breath permeated the room. Nero's back was toward the door when I opened it, so he was probably unsure how much I had seen. In any case, I represented a potential threat to his already tarnished reputation.

As you read this letter, you are probably wondering why I am writing this from Poppaea's bedroom instead of leaving the palace to return home to our apartment or to stay with some of our friends. First of all, I owed it to Poppaea to try to revive her and possibly save her unborn child. When I couldn't, I felt obligated to stay with her body.

Secondly, I knew Nero could track me down no matter where I hid. He has probably already notified his guards to stop me at the palace gate. Even if I were able to escape the palace, I wouldn't want to jeopardize the lives of our friends who might try to help me. There has been too much bloodshed already.

So, I sit here writing to say I love you. I pray that God protects me from harm if it is His will. But I know that even if Nero takes my life, I will be with Jesus in Heaven. My sins are forgiven, paid for by his suffering and death on the cross. Our resurrection is assured by his resurrection. You and I will be together again in the Heavenly kingdom where there will be eternal joy.

I hope that this letter will provide you some closure if my death is imminent. I am hoping for the best but prepared for the worst. Always remember that I love you more than anything on earth. I know you feel the same way about me.

Your loving wife,

Abigail

After reading the letter, Simon broke down and cried uncontrollably. He now had to find out what had happened to Abigail. He prayed she was still alive. That afternoon, Simon paid another visit to Mamertine Prison and waited outside until the Captain of the Guard emerged.

"Sir, I hate to bother you," apologized Simon, "But I am looking for someone who entered the prison a few days ago."

"Don't waste my time," the Captain replied with a tone of

distain. "Hundreds of people come and go through those doors every day. I don't keep track of everyone."

"This person is a woman. In fact, she is my wife. Her name is Abigail. The day that Nero announced that his wife and unborn child had died, she was taken here. As far as I know, she never left the prison. I need to know if she is being held in one of the cells."

"You must be misinformed. No women are jailed here. Even if she were, I wouldn't provide any information to you or anyone else without permission from the Emperor. This prison is reserved for enemies of the state, and the status of prisoners is confidential."

"I understand the need for confidentiality. But we are talking about my wife. If she isn't here, can you tell me if she was taken somewhere else?"

"As I said, information regarding our prisoners is confidential, whether they are housed here at the prison or not."

Simon put his hand on a bag of coins tied to his belt. "If someone wanted to locate a Roman citizen who was wrongly charged with a crime they didn't commit, would you consider helping them? You would be providing information about an innocent citizen and not an enemy of the state. Further, you would be rewarded handsomely for your assistance. No one else would know that you cooperated."

The Captain of the Guard was no stranger to bribery. For sizeable sums of money, he spared the lives of several senators whom Nero had sentenced to death. In order to disguise his actions, the Captain executed two petty criminals and battered their bodies beyond recognition. On orders from Nero, he paraded the bodies around the city to show what corrupt senators should expect. The senators who escaped the death sentence fled the country and spent the rest of their lives in permanent exile. No one was the wiser, and the Captain of the Guard was significantly richer.

"I generally don't like to deal in hypotheticals. However, if I were to do a favor involving an innocent citizen, what type of reward could I expect?"

"I am not a rich man, but my wife is the most important person in my life. I will pay any amount you ask if you help me find her, even if it takes the rest of my life to do so."

"The love you have for your wife is admirable. It shows strength of character that I rarely see in my line of business. I wouldn't be surprised if you were a Christian. Many of them have passed through this prison and, in spite of the prospect of beatings and death, they never stopped trusting in their God. I don't need your money, and I suspect that it wouldn't be much. Unfortunately, the answer you are looking for is not what you were hoping for."

"You are frightening me. But I still need to know even if it breaks my heart. Please tell me what happened to her."

"We received a woman prisoner who had been tried before Nero. I don't know the charges that were brought or why a guilty verdict was reached. All I know is that I was ordered to execute her and bury her body in the field reserved for nameless criminals. Is there anything else you need to know?"

Simon sobbed unabashedly. After regaining control, he asked, "How did she die? Was she beaten before you killed her? Where was she buried?"

"She was not beaten. The orders were to execute her. Her death was quick. She declared herself to be a citizen of Rome.

This required us to behead her rather than using a drawn-out method such as crucifixion which is reserved for non-citizens."

"You say that with a lack of emotion. With all due respect, how do you live with yourself? My wife did nothing other than serve her mistress faithfully. You and Nero have murdered an innocent woman."

"You will have to take that up with the Emperor. As for me, I am making a living for myself and my family. When I leave this prison each afternoon, I don't look back."

The Captain sent one of his guards with Simon to the field where Abigail was buried. The plot of land served as an unmarked mass graveyard for victims of the Roman justice system. In Judaea, it would have been called a potter's field. There was no way to identify the exact spot where her body lay, but knowing the general location provided partial closure.

Simon remained there until evening, alternating between tears of sorrow and praise to God for the time he had been given with Abigail. At another time in his life, the former Zealot would have sought revenge against everyone involved. Now, because of what Jesus taught, Simon prayed for strength to forgive those who had taken Abigail's life.

Three months after discovering Abigail's fate, Simon and Peter moved from the safe house back into the city. There was a chance that Nero might be looking for them, but by this time the persecution of Christians had been largely suspended. Speculation about Nero's involvement in the Great Fire was no longer an issue to most of the citizenry. Nero's focus turned to suppression of revolts springing up throughout the Empire in reaction to his egregious taxation policies.

It didn't take long for Simon to conclude he couldn't remain in Rome any longer. He tried to stay busy doing the work of the church, but every night he returned to an empty apartment. He firmly believed he would be reunited with Abigail in Heaven, but he couldn't shake the grief and depression that was slowly engulfing him.

"Peter, I need to get away," Simon confessed. "I can't go anywhere in Rome without triggering memories of Abigail. From the time we met until now my world revolved around her. I don't know how I can stay here when I am constantly reminded of our life together and the tragic way she died."

"I empathize with your pain," replied Peter. "As you might have heard, my wife died several years ago while we were living in Jerusalem. That is part of the reason I decided to come to Rome. Like you, I had a difficult time carrying on without her. We deeply miss our wives, but we both know their souls are now with Jesus in Heaven awaiting the resurrection of their bodies at his second coming. That knowledge gives hope going forward, but it can't fully erase the emptiness we feel.

"You have been here in Rome for nearly twenty years, and the church has experienced outstanding growth and unification under your leadership. Given the circumstances, no one could fault you for leaving the congregation here to minister elsewhere. Where are you planning to go?"

"I would like to return to Jerusalem to assist the Apostle John. After you left there to come to Rome, John was the only Apostle still there. The others are spreading Jesus' message in other locations or unfortunately have been martyred. Although there are fewer Christians in Jerusalem than in Rome, John must deal with opposition that is more hardcore. The Sanhedrin in Jerusalem tends to be more orthodox than leadership in Rome and more apt to actively oppose Christians."

"If you leave for Jerusalem, would you ever consider returning to Rome?"

Simon thought for a moment and replied, "Honestly, I don't think so, but it would ultimately be up the Lord. Paul told me about several instances in which Jesus redirected him from his original plans. My biggest regret will be leaving all my Christian friends whom I have come to know and love. But Abigail's death continues to haunt me. I need to restart my life somewhere else where I can continue to serve the Lord with peace of mind."

"You certainly have my blessing, Simon. I suggest you spend more time in prayer to make sure this is the direction in which God wants you to go. If you still feel positive about leaving, then by all means do so."

The following week, Simon booked a sea voyage to Jerusalem. The entire congregation in Rome traveled to Ostia to send him off. The parting was tearful, but Simon knew that the church would thrive under Peter's leadership.

Prayers were offered to bless Simon's endeavors in Jerusalem and wherever else God might lead him. As the ship pulled away from the dock, Simon looked back wistfully and thanked God for the opportunity to share the love of Jesus with the people of Rome and for the tremendous joy that Abigail had given him.

Chapter 18

REBELLION

Simon stopped in his tracks. As he approached the marketplace in the center of Jerusalem, dozens of Roman soldiers in full battle gear marched past him. Soldiers on patrol were a common sight in the city, but this was clearly different. The standard bearer's flag was unfamiliar. Simon concluded that these troops were from somewhere other than Jerusalem.

When the soldiers reached the middle of the marketplace, they came to a halt. Seconds later a trumpet sounded. Simon recognized the sound immediately. While in Rome he had heard it often during periods of civil disobedience. It was a signal to attack.

The soldiers pulled swords from their scabbards, charged into the crowd, and struck down anyone within reach. Shoppers and vendors scattered, stumbling over each other in an effort to escape. Screams filled the air and blood flowed in the street.

Simon turned and ran as fast as he could from the carnage taking place. By the time he reached his apartment, his heart was nearly beating out of his chest. After catching his breath and calming himself down, Simon thanked God that he had not gone to the marketplace earlier. He also prayed for those who were wounded and for the families of those who had been killed.

Simon couldn't believe what he had witnessed. When he arrived almost a week earlier, there was no indication of trouble brewing. After a month-long sea voyage from Rome to Caesarea Maritima followed by a sixty-five-mile overland trip to Jerusalem, Simon spent the first two days looking for housing. He found a modest apartment in the Lower City where many in the Christian community resided. That morning, he intended to buy food and other necessities for his new home, but his trip to the marketplace was cut short by the violence.

Simon hadn't informed the believers in Jerusalem that he was coming. After his days as a bully in synagogue school ended, Simon no longer enjoyed being the center of attention. He had planned to contact his fellow Apostle John after getting completely settled in, but Simon decided to pay John a visit that evening. He needed to find out what had happened at the marketplace.

John welcomed Simon warmly and expressed surprise that

Simon had come to Jerusalem unannounced. They exchanged pleasantries before moving on to more weighty topics of conversation.

"Peter sends you his greetings from Rome," Simon began. "The situation there has improved now that persecution of Christians has become a lesser priority for Nero. You might have heard that my wife, Abigail, was a casualty of his cruelty. It was a devastating loss for me. That is the primary reason I returned to Jerusalem. It was too painful to remain where memories of my deceased wife were constantly triggered."

"Yes, I did hear, and I am so sorry for your loss," John sympathized. "But I know you are comforted knowing that Abigail's soul is in Heaven with our Lord. You said that her death was the primary reason you left Rome. That implies there are other reasons."

"There is an additional factor. I came to offer my assistance in the administration of the church in Jerusalem. You and Peter are considered the leaders of the worldwide church. Now that Peter is in Rome, I imagine you might need help dealing with local issues."

"I welcome your support, my friend. We have a strong leadership group here in Jerusalem, but none of them knew Jesus personally as you and I did. I could use another voice who can provide eyewitness testimony of Jesus' life, death, and resurrection. Also, I have heard reports on your success in expanding and unifying the church in Rome. That experience will be invaluable in administering the Jerusalem church as well."

"I'm pleased that you feel I can be of help. I should have asked your opinion before leaving Rome, but I was planning to come here in any case. I look forward to assisting you in any way I can. By the way, what happened at the marketplace this morning? I was on my way there to buy supplies for my apartment and saw Roman soldiers attack innocent men and women. I was hoping to find out what caused the unprovoked assault."

"About a year ago, Nero appointed a man named Gessius Florus as procurator of the province of Judaea. It's rumored he got the job because his wife was a friend of Nero's wife, Poppaea. In any case, Florus was unfit for the job. His attitude toward the Jews was hostile from the beginning. He came here from Greece and has consistently showed favoritism to the Greeks over the Jews throughout the province."

"Do you have an example of Florus' preferential treatment of Greeks?"

"The most blatant incident happened three months ago in Caesarea Maritima. As you are aware, the capital of Judaea was moved there from Jerusalem shortly after Herod the Great died. That was about the time that you and I were born. Gessius Florus governs from there, and the majority of the city's residents are Greek.

"The largest synagogue in Caesarea Maritima is located next to a Greek commercial building. The owners of the building resented being located so close to a Jewish place of worship, but neither party could reach a satisfactory agreement to buy out the other. The impasse reached a fever pitch when the Greeks began offering pagan sacrifices on the steps of the synagogue. The Jews were outraged at this sacrilegious act and appealed to the city magistrates to stop the Greeks from defiling their holy place.

"Their appeal landed on deaf ears, so the Jews appealed to Gessius Florus. An audience with Florus did not come cheap. The Jewish community had to raise eight talents of gold in order to meet with him. Since a talent of gold is equal to twenty years of a laborer's wages, it is clear the Jews were desperate to end the desecration of their synagogue. Shortly before the scheduled meeting, Florus left the city without notifying the Jewish representatives. The meeting has not been held to this day, and Florus has not returned any of the money."

"I can understand how this incident and others like it must have caused resentment on the part of Jews. I can also understand how Florus must have been upset that the Jews were blaming the Greeks. But none of those issues should result in the massacre of innocent people," Simon reasoned.

"You are correct," admitted John. "The primary obstacle to peaceful coexistence between Jews and Romans is the burdensome level of taxes that Florus has imposed. He claims his actions are directed by Nero in order to rebuild Rome after the fire. However, it was discovered that Florus was funneling a large percentage of the tax collections into his own pocket. In any case, whether the funds were diverted to Florus or sent to Rome for building projects, the tax money was not being used to improve the lives of the people living in Judaea. Jewish leadership petitioned the Roman government to ease the tax burden and to replace Florus, but to no avail."

"Excessive taxation by Rome has always been a thorn in the side of Jews," noted Simon. "Something extraordinary must have happened to cause the incident this morning. What triggered the random killing by the Roman soldiers?"

"Two months ago, the Sanhedrin received a demand from Florus to remit seventeen talents of gold from the Temple treasury, presumably to fund a cash shortage in Rome. His demand was unanimously rejected due to the outrageous amount and, more importantly, because funds in the treasury are designated solely for the maintenance of the Temple."

"I imagine that refusal didn't sit well with Florus."

"No, it didn't. A few days ago, Florus and three cohorts of his soldiers, 1,440 in total, marched to Jerusalem. This morning during the daily sacrifices, Florus and several hundred of his men attempted to gain access to the Temple in order to seize funds in the treasury. Eleazar ben Ananias, who serves as Captain of the Temple, ordered the Temple guards to block the Romans from entering."

"I'm not familiar with Eleazar ben Ananias," Simon confessed. "He must have been appointed since I left for Rome."

"Eleazar is the son of the former high priest Ananias. Ananias was the high priest when the Apostle Paul was arrested on the false charge he brought a Gentile into the Temple. Before Ananias stepped down as High Priest, he appointed Eleazar as his second in command.

"As the Captain of the Temple, Eleazar oversees a total of 7,200 Levites who guard the Temple and the sacred scrolls stored there. They are divided into twenty-four shifts each of which serves two weeks a year. At any one time, 300 Temple guards are present in the Temple working around the clock. They have pledged to defend the Temple and its sacred documents from anyone attempting to destroy them, including the Romans.

"Eleazar is one of several young priests who have diverged from the politics of the older generation. The aging members of the Sanhedrin, particularly the Sadducees, have been willing to let Rome dictate Jewish religious practices in in exchange for personal wealth and political power. The new generation wants to preserve Jewish religious beliefs and traditions without interference from Rome. I'm not surprised that Eleazar would take such a bold stand against Florus."

"What happened when Eleazar prevented Florus and his troops from entering the Temple?"

"The Roman soldiers were outnumbered, so they waited outside the Temple for reinforcements. During the standoff, some of the young priests threw coins at Florus to mock his penchant for greed. Embarrassed and frustrated by his failure to gain entry, Florus ordered his soldiers to retreat from the Temple Mount to the marketplace before reinforcements arrived. They conducted the attack that you witnessed."

"I didn't return to see how much damage was done. Do you know how many casualties there were?"

"Several hundred men and women were killed this morning. The carnage continued this afternoon in different parts of the city. Hundreds more were killed. I believe the worst isn't over yet. Florus will continue to punish Jerusalem for disobeying and embarrassing him."

"When do you think this assault will end?"

"I don't think Florus will try to seize control of the entire city, at least not now. There aren't enough Roman soldiers to accomplish that. He will probably continue doing damage until his anger subsides. Then he and his troops will return to Caesarea."

"Do you have any information on Christian casualties?"

"Most Christians live in the Lower City. After the massacre in the morning, the Roman soldiers concentrated on the Upper City where the wealthy Jews live. I don't believe our community of believers was impacted at all."

"I can see why the situation here has deteriorated so quickly," observed Simon. "I'm not surprised that money issues triggered the unrest. After Nero drained Rome's treasury, the only way to replenish it was to increase taxes throughout the Empire."

"Judaea can't be the only province that is feeling the tax burden," John proposed.

"That is correct," Simon replied. "Taxation policies have sparked uprisings in Gaul, Britain, and Germania. The Roman army quickly crushed them. The province of Judaea appears ripe for a similar rebellion. I'm afraid incidents like the one today will trigger a bloody war which the Jews have no possibility of winning."

Later that evening, John called a meeting of Christian leaders. After introducing Simon to the group, he asked for any new information regarding the marketplace attack. To the relief of everyone present, it was confirmed that none of Jesus' followers had been killed or injured in the melee. The meeting ended with a prayer for peace and thanksgiving for the protection God had provided.

John's predictions regarding duration and severity of the fighting proved accurate. During a week of chaos, nearly 3,600 Jews lost their lives, 2,000 of whom were crucified. After Florus convinced himself that the Jews had been sufficiently punished, he ordered most of his troops back to Caesarea, leaving several hundred behind to assist the local Roman garrison in preserving order.

Instead of being intimidated by Florus' military capability, the Jews were emboldened by his withdrawal. Residents of Jerusalem, aided and encouraged by the Zealots, destroyed several Roman government buildings. Showing disdain for the Roman army, they captured the Antonia Fortress and executed the 480 Roman soldiers stationed there.

These actions were sufficient to provoke Nero's anger. However, the act of defiance that captured the most attention in Rome did not involve destruction of property or military losses. Eleazar ben Ananias, the Captain of the Guard who prevented Florus from entering the Temple, persuaded his fellow priests to discontinue Temple sacrifices made on behalf of foreigners.

During the early years of Roman rule, Emperor Caligula regarded himself as a god who should be worshipped. He demanded that the Jews offer daily sacrifices to him in the Jerusalem Temple. The Jews, who worshipped only one God, would not condone such sacrilege and threatened rebellion. In a spirit of compromise, Caligula agreed that making sacrifices to the Jewish God on his behalf was an acceptable alternative. This practice continued uninterrupted until Eleazar put a stop to it. This affront to the authority of the emperor signaled to Nero that the Jews no longer considered themselves subject to Roman rule.

While Florus was attacking Jerusalem, hostilities were taking place sixty miles south of the city. An extreme faction of Zealots called Sicarii carried out a surprise raid on the Roman fortress of Masada and executed the Roman soldiers stationed there.

Masada was a one of several fortresses constructed by Herod the Great to provide refuge in the event he needed to escape from Jerusalem. Herod chose this location because it was seemingly impenetrable from all sides. Located on an eighteen-acre plateau, the cliffs that surrounded the fortress rose 1,300 feet from the desert floor.

The entire plateau was encircled by a thirteen-foot-high wall interspersed with towers that allowed defenders to shoot arrows, throw rocks, or pour burning oil on attackers. Three narrow winding paths led from the base of the cliffs to massive gates at the summit.

In addition to two elaborate palaces, Masada's infrastructure included storage buildings filled with large supplies of food and weapons, cisterns to collect rainwater, and living quarters for the troops stationed there. The capture of Masada gave the Zealots a stronghold near Jerusalem that was nearly impervious to direct attack or prolonged siege.

After Florus withdrew and the Jews retained control of the city, Jerusalem experienced a short period of uneasy calm. The cessation of hostilities allowed Simon to travel to Bethany, the town where he was born and raised. Bethany was located two miles southeast of Jerusalem and was the home of Mary and Martha, sisters of his deceased friend Lazarus.

Simon had lost touch with the women during his stay in Rome. He was now sixty-one years old, the same age Lazarus would have been had he lived. If his memory were accurate, Martha would be sixty-five and Mary sixty-three. He prayed he would find them in good health.

Simon's first stop was the Bethany Inn which Mary and her husband, Caleb, owned. He was told by the new proprietor that Caleb died several years earlier. Soon after her husband's death, Mary sold the business to him. He believed she still lived in Bethany.

Simon next visited the house where Lazarus and his sisters were raised. Martha lived there and operated her father's pottery shop on the property after he died. He discovered that a man and his family purchased the house five years earlier. The new owner told Simon that Martha lived in a house nearby on the road to the synagogue. He believed she lived there with her sister.

The synagogue was situated at the top of a hill, the highest point in Bethany. As he walked up the road, Simon recalled his daily trek to synagogue school until he graduated at the age of fifteen. He remembered with regret his early years as a bully to his classmates, including Lazarus. Unpleasant images were offset by fond memories of the friendship that later developed between the two of them.

"I can't believe it's you," Mary exclaimed. "We knew you relocated to Rome and were worried that you might be caught up in the persecution of Christians there."

"I'm so happy to see you again," declared Martha. "Quite a few things have changed since you brought us back from Damascus years ago. Caleb died and Mary sold the inn. I got tired of making pottery, so I sold the shop and the old house which was too big. We both live here rather comfortably. The money we received from selling everything should last the rest of our lives, God willing."

"Come in and relax," Mary offered. "You are welcome to stay with us while you are in Bethany. We want to hear what has happened since we last saw you and what your plans are for the future."

For the rest of the day and into the evening, Simon recounted the events of his life over the past thirty years. Mary and Martha expressed their sympathies over the death of his wife and congratulated him on his accomplishments with the church in Rome.

"I give all credit to God for any successes that were achieved in furthering His kingdom," Simon said. "I know that Abigail is with Jesus in Heaven and I look forward to being reunited with her when my life here is done."

"What are your plans going forward?" asked Martha. "Will you stay in the area or are you just passing through?"

"My immediate plans are to remain in Jerusalem and assist the Apostle John in administering the church there. Shortly after I arrived a serious impasse between Jews and Romans resulted in violence by both sides. We have a large community of Christians in the city, and I don't want any of us to be harmed. Perhaps I can help to calm things down."

"We're a bit isolated here in Bethany," remarked Mary. "We don't know much about political discord in Jerusalem. How bad is it?"

"The violence I spoke about was provoked by procurator Gessius Florus. Zealots have gained significant influence throughout the province of Judaea, and they are committed to fighting for independence from Rome. If anything happens that might endanger the residents of Bethany, I will move you to safety just as I did after your brother was murdered."

Chapter 19

JEREMIAH

After becoming aware of the worsening situation in Judaea, Emperor Nero concluded that Gessius Florus was incapable of quelling the unrest. He ordered Cestius Gallus, the procurator of Syria, to suppress the Jewish uprising. Gallus led an army of 30,000 troops from Antioch in Syria to Jerusalem. On the way south, his army wreaked havoc throughout Galilee, destroying several towns and cities and murdering many of the residents.

After Cestius Gallus and his army arrived at Jerusalem, he attacked the northern section of the city. His men broke through the city wall and made their way toward the Temple where the Zealots, led by Eleazar ben Simon, and the Temple Guard, led by Eleazar ben Ananias, made a last-ditch effort to save the sacred place of worship. For nine days the defenders of the Temple, outmanned by Gallus' soldiers, fought with such intensity they were able to drive the Roman forces out of the city.

Realizing that winter was approaching and that his current detachment of soldiers would not be able to overcome the Jerusalem defenders in a timely manner, Gallus decided to return to Syria with his men to regroup and make plans to attack again the following spring.

Eleazar ben Simon was not content to let the Romans leave quietly. He and his fellow Zealots followed Gallus' army northward and ambushed them at a narrow mountain pass called Beth Horon. The attack caught Gallus and his troops by surprise. More than 5,000 soldiers under his command were killed. Those fortunate enough to escape carried their wounded with them, leaving nearly everything else behind. The Jewish rebels became beneficiaries of a trove of Roman uniforms, body armor, weapons, and equipment which could be used in the event of another attack on Jerusalem.

Two months after Cestius Gallus and his soldiers limped back to Syria, the Apostle John stopped by Simon's apartment. "Hello, my friend," greeted Simon, "To what do I owe the pleasure of your visit?"

"I came here today to inform you of developments that could impact our Christian community in Jerusalem. Rome has been relatively silent lately. I wondered why Nero hadn't reacted to

Cestius Gallus' failure to take control of the city. I just learned the answer. Soon after he returned to Syria, Gallus was found dead. Officials there say he died of natural causes, but I'm not convinced that was the case. Nero was extremely unhappy with his performance, particularly the massacre of Roman troops at Beth Horen."

"How does that affect us?" asked Simon.

"I fear we are going to pay for the actions of out-of-control Jews. Both Florus and Gallus jeopardized the tenuous relationship between Rome and Judaea. The failures of the Roman procurators emboldened the Jews, particularly the Zealots, to promote all-out war to achieve independence.

"I just found out that Nero has sent one of his top generals, Vespasian, to quash a potential full-scale rebellion. He and his army recently landed in the Mediterranean port city of Ptolemais in northern Galilee. From there they marched to Antioch in Syria where they are preparing to invade Judaea.

"Vespasian currently commands three legions along with a number of auxiliary troops from Syria. Altogether there are 60,000 soldiers at his disposal. His son, Titus, serves as second in command. Without a doubt their primary target is Jerusalem. It might be a good time for Christians to leave the city."

"I'm not surprised," Simon remarked. "Nero would never allow insubordination by a small province like Judaea. It would ruin his reputation throughout the Empire. I have a feeling that unless an offer of peace is made by the Jews before Vespasian gets to Jerusalem, the city and its residents will not survive."

"I agree with you. I understand that the Sanhedrin feels the same way. They attempted to communicate with Roman authorities in both Syria and Rome to ease the tension. When their peace initiatives were not successful, they sent an envoy named Josephus to Galilee to fortify its cities and towns against attack. He is working with the residents of the larger cities there to strengthen their fortifications and fill their storerooms with food in the event of a siege. They don't expect the Galileans to stop the Romans, but it is hoped they can slow Vespasian's army as it heads south."

"I'm encouraged by what the Sanhedrin is trying to do," Simon replied. "Peaceful coexistence with Rome is the only way for the Jewish nation to survive. Unfortunately, that will be difficult given the political climate in which Zealots and most ordinary citizens are intent on war. Perhaps when people are aware that the Roman army is on its way, they will recognize the need to negotiate. If peace can't be achieved through negotiation, fighting or surrendering would be the only two options remaining. Now, more than ever, Christians need to trust that God will look after us."

A week after John visited Simon, Simon appeared at John's door. Before John could greet him, Simon exclaimed, "Do you remember suggesting it might be time for Christians to leave Jerusalem? I agree with you that the time is now."

"I wasn't completely serious. Vespasian's army hasn't left Syria yet. What makes you think we need to leave now?"

"Last night I had a vision. I was wide awake when an angel of the Lord appeared to me. He asked if I was familiar with the prophet Jeremiah. I replied that I had read his writings in synagogue school and heard portions of them read in Sabbath worship. The angel then announced that God wants me to imitate what Jeremiah did 600 years ago. Before I could ask what he meant, the angel disappeared. I came here today to discuss with you what the angel told me."

"It's been a while since I studied the prophet Jeremiah," John admitted. "I remember that he was sent by God to warn the Jews that the destruction of Jerusalem was imminent and they would be taken into exile in Babylonia. Jeremiah's prophesy was fulfilled, just as God revealed to him. If that is what the angel meant, God is telling you that Jerusalem will be destroyed by the Romans and that you need to warn the Jews this is going to happen."

"I'm not sure the angel's message was as clear-cut as that," Simon remarked. "You identified the main message, but there might be more to it. Jeremiah also gave the Jews a way out of the mess they had created. He said that God had lost patience with them because they were continually disobedient, primarily in their worship of idols.

"However, God said that He loved them despite their wrongdoing, and that He still considered them His people. If they repented of their sins and changed their ways, He would forgive and not punish them. Perhaps if the Jews can be convinced to repent of their wrongdoing, destruction of Jerusalem can be avoided."

"Have you considered whom you are going to warn and what are you going to tell them?"

"With regard to whom I will warn, there are two major players in Jerusalem. One is the Zealot party, and the other is the Sanhedrin. They are on opposite sides politically. The Zealots want to lead the country into a war for independence, and the Sanhedrin wants to maintain the status quo. I plan to reach out to the Zealots first because they currently have the most influence in determining which direction the city goes.

"Regarding what I will tell them, both groups need to hear that disaster is near and that a true change of heart is required to avoid it. That change must include repenting of their sins and believing that without God' grace through faith in Jesus there can be no forgiveness."

"I think you have identified what you need to tell them," agreed John. "If they reject that message, their fate is sealed."

"What are the implications of the angel's message for Christians?" asked Simon. "In Jeremiah's day, people could only look forward to Jesus' coming. We have witnessed his life, death, and resurrection. Should Christians who believe that Jesus is the promised Messiah suffer the same fate as those who have not believed? I think not. That is why I am advocating that Christians leave Jerusalem as soon as possible."

"I agree with you," John said. "But don't you think we should wait to leave until you have reached out to the Jews who are in charge as you just indicated? If they accept your message, we will not have to leave. If they reject your message, then it will be time for Christians to move to a safer location."

"That is a great point," Simon replied. "We should wait. Interestingly, Jeremiah's prophesies of gloom and doom were not well received by his audience. He was rejected by royalty, common folks, and even his own family. He was beaten, imprisoned, and thrown into a dry well to die. I hope God doesn't require me to imitate that part of his life."

"Eleazar ben Simon! It's been nearly forty years since we last saw each other."

"Simon, my old friend, I almost didn't recognize you. It's a shame we lost contact, but I see that time has been kind to you."

"You look good for an old man as well. I understand that you are now the leader of the Zealots in Jerusalem."

"You might say that. Just as it was when you joined, the Zealots have no formal hierarchy. However, I am one of the primary decision makers. Seniority has its privileges, and I am the most senior member. I have the backing of my fellow Zealots in the city and surrounding area. Other Zealot factions exist in regions such as Galilee, but Judea has the largest membership."

"Your advancement is impressive. By the way, I heard about another Eleazar, son of former High Priest Ananias, who serves as Captain of the Temple Guard. Apparently, Eleazar ben Ananias stood up to Gessius Florus when he tried to enter the Temple. Do you know him? It sounds like he would make a good Zealot."

"Yes, I know him. His Temple Guard and my Zealots drove the forces of Cestius Gallus out of Jerusalem. He and the other young priests are very protective of Jewish religious practices and the sanctity of the Temple. They have that in common with the Zealots. However, I understand that Eleazar ben Ananias is opposed to going to war against the Romans as are most of the Jewish religious leaders. That is where he and I differ."

"At this point, you are probably wondering why I asked to meet with you."

"I thought you were going to ask about rejoining the Zealots."

"When I was young and passionate about independence from Rome, I was a committed Zealot. But my life went in a different direction after I met a rabbi named Jesus. His philosophy is to love everyone, even our enemies. I'm afraid that it isn't compatible with Zealot ideology.

"In any case, I came here to warn you and the rest of Jerusalem that danger is imminent. As I'm sure you already know, General Vespasian is in Syria preparing his troops to invade Judaea. Nero wants to restore order before current unrest escalates into full scale rebellion. Jerusalem will be his primary target."

"I am aware that the Romans are preparing to attack us, but I am not afraid of them. They are playing into our hands. We want independence from Rome and that is what we will accomplish. Their army is not invincible. A short while ago, I led the Zealots to victory over Gallus' forces at Beth Horon. We killed 5,000 of their soldiers and recovered a huge number of weapons and equipment that will help us defeat Vespasian. However, the biggest advantage we have is that God is on our side. The Jews are his chosen people, and He will lead us to total victory."

"What if I told you that God might not be on your side?"

"What do you mean? You are a Jew. That is blasphemy."

"I am a Jew by birth but now consider myself a Christian. I follow Jesus, the Messiah promised long ago. The Jews were chosen by God to be the ancestral line from which Jesus was born. Now that the Messiah has come, all people, Jews and Gentiles alike, have been chosen by God to be His people. Everyone who believes in what Jesus has done for them will be saved and live with God forever in Heaven."

"Years ago, I heard talk about a rabbi named Jesus from Galilee who allegedly healed sick people. But that Jesus couldn't have been the Messiah since he died without freeing Jews from Roman rule. As far as I'm concerned, that is the only requirement the true Messiah must fulfil."

"I understand why you think that way. Immediately after Jesus was crucified, the hope of his followers that he was the Messiah appeared shattered. While he was with us, we were certain Jesus was the one who would restore David's kingdom. We had ample reason to believe after being eyewitnesses to his miraculous powers.

"You heard that Jesus healed a few people. That is a gross understatement. In the presence of many witnesses, including me, Jesus cured leprosy, blindness, deafness, paralysis, blood disorders, and deformities. He cast evil spirits out of individuals who were demon possessed. People were healed simply by touching his garments.

"Jesus' miracles went beyond healing. At a wedding celebration he turned gallons of water into wine. Later he fed thousands of people with only a few fish and some small loaves of bread. Even more astounding, he raised my friend Lazarus from the dead after his body had decomposed for four days in the family tomb.

"Jesus did so many unbelievable things that I sometimes took his miracles for granted, but there was one that I will never forget. During Jesus' ministry we often sailed to our next destination instead of walking. One night our boat was caught in a furious storm on the Sea of Galilee. We were certain we were about to drown. Jesus was tired from a day of teaching and was sleeping in the back of the boat. We woke him and implored him to help us navigate the storm. Instead, he commanded the wind and waves to be still. Immediately, the storm ceased as if it had never occurred.

"All of these displays of his power caused us to believe that Jesus was the Promised One who would liberate our nation. If Jesus could command the weather, he could certainly destroy legions of Roman soldiers with lightning and hail. We planned to crown Jesus as our king just as his ancestors David and Solomon had been."

Eleazar listened intently, paused a moment, and responded, "If what you just described is even close to being true, I understand why you thought that Jesus could be the Messiah. However, you said your hopes appeared shattered after he died. What caused you to have faith in him after his death?"

"If you have a difficult time believing that Jesus performed miracles, you are going to have a harder time accepting what I tell you next. Three days after Jesus died, God raised him from the dead. Jesus appeared bodily to me and the other disciples. He showed us the wounds from his crucifixion, so we knew it was him. Later he showed himself to hundreds of people in Galilee. For the next forty days, Jesus remained with us until he ascended to his home in Heaven."

"You are correct. Your story does sound unbelievable. But even if it has a shred of truth, I don't understand why you continue to think Jesus is the Messiah. He still hasn't restored our independence."

"That is because the Messiah whom you and I were expecting was not the Messiah that God promised us. Jews have been looking for a warrior king who would reestablish the nation's former glory. When the prophet Isaiah foretold that God was sending a Redeemer, he was talking about redemption from the consequences of our sinfulness and not from the country's enemies.

"During our time together, Jesus predicted that he would suffer, die, and then rise again after three days in the grave. We ignored those predictions because we couldn't accept that he would leave us before accomplishing what we expected of the Messiah. Once Jesus died and rose again, he made it clear to us that he had completed the mission assigned by God. He endured the punishment we deserve for our sins so we could stand guiltless before God on the Day of Judgement. Jesus' sacrifice for the sins of all mankind is the true test of the Messiah.

"Eleazar, my warning to you is that unless the Jewish people repent of their sins and believe in Jesus as their Savior from sin, you and your city will meet the same fate as your ancestors in the days of Jeremiah the prophet. I bring this word directly from the angel of God who appeared to me in a vision. God still loves the Jewish people and has given you this opportunity to be saved from destruction. I pray that you take it."

"Simon, I believe that you are sincere in your beliefs. However, as a Jew who is faithful to the traditions of our people, I can only conclude that you have somehow been deceived. Therefore, I will disregard your warning and give you mine. If you or your Christian friends collaborate with the Romans in any way, the Zealots will consider you to be our enemy just as we view our Roman oppressors and anyone who supports them."

Disappointed that he made no inroads with the Zealots, Simon turned his attention to Jewish religious leaders. The Sanhedrin maintained a high level of credibility with most Jews even though their political influence was being usurped by the Zealots.

Persuading the Sanhedrin to heed the angel's warning would require a complete reversal of their belief system. However, Simon was willing to try.

Simon chose Nicodemus to be his initial contact. He was surprised to learn that Nicodemus was still a member of the Sanhedrin. During Jesus' ministry, Nicodemus came to faith through the Holy Spirit. He kept his relationship a secret over the years in order to advocate for Jesus and his followers whenever possible.

Simon visited Nicodemus at his home in the Upper City. From the street his residence appeared spacious. The neighborhood was quiet and well maintained. These were qualities befitting a member of the Sanhedrin.

"Hello, my name is Simon. We have never been formally introduced, but I was a good friend of Lazarus. He and I grew up together in Bethany. I was at the Jerusalem prison with him the night he died. I was also one of the disciples who followed Jesus during his three years of ministry."

"Yes, I recognize your name. Lazarus spoke highly of you before his tragic death. He came to my home to learn about the condition of his sisters after they were arrested by Saul. I told him they were being used as a ploy to capture and execute him. Unfortunately, Saul's plan succeeded."

"I blame myself for what happened. Although it was Lazarus' decision, I advised him to storm the prison to free Mary and Martha. The night he died, I promised Lazarus that I would get his sisters to safety outside of Jerusalem. That vow led me to Damascus where I witnessed Saul's conversion to faith in Christ. I baptized Saul that day and later helped him escape from the Jews who were going to kill him."

"You shouldn't be so hard on yourself regarding Lazarus' death. Saul would have continued to pursue Lazarus until he found him. However, I'm pleased to know you were a participant in Saul's conversion. It was quite a shock to the Sanhedrin. When Saul's men returned and announced that he was now a follower of Jesus, members of the Sanhedrin were furious. I was glad to hear that he had come to faith. I understand he now goes by the name Paul."

"Yes, Saul now uses the Roman version of his name. I imagine that is because he is dealing primarily with Gentiles. He tirelessly preaches Christ crucified throughout the Roman Empire in spite of beatings and imprisonment."

"God certainly works in unexpected ways," Nicodemus observed. "Who would have guessed that God would turn an adversary like Paul into one of the outstanding spokesmen for Christianity? Now let's discuss why you came to see me today."

"I am here to ask for your help. A little background might help. I left Jerusalem thirty years ago to live in Rome. The Christians there requested an Apostle to help organize and unify the church. I planned to stay there until I died, but my wife Abigail was executed by Nero to cover up the murder of his wife. I couldn't go anywhere in Rome without the memories of our life together haunting me.

"I returned to Jerusalem several months ago to assist the Apostle John with the administration of the church here. It didn't take long to realize that the province of Judaea was butting heads with the Roman authorities. As I'm sure you already know, matters have become worse to the point that Nero sent his favorite general, Vespasian, to suppress the unrest here.

"John and I are very concerned about the safety of Christians in Jerusalem. We have considered relocating everyone to a location that the Roman army will not attack. In the meantime, I had a vision in which an angel of the Lord charged me with imitating the prophet Jeremiah. As you recall, Jeremiah warned the Jews that their destruction was imminent unless they repented of their evil ways and became obedient to God again. Apparently, what God wants me to do is convince the Jews to repent and turn to Jesus in order to be forgiven. In that case, Jerusalem would not be destroyed.

"I have already visited Eleazar ben Simon, leader of the Zealots, to urge him and his followers to look to Jesus for forgiveness but without success. The Sanhedrin also has significant influence with the local population, so I feel obligated to reach out to them as well. Is it possible for me to get an audience with the Sanhedrin?"

"It is possible but not probable. A few members other than me have become believers. But the majority are the same ones who condemned Jesus to death and commissioned Saul to persecute his followers. However, I can try to get you an audience with the full body of the Sanhedrin. If they agree to a meeting, hearing your message will at least give the Holy Spirit an inroad to bring them to faith."

A week later, Simon stood before the Sanhedrin in the same room where Jesus had been questioned the night before he was crucified. The High Priest, Phannias ben Samuel, presided over the meeting and sat on the same elevated seat that Caiaphas had been sitting while interrogating Jesus.

"Members of the Sanhedrin," Simon began, "As scholars of the Scriptures, you are all familiar with the story of the prophet Jeremiah. The people of Judah had forsaken God by worshipping idols and abandoning the Mosaic Law. Jeremiah was sent by God to warn Jerusalem that the city would be destroyed unless they repented of their sins and changed their sinful ways.

"God had run out of patience and was ready to allow the Babylonian army to level the city and take the residents into exile. Yet He still loved his chosen people and provided the opportunity to avoid destruction. They didn't listen to Jeremiah, and you know the result.

"Today I have a similar warning. God has revealed to me that the city of Jerusalem will soon be destroyed by the army of Rome unless you repent and change your ways. The change I am talking about does not refer to the worship of idols. It does, however, involve changing your belief system.

"I mentioned that the Jews are God's chosen people. Have you ever asked yourselves why they were chosen? Was it because they were better than anyone else? I think not, given the number of times that Jews have deserted God and worshipped false gods.

"I have the answer for you. After Adam and Eve sinned, God promised that one of their offspring would crush the head of Satan, and Satan would strike the heel of their offspring. That was the first reference to the coming of the Messiah.

"Throughout Jewish history, God continued to foretell the coming of the Messiah through prophets such as Isaiah. The Messiah would come from the lineage of Abraham and his heirs, including King David. In other words, God chose the Jews to be the people from whom the Messiah would emerge. That is why God allowed them to exist in spite of their disobedience.

"Unfortunately, the Jews failed to recognize the Messiah when he came. His name is Jesus, and he is the Promised One. Satan bruised Jesus' heel when he convinced the Sanhedrin to condemn him to death. Jesus bruised Satan's head when he died on the cross to earn forgiveness for everyone who believes in him. Jesus was the ultimate victor.

"I'm sure that this is not pleasant for you to hear. But like the Jewish leaders in Jeremiah's day, you need to change in order to avoid the killing of hundreds of thousands of Jews, including yourselves. The necessary change is for you to believe that Jesus is the Messiah and to rely on him alone for forgiveness of your sins.

"Your efforts have never been enough to please God. Neither have sacrifices made in the Temple. Jesus became the final and only sacrifice necessary for us to be saved from eternal punishment and separation from God."

The room was quiet during Simon's speech, but immediately after he finished, pandemonium broke out. The High Priest was apoplectic. His face turned bright red, and he trembled with anger. "You have blasphemed God and his anointed representatives," he screamed. "You accuse us of killing the Messiah even though everyone knows the Messiah has not yet come. Jesus was a fraud. He was condemned for falsely claiming to be the Messiah. He was a danger to the Jewish nation just as you are now. What more do you have to say for yourself?"

"I see that you are committed to the destruction of Jerusalem," Simon replied. "I can do nothing more than warn you of what is about to come. If you don't listen to what I have told you, you and the rest of Jerusalem will suffer the consequences. I pray that God's Spirit can change your hardened hearts."

"I am confident that God will not allow the destruction of Jerusalem," the High Priest responded. "The city houses the Temple in which He lives. However, the Sanhedrin is not sitting back waiting for God to act. We are actively working to avoid going to war.

"Along with several moderate city leaders, we formed a provisional government to restore the relationship we used to have with the Romans. The head of the provisional government is a former High Priest, Ananus ben Ananus. He has communicated with Roman authorities in Syria and Rome to ease the tension. It appears that progress toward peace is being made."

Simon replied, "I congratulate the Sanhedrin's pursuit of peace and encourage you to continue doing so. Unfortunately, that might be difficult in this political climate. Zealots are intent on war and are gaining in popularity with the public. Despite your efforts to avoid a violent confrontation, political momentum favors the Zealots."

"I should have you jailed for blasphemy, but I won't," remarked Phannias ben Samuel. "I believe you want peace as much as we do. However, don't expect the Sanhedrin to take your warning seriously. Believing that Jesus is the Messiah would betray our Jewish roots and traditions. When this matter is settled peaceably, we invite you to return and apologize for offending us with your lies and false accusations."

After his meetings with Eleazar ben Simon and the Sanhedrin, Simon visited John at his home. "I've met with the two parties that could change the outcome of what is about to happen. The

Zealots favor war and the Sanhedrin favors peace. The Zealots appear to have the advantage at this point.

"In any case, neither group consider the warning I gave them as legitimate. Both have pledged to ignore it. Since the Zealots think that they can't lose a war and the Sanhedrin believes they can negotiate peace without war, they have no reason to change their belief system and acknowledge that Jesus is the Messiah. It appears that the destruction of Jerusalem is inevitable."

"I prayed that this day would not come, but it now appears to be time to evacuate Christians from the city," replied John. "If any of our number decide to stay, I plan to remain here to support them."

"I respectfully disagree with you, John," pleaded Simon. "When James, the brother of Jesus, was stoned to death several years ago, you and Peter assumed the primary leadership roles in the church. Peter has decided to stay in Rome, so you are the only leader left in this part of the world. For the welfare of the church here and at large, you need to leave Jerusalem as soon as possible."

"Where can we go to be safe from the Roman army?" asked John.

"There are a few destinations that make sense," Simon replied. "Antioch in Syria would be an excellent choice if Vespasian's troops could be avoided on the way north. The Christian congregation there is sizeable, and they would welcome us warmly. Egypt would be another good option. Several Egyptian cities including Alexandria have significant Christian populations.

"However, the location I recommend is Pella, a city east of the Jordan River and south of the Sea of Galilee. It is located outside of Judaea in the Decapolis region about sixty miles from here. It is unlikely that the Roman army will strike beyond the border of Judaea, and the proximity to Jerusalem would enable Christians to easily move back when hostilities are over."

"I've traveled through Pella several times," noted John. "It appeared to be a city with enough jobs and housing to accommodate us until we can return. Let's present your suggestion to our congregation."

The following evening Simon and John gathered the membership together to encourage all who were willing and able to relocate temporarily to Pella. Simon emphasized that the threat to their safety was both real and imminent. He reminded them that Jesus predicted the destruction of Jerusalem and said that it would be a sign of his second coming. John promised to accompany them to Pella and continue to provide apostolic leadership.

The families at the meeting heeded the warning and left with John for Pella. Simon made sure that Mary and Martha went with them. Only ten Christian men remained in Jerusalem. Nine opted to stay behind to protect believer's homes and businesses from vandalism. Simon was the tenth. He felt obligated to imitate the prophet Jeremiah who continued to urge repentance until Jerusalem was destroyed.

PREPARATION

Jewish losses mounted in Galilee as the Roman army advanced southward from Syria. Refugees fled to Jerusalem in hopes that the city walls would keep them safe. Jerusalem was thought to be invincible in large part because of its location. The city was surrounded on three sides by steep cliffs dropping 200 feet to the valley below. The Kidron Valley protected the eastern exposure, and the Hinnom Valley safeguarded the southern and western exposures. Only the north side of the city was at roughly the same level as the surrounding land.

The city's entire 350 acres were encompassed by a massive limestone block wall that measured over two and a half miles long and averaged forty feet high and ten feet thick. In case the outer wall was breeched, internal walls divided Jerusalem into sections that could be defended independently.

Another reason that Jerusalem was considered a safe haven was the availability of clean water. Historically, when a hostile army met resistance from a city it could not quickly overcome, the army laid siege to it. Jerusalem had a source of water to outlast a siege thanks to a construction project completed 800 years earlier.

During the reign of King Hezekiah, Judah's thirteenth king, King Sennacherib of Assyria threatened to attack Jerusalem. Anticipating a lengthy siege, Hezekiah made plans to store food and secure a reliable water supply.

Jerusalem was built over a natural spring of clean water that surfaced intermittently from a cave below the surface. When rains came, the cave filled with water which escaped upward and flowed onto the land above. The gushing water feature was called Gihon Spring.

Prior to Hezekiah's reign, the spring was located just outside Jerusalem's east wall near the drop-off into the Kidron Valley. Some of the water was diverted into the city and some was allowed to run into the valley below for irrigation purposes. In order to deprive Sennacherib's army of a source of water near the city, Hezekiah extended the east wall of Jerusalem to encompass Gihon Spring.

However, water flow from the spring was intermittent based on the amount of rainfall. To guarantee the availability of water when the spring was not flowing, Hezekiah carved an underground tunnel that fed water from the Gihon Spring into a huge man-made reservoir in the southern portion of the city called the Pool of Siloam. The Pool of Siloam provided a secure supply of drinking water and also served as a ritual purification site for Jews visiting the Temple.

Hezekiah's strategy ensured that Jerusalem had a sufficient source of water to survive the siege that followed and helped prevent the city from being captured by Sennacherib. Eight centuries after the Assyrian attack, the Gihon Spring and the Pool of Siloam continued to provide a clean and reliable water source within the walls of Jerusalem.

During Vespasian's six-month campaign in northern Judaea, over 100,000 Galileans were killed or sold into slavery. Jews fled Galilee in large numbers while Vespasian's legions were making quick work of the outmatched Jewish resistance comprised primarily of Zealot fighters. Despite decades of experience in local skirmishes with Roman soldiers and sympathizers, the Zealots were no match for Vespasian's army.

The leader of the Galilean Zealots was John of Gischala. He and his contingent of 4,000 men battled Vespasian's troops valiantly for six months until only the city of Gischala, John's hometown, remained standing. Roman troops encircled Gischala and demanded an immediate surrender. John requested a one-day reprieve to observe the Sabbath and used the delay to escape under cover of darkness to Jerusalem along with his fellow Zealots.

After the arrival of John of Gischala in Jerusalem, the city was home to two factions of Zealots under two separate leaders. In order to prepare the city to defend itself as the Roman army approached, it would be critical for Eleazar ben Simon and John of Gischala to work together.

The first project that the two Zealot leaders tackled was the elimination of the provisional government set up by the city in conjunction with the Sanhedrin. Simon had learned about this governing entity when he spoke before the Sanhedrin. Ananus ben Ananus, leader of the government, made prior peace overtures to Rome and Syria but received no response. Now he planned to send envoys to Vespasian to express remorse for past actions and offer to pay reparations for damage done by the rebels.

The Zealots learned about Ananus' plans toward peace and vowed to stop his efforts. The provisional government was equally opposed to the Zealot's intention to wage war. Differences of opinion turned into violence.

The provisional government was in control of most of the city while the Zealots were confined to the Temple Mount. One afternoon the two Zealot factions met in the Temple. As the Zealots exited the Temple into the outer courtyard, they were met by a mob of armed Jews led by Ananus bin Ananus. He and the other provisional government leaders had convinced a significant number of moderate Jews that the Zealots needed to be driven out of Jerusalem.

The two sides clashed in heavy fighting. Ananus' supporters gained the initial advantage. The Zealots retreated into the Temple and were able to hold their ground until nightfall. Despondent after failing to banish the Zealots from the city,

Ananus and his men withdrew from the Temple Mount. The element of surprise was no longer available to them.

Back inside the Temple, John proposed a strategy to eliminate the provisional government and take over the entire city of Jerusalem. He suggested to Eleazar that they enlist Simon bar Giora and his followers to join them. Simon bar Giora was the Zealot credited with capturing Masada. He and his men now controlled Masada as well as the surrounding countryside.

Simon bar Giora agreed to assist his fellow Zealots. He and the majority of his men left Masada and headed toward Jerusalem. Ananus ben Ananus learned of the Zealot's plan and ordered the city gates to be shut. No one was allowed to enter or leave without his permission.

Simon bar Giora encamped outside city walls and waited. Although the Zealots inside were confined to the Temple Mount, on a stormy night they were able to bypass Ananus' sentries and open one of the city gates.

Once inside the city walls, Simon bar Giora's men captured and killed the leaders of the provisional government including Ananus. The entire city was now under the control of three Zealot factions. Eleazar ben Simon's 2,400 men combined forces with John of Gischala's 6,000 followers to occupy the Temple Mount and the Lower City. Simon bar Giora, with 16,000 men under his command, occupied the rest of Jerusalem. Moderate leadership seeking peace had been eliminated, and war with Rome was now inevitable.

"John, have you heard?" exclaimed Simon. "Peter and Paul were executed by Nero." Simon had traveled to Pella to deliver the news to his fellow Apostle personally.

"Are you sure?" responded John. "Peter remained in Rome after you left, but I thought Paul went to Spain after his release from prison."

"Apparently Paul returned to Rome shortly after I set sail for Jerusalem. When Nero heard he was back, he ordered Paul's arrest for allegedly violating an agreement made when he released Paul from prison. Before he left Rome for Spain, Paul shared the specifics of the agreement with me. It stated that Paul would not return to Jerusalem, but there was no mention of Rome. Nero wouldn't admit his mistake and imprisoned Paul. The Jews convinced him to arrest Peter too."

"Were they given a trial? Wouldn't the truth about the agreement exonerate Paul?"

"I'm familiar with trials before Nero. He is judge and jury. No one would be allowed to corroborate Paul's side of the story because it would contradict Nero. In any case, throughout history the emperor always has the final say."

"How were they executed?"

"Paul was a citizen of Rome and therefore entitled to a swift death. He was beheaded. Peter wasn't as fortunate. He was crucified, the most gruesome punishment that Rome can inflict on convicted criminals. Similar to what Jesus went through, Peter must have suffered for hours before he died. Out of respect for Jesus, Peter asked to be hung upside down."

"I'm grateful that you told me in person. I know that their souls are with Christ in Heaven, but I can't help being extremely upset. Peter and Paul were men of tremendous faith and good friends to both of us. We have lost two stalwart evangelists and leaders who gave their lives for our Lord. I pray that their work will not be in vain."

"You don't need to worry about that. The prophet Isaiah wrote that God's word will not be proclaimed in vain but will achieve the purpose for which it was intended. Both Peter and Paul proclaimed the message of God's love for the world by sending Jesus to save us. That is a lasting truth that will never cease to be spoken."

"After the untimely deaths of Peter and Paul, I'm thankful that you encouraged me to leave Jerusalem. I'm not afraid to die, but it is important for remaining Apostles to stay alive. We are the only ones who can provide personal details of his life with us. I plan to document my recollections in writing. You might consider doing that as well."

"I'll consider it, but I am not a proficient writer. However, I will joyfully serve God in any manner He wishes. My prayer is for you to continue caring for the Christians in Pella and provide leadership to believers throughout the world. May God bless you and grant you a long and purposeful life."

A few weeks after visiting John in Pella, Simon received an excited visitor at his apartment in Jerusalem. "Nero is dead! He killed himself rather than being tortured and executed by the Roman Senate," exclaimed Yosef. "As soon as I heard, I ran here to let you know. I imagine this is good news for you."

Yosef was one of the ten believers who remained in Jerusalem. Simon first met him in Damascus over thirty years earlier. Yosef, who was a young man at the time, was instrumental in getting

Saul safely out of the city.

Yosef moved to Jerusalem shortly after Simon brought Mary and Martha back to Bethany. He became an active member of the Christian community and worked as a security guard at the prison where Lazarus had been killed.

"My first emotion was elation," admitted Simon. "Nero was Satan incarnate. Not only did he kill Peter, Paul, and my wife, but he also murdered thousands of other Christians who did nothing to deserve death. Nero thought only of himself and had no regard for Christians, Jews, or even his own citizens. However, my elation is tempered by fear that a new emperor might be as bad or worse than Nero."

"You left Rome recently. Is there any consensus on who the new emperor might be?" Yosef asked.

"To my knowledge, Nero had no male heirs," replied Simon. "Even if he had a son, I don't believe the Roman Senate would put him in power given Nero's unpopularity. In my opinion there are probably four legitimate rivals for the throne. I wouldn't be surprised if civil war broke out until a victor emerges. That would not be unprecedented given historical transitions of power in Rome."

During the year following Nero's demise, civil wars and palace intrigue took place in Rome. Three emperors came to power, and each lost their life shortly thereafter. The first of the three, Servius Galba, was beheaded by his successor after ruling for six months. Marcus Otho, Poppaea's second husband prior to her marriage to Nero, was next and ruled only three months before committing suicide to avoid being executed. The third emperor, Aulus Vitellius, was murdered in Rome by supporters of General Vespasian eight months after taking office.

The unrest in Rome created a temporary slowdown in the fighting in Galilee. Vespasian paused his campaign to solidify his bid to become the next emperor. Not surprisingly, following the death of Vitellius, the Roman Senate proclaimed Vespasian as the fourth emperor to succeed Nero.

Before leaving for Rome to assume his new role, Vespasian appointed his son Titus to be commander of the army in Judaea. Titus held his troops in abeyance until he received orders from the new emperor, his father. The delay in fighting provided Jerusalem with the opportunity to bolster its defenses prior to a probable attack.

Unfortunately, instead of working together, the three Zealot factions that controlled separate parts of the city spent much of their time fighting each other. Most of the food storage facilities that had been built to withstand a siege were destroyed during the conflict. The feuding between Zealot factions served to further weaken a city that was already extremely unprepared for an attack by the Roman army.

Chapter 21

SIEGE

Passover was observed in mid-April the year after Vespasian became emperor. Despite the possibility of an attack on the city, Jews from all over the Empire, emboldened by a lull in activity by the Roman army over the past eighteen months, traveled to the Jerusalem Temple as the Torah required them to do.

During the weeks prior to the Passover celebration, the population of Jerusalem and its environs normally ballooned from about 30,000 permanent residents to approximately 150,000. Not all visitors stayed within the city walls. Many of the pilgrims camped near Bethany or the Mount of Olives. However, the influx of Jewish refugees escaping the fighting in Galilee added thousands more to an already overcrowded situation.

At sunrise four days before the Passover meal, sentries stationed on the northernmost wall of the city noticed a cloud of dust on the horizon. As the cloud moved closer and grew in size, it became evident that this was not merely a wind event. The Roman army was bearing down on Jerusalem. The Jewish sentries sounded their horns, warning of an upcoming attack. Within minutes, 20,000 defenders, primarily Zealots, ran to their battle stations atop the city walls.

Earlier in the year, General Titus received orders from Emperor Vespasian to stamp out the rebellion in Judaea once and for all. The political climate in Rome had finally stabilized. Unlike his three predecessors, Vespasian was able to consolidate support within both the Senate and the military. However, he needed a military victory to solidify public favor.

Emperor Vespasian reasoned that if Jerusalem could be captured and destroyed quickly without significant Roman casualties, the entire Roman Empire would realize that rebellion against Rome is a losing proposition. He also understood that if he failed to quell the rebellion, he would face a public relations nightmare that could prompt other provinces to revolt. He had no choice but to win.

Titus took his father's orders to heart. After destroying the remaining cities and towns in Galilee, Titus and three of his legions wintered in Caesarea Maritima, located about seventy miles northwest of Jerusalem. Another legion wintered in Jericho, located about sixteen miles to the northeast. The Roman army prepared for an all-out assault on Jerusalem, the last major Jewish stronghold in the province of Judaea.

Victory over Jerusalem was not a certainty even though the

Roman army outnumbered the rebels by a factor of three to one. The city was built to withstand nearly any direct assault. It was perched on a hill surrounded by valleys on three sides, every direction but the north. The oldest sections of Jerusalem, called the Upper City and Lower City, were encircled by walls as high as sixty feet and as wide as fifteen feet.

As Jerusalem's population grew, additional residential areas were constructed to the north named the Second City and the New City. These were encircled by a second and third wall built as sturdy as the first. All three of the walls were topped with wide battlements that enabled defenders to bombard invaders below with spears, rocks, and hot oil. Rows of archers shooting from the battlements could rain down a barrage of arrows on attackers approaching a good distance from the walls.

Despite Jerusalem's seemingly impenetrable defenses, decades of empire building allowed Roman army engineers time to develop methods to overcome the highest and thickest walls. Standard procedure began by hurling large rocks from catapults positioned out of range of the defenders' arrows. The rocks weighed sixty pounds or more and flew distances up to 1,000 feet at tremendous speed. Catapults were most effective when aimed at the top layers of the wall. Rocks that hit their targets shook the battlements, intimidating and often killing the defenders stationed there.

While catapults were softening the walls, siege towers and siege ramps were constructed to enable battering rams to complete the breach. A Roman battering ram consisted of a thick log suspended by ropes from a large beam beneath the roof of an enclosure similar to a wooden shed on wheels. The ends of the battering ram stuck out from both ends of the protective enclosure. A large iron likeness of a ram's head was secured on the forward end of the log, hence the name battering ram. The log was swung so that the iron end of the battering ram pounded the wall until it was breached.

Siege ramps, inclined piles of dirt, were built adjacent the wall previously weakened by catapult blows. Battering rams were rolled up the ramps to reach the wall. Soil removed from nearby fields was used to form the siege ramps. A level area was formed at the top of the incline to provide a level space for the battering rams to operate.

Siege towers provided limited protection for soldiers building siege ramps. Made of wood, equipped with large wheels, and covered with fireproof coatings, the towers were built higher than the city walls. After completion, the siege towers were rolled near the siege ramps being constructed. A dozen Roman archers stationed at the top of the towers shot arrows downward toward the defenders on the battlements, limiting the ability of the defenders to slow siege ramp construction. In addition, much of the ramp building was done at night.

Once battering rams created sufficiently wide openings in the damaged wall, Roman soldiers and auxiliary troops stormed up the ramps, through the breach, and into the city. Once inside the walls, complete victory was virtually guaranteed.

Until Titus and his army appeared on the horizon, clashes between the three factions of Zealots fighting for control of the city continued. However, once the Roman army arrived at the city's outskirts, the entire population of Jerusalem united as one.

Reports from Galilee of cities and towns destroyed and residents annihilated indicated that the Roman army would show no mercy to anyone in Jerusalem regardless of their involvement in the rebellion. Surrender might save some lives, but the best they could expect was a lifetime of slavery.

The only feasible option for those trapped in the city was a furious full-scale defense. If the Roman army withdrew, even temporarily, those who desired to flee Jerusalem might be able do so. Any pause in the fighting would give defenders additional time to repair walls and replenish food supplies.

The morning that the Roman army was spotted on their way to Jerusalem, Simon was holding a worship service in Yosef's home. It was Sunday, the day after the Sabbath, the Jewish traditional day of rest. Years earlier, Christians in Antioch began worshipping on Sunday rather than Saturday to commemorate the day of the week Jesus rose from the dead. Christians throughout the Empire adopted the practice, and Sunday was set aside for worship, breaking bread, fellowship, and prayer.

Shortly after the Scripture readings and singing and prayers were completed, trumpets blasted from the north wall of the city. A look of fear was etched on each of the ten faces after hearing the designated warning. All eyes turned to Simon, the only remaining Apostle in Jerusalem.

Sensing the need for leadership at this moment, Simon spoke up, "Brothers, this could be a false alarm or a real emergency. In either case, we need to pray for God's help and guidance. Jesus promised to be with us always, even to the end of the world. If it is his will, we will be protected from any harm or danger that presents itself. I suggest you all return to your homes. I will find out what is happening and report back to you. God willing, we will meet back here again this evening."

Simon remained in Yosefs house after the worship service ended. "Yosef, you have shown outstanding leadership in our congregation. We all hold you in high regard. I would like you to assist me during difficult times ahead. I need someone younger to work with me. If you are willing, I would welcome your help."

"Nothing would please me more. I appreciate your confidence in me and will do my best to be of service."

"The first thing I'd like you to do is accompany me to find out why the trumpets sounded. Then we can decide what actions to take, if any."

"Certainly, there is nothing I wouldn't do for you and my Christian friends."

"When I was a child in synagogue school," Simon recalled, "my classmates and I would pretend that we were fighting the Roman army. Even then, Romans were oppressing Jews with high taxes and corrupt rulers. More than fifty years later nothing has really changed except that we are no longer children pretending to do battle. We are grown men fighting for our lives."

Simon and Yosef hurried to the third wall of the New City from which the warning blast had come. After climbing onto the battlement, Simon quickly realized that this was not a false alarm. Tens of thousands of Roman army troops were setting up camp about a mile northwest of the city. Another contingent of soldiers was establishing a camp on the Mount of Olives about a mile east of Jerusalem.

"It appears that the estimates of Roman troop strength we heard about were accurate," noted Yosef. "There must be 50,000 to 60,000 soldiers."

"I'll venture a guess that they aren't all Roman legionnaires," offered Simon. "If the Romans are true to form, the majority of those troops are mercenaries and soldiers from nearby countries allied with Rome. The auxiliary troops are the ones who will do most of the dirty work like building siege ramps. They will also do much of the fighting. But the Roman army will take credit for victory and take most of the plunder back to Rome."

"How many trained soldiers do you think remain in Jerusalem?" asked Yosef.

"I spoke to Eleazar ben Simon not long ago. The three Zealot factions have nearly 25,000 fighting men between them. Fortunately, they are relatively well equipped because four years ago the Zealots captured a trove of weapons, equipment, and uniforms from Cestius Gallus at Beth Horon. Ironically, the weapons and equipment used by the Roman army to kill Jews will now be used against them."

As the day wore on, Jewish defenders stationed at the walls could do nothing more than watch from a distance as the Romans built their encampments. Simon and Yosef remained on the battlement the rest of the day to gather information they would report to their fellow Christians that evening.

Late in the afternoon, trumpets sounded another warning. Watchmen spotted several hundred horsemen riding from the northwest encampment toward Jerusalem. The cavalrymen halted their horses just out of reach of the archers' arrows.

Several soldiers dismounted, appearing to evaluate sections of the city wall. After a brief discussion, they remounted, and the entire detachment rode east toward the camp being set up on the Mount of Olives.

"It appears that the Romans are reconnoitering the city," observed Simon. "I can't imagine them attacking from any direction other than the north or northwest. The terrain is too steep in the valleys that surround the rest of Jerusalem."

"I agree," Yosef responded. "There are several places that could be targeted along the northern wall, especially near the wooden gates. The Romans have equipment that can breach most walls, but I'm not sure they can breach ours."

From their position on the battlement, Simon and Yosef observed several hundred Zealots assembling near the northwest gate. John of Gischala was giving orders to his troops. The gate was opened briefly, and the men disappeared into the trees and underbrush several hundred yards outside the wall.

"It appears that John's men are setting up an ambush," observed Simon. "When the horsemen return to their camp northwest of the city, they will pass this way, and the trap will be sprung." As predicted, just before sunset, the cavalry returned from the camp on the Mount of Olives. As the riders approached, the glare of the setting sun provided additional cover for the Jews waiting in ambush.

At a signal from John of Gischala, the Zealots sprang from their hiding places and attacked. Several horses, frightened by the shouts of the attackers, reared up on their hind legs and flung their riders to the ground. Most of the cavalrymen managed to stay on their mounts and bolted away toward the Roman camp. Those who could not escape fought bravely. The Romans had been taken completely by surprise. As the battle raged, it was evident that the Zealots held the advantage.

Simon and Yosef noticed that the fiercest fighting centered around one of the Roman horsemen who had fallen. The other soldiers were clearly trying to protect him and provide an opportunity for him to escape. After a supreme effort on his part and that of the others nearby, he managed to mount a horse and gallop away. When the battle was over, fifty Romans had been killed or captured versus only five casualties sustained by the Zealots. Later that day, John of Gischala informed his men that General Titus had nearly been ensnared in their trap.

Simon met with the remaining Christians that evening. Throughout the day they heard rumors about what was happening, most of which were inaccurate. Word on the street said that Roman forces ranged anywhere from 100,000 to one million soldiers. Other reports alleged that the Zealot defenders had routed the Romans and the enemy had retreated. With all the misinformation swirling around, Simon was anxious to provide them with the truth.

"Brothers in Christ, I won't try to sugar coat what is happening. The Roman legions along with their auxiliaries are camped to the northwest and east of the city in large numbers. The best estimate of enemy strength available right now is 60,000 troops including both infantry and cavalry. This is in contrast to Jerusalem's combined forces of 25,000 Zealots and 10,000 other trained Jewish fighters, not counting untrained residents and visiting pilgrims who are willing to fight.

"If we consider numbers alone, it appears that Jerusalem will soon be overrun by the Roman army. However, we need to remember that God, not man, is in control of our destiny. Throughout the history of Israel, God has given His people victory in the face of overwhelming odds. But don't misinterpret what I am saying. I am not guaranteeing miraculous deliverance from the Roman army. Instead, I want all of you to be confident that God is in control of this situation and will be with us no matter what the outcome happens to be. May His will be done.

"When we look back at the history of the Jewish people, it would be easy to conclude that God blessed them when they obeyed Him and punished them when they disobeyed. I contend that what has happened to God's chosen people from Abraham to the present day was not the result their obedience or disobedience. Instead, God had a plan that depended on their survival. From the moment that Adam and Eve sinned, God set in place the steps that would bring mankind back into that original perfect relationship with Him. The vehicle to accomplish this was His chosen people, the Jews.

"Most of you are Christians of Jewish ancestry just as I am. As such, you are all familiar with how God carried out His plan. He sent Jesus, descended from Abraham, Isaac, and Jacob as well as King David, to save all mankind from the consequences of their sins. Jewish history is not just a series of random events or God responding to the obedience or disobedience of men. Instead, Jewish history is actually the fulfillment of God's purposeful plan to send a Savior. It is a perfect illustration that God is in control, whether we realize it or not.

"You might be thinking, how does this history lesson apply to the situation we are in right now? None of us knows for sure what will result when the Roman army attacks. We have no idea whether we will live or die. The uncertainty causes anxiety and confusion. We are tempted to rely on the strength of our troops or to abandon hope completely.

"Right now, we need to trust that God is in control. The immediate benefit is freedom from fear. Uncertainty about the short term is replaced by certainty regarding the long term. We can be certain that all who believe in Jesus will be resurrected on the Last Day and live with God forever in Heaven. Regardless of the outcome of the battle to come, we can be sure that God is in control. We are the beneficiaries of the plan of salvation that Jesus has completed. God's love and mercy will not leave us now or ever. I repeat, may His will be done."

During the following week, Jewish fighters on the city walls could only watch as the Roman soldiers prepared for the assault. It was apparent that Titus had decided to breach the outer wall on the northwest side of the city north of Herod's palace. This portion of the third wall had been completed recently and was presumed by Titus to be the most vulnerable.

A breach at this location would provide entry to the New City and access to the interior wall leading to the Second City. After breaching the interior second wall, the troops could work their way east to the Antonia Fortress and the Temple Mount and south to the Second City. From there they could breach the interior first wall leading to residential and business areas in the Upper and Lower Cities.

Once the targeted site was chosen, the Romans began to

weaken the wall with rocks thrown from catapults. The catapults were positioned out of range of Jewish archers, but close enough to deliver accurate results. Every rock that found its target made a deafening crash that shook the wall and showered debris on the Jewish soldiers standing nearby.

While the wall was being battered, the Romans cleared all trees and other vegetation growing within a mile of the city. This served two purposes. The first was to detect the approach of Jewish fighters in the event of a counterattack. Titus had narrowly escaped an ambush by Jews who hid behind trees and hedges growing outside the city wall. In another instance, Jewish fighters emerged from thick vegetation to conduct raids on the Mount of Olives camp. Without vegetation to conceal them, Jewish fighters would be at a disadvantage.

The second purpose was to provide materials necessary to build siege towers. The Roman army brought most of their food supplies and weapons with them, but the wood used to construct siege towers was sourced locally when available.

Once three siege towers were constructed, the following week was spent building three siege ramps. As workers hauled dirt to construct the ramps, Jewish fighters on the battlements shot arrows and threw rocks at them. To counter this tactic, Roman archers in the siege towers rained arrows down on them. In a final effort to stop construction, the Jews sent fighters out of the city gates to attack enemy workers on the ground, but they were driven away by Roman infantry and forced to retreat back into the city walls.

Two weeks after the Romans arrived, all three siege ramps were completed. Battering rams were rolled up the ramps and placed next to the wall. The roof and sides of the battering ram enclosures protected the soldiers inside as they rocked the iron ram head back and forth into the wall. Large chunks of limestone flew in every direction. Cracks turned into gaping holes as the battering rams worked their way through the bulwark.

By late afternoon two of the three battering rams had completely breached the wall and the third was within a few yards of breaking through. Realizing that they could not stop the Romans from entering the New City, the Jewish fighters abandoned their positions on the outer third wall and retreated into the Second City where they took positions on the interior second wall. Residents of the New City had previously fled into safer sections of Jerusalem.

Roman troops were poised to rush into the northernmost section of Jerusalem. Once the final battering ram broke through, hundreds of troops ran through the three openings shouting loudly and brandishing swords and spears. What they found was an empty shell of a community devoid of any humans. A few donkeys and stray dogs were the only signs of life.

Titus entered the New City and gave orders to set up a fortified camp within its walls. He gave orders to tear down the homes and businesses and reduce them to rubble. While some soldiers worked to establish the camp, others shifted their focus to the interior second wall which would provide access into the Second City.

It took only four days to breach the interior second wall. Jewish resistance was surprisingly soft. Romans quickly constructed two siege ramps without the aid of siege towers. Battering rams were rolled up the ramps and went to work pounding the rows of limestone block. When one of the battering rams broke through, instead of waiting for the breach to widen further or waiting for the second battering ram to complete its job, impatient Roman soldiers streamed through the narrow opening into the Second City.

Once inside, the Romans viewed a scene reminiscent of their entry into the New City. Jewish fighters had abandoned their positions on the second wall, and the streets were deserted. Believing that the Jewish troops had retreated to the interior first wall leading to the Upper and Lower Cities, Roman infantry surged ahead through the Second City streets.

Suddenly, Jewish fighters attacked from behind houses and businesses that lined the streets. They had lured the Romans into an ambush with no way out. The soldiers that rushed into the Second City were outnumbered and outflanked. Many lost their lives in close combat on the cramped streets.

Fearing a complete massacre, Romans soldiers retreated toward the interior second wall through which they had come. However, the opening was too narrow for more than a handful of men to pass through at a time, and the Jews were able to kill many of the stragglers before they were able to escape.

Emboldened by their success, Jewish fighters followed the retreating Romans soldiers into the New City and continued the slaughter. The battle continued for the remainder of the day and into the night. By the next morning, reinforcements from Roman camps outside the city arrived and were able to push the Jews back into the Second City.

While they retreated, the Jews destroyed the two battering rams and rebuilt the sections of the second wall that had been breached. Jewish fighters resumed their positions on the second wall leaving General Titus frustrated and even more determined to destroy the entire city.

STARVATION

Six weeks had passed since the Roman army reached Jerusalem. No progress was made by either side since the Romans recaptured the New City. Pleasant weather in April turned into intense summer heat of June. Titus realized that his efforts to quickly conquer the city had failed. He would have to resort to a war of attrition.

Titus ordered his men to build an earthen wall of circumvallation to completely encircle the city. The plan included thirteen towers evenly spaced around the perimeter of the wall to be manned by Roman soldiers. In order to distract his men from the recent setbacks suffered at the hands of the rebels,

Titus announced a competition between the legions. The group that built their section of the wall fastest would be rewarded. In response, his men completed the entire five miles of earthen wall in only three days.

This change in strategy completely changed the complexion of the battle for control of the city. Although the city's inhabitants had plenty of water supplied by the Gihon Spring, Titus knew that Jerusalem's food storage had been nearly depleted during the infighting between Zealot factions. He also surmised that the addition of Passover pilgrims and refugees from Galilee made the food situation more tenuous.

Until the wall of circumvallation was built, daring Jews could sneak out of the city at night largely undetected by the Romans. Once outside the gates, they foraged for foodstuffs such as wheat, grapes, and dates which they brought into the city. After the earthen wall was in place and enemy guards were posted around the perimeter, any Jews venturing out of the city were captured and killed.

Titus' efforts to conquer the city by force had been unsuccessful. Starvation now became his most effective weapon. His men could let hunger run its course while sitting back out of danger. Even though victory would take longer to achieve, as time passed it would be much easier to deal with a famished group of Jewish fighters.

Simon could see worry etched on the faces of his fellow Christians. The siege was taking a toll. Ten weeks earlier the Romans had completely cut off the supply of food from outside the city. Before then, the men were healthy and vital. Now their faces were gaunt, and clothes hung loosely from their bodies.

The believers who remained in Jerusalem relied on God and each other for support. Early on, a few had some wheat and oil to make bread. Others had small supplies of beans, dates, and figs that were not subject to spoilage. Those who had food shared it with those who had none.

As time passed and supplies dwindled, meals became meager and eaten less frequently. Despite the dire circumstances, believers continued to worship regularly. The men sang praises to God with as much vigor as before the siege. Prayers of thanks were mixed with prayers for deliverance.

After the bread was gone and the supply of wine had run out, they could no longer eat and drink the meal Jesus had instituted. However, the men continued to commemorate his sacrifice for their sins on the cross. Jesus' suffering made their suffering endurable. His death and resurrection made the specter of their death, followed by eternal life with him in Heaven, eagerly anticipated.

For many others trapped in the city, desperation overcame basic decency. Some killed their pets for food while others boiled leather to get some form of nutrition. In a horrible instance of depravity, a young mother smothered her infant son to death and then cooked and ate him. When the authorities found out what had happened, they were so appalled that no punitive action was taken against her.

Desperation also drove starving individuals and families to attempt escape from the city despite the consequences. Once outside the walls, runaways were captured and hung on crosses placed atop the wall of circumvallation. Those who attempted to surrender rather than escape were also crucified. From the city battlements, observers could see the corpses of hundreds of their countrymen and women rotting in the sun.

As the siege wore on and more people died, Simon obtained a scroll containing the writings of Jeremiah. He wondered if he and John missed something while interpreting the angel's message. As far as Simon could tell, he had accurately followed Jeremiah's example. As he read further, Simon discovered something that he missed.

In a final effort to save His people, God told Jeremiah to tell King Zedekiah to surrender to the Babylonians. If he did, Jerusalem would not be destroyed, and the king and his family would be spared. However, if the king refused to surrender, the city would be burned to the ground, and he and his family would be killed. Zedekiah was too afraid to follow God's directive and suffered the consequences. For his efforts to warn Zedekiah, Jeremiah was imprisoned until the city was destroyed.

Simon decided to make one more appeal to Zealot leadership. This time he spoke to Simon bar Giora who commanded the largest number of Zealots and controlled the largest areas in the city. They met in Herod's palace which Simon bar Giora had appropriated for his headquarters. The plush accommodations belied the fact that the Zealots were starving as badly as the rest of the city.

"My name is Simon. I am a Christian and a former member of the Zealots. I come to you today with a message from God, similar to the one that the prophet Jeremiah delivered to King

Zedekiah. Jerusalem is about to be destroyed by the Roman army. God has lost patience with you and the rest of the Jews. You have refused to repent of your sins. More importantly, you have not accepted Jesus as the Messiah.

"However, God still loves his chosen people and has provided you with one more chance to avoid annihilation of the city and its people. You and the other Zealot leaders must surrender to General Titus immediately. If you do, Jerusalem and its people will be spared. If not, your fate will be sealed."

Simon bar Giora sat wide-eyed as Simon spoke. When Simon finished, Simon bar Giora burst out in laughter. "Who let this maniac into our presence?" he asked the other Zealots in the room. "He just wasted two minutes of my time. Surrender is not an option especially when we are winning. This man claims to be sent by God, but he is clearly speaking on behalf of Satan. God gave Eleazar ben Simon a victory against the Romans at Beth Horan, John of Gischala escaped from under Vespasian's nose, I captured Masada. Our fighters have made the Roman soldiers look foolish time and time again. Let's move on. What should we do with Simon the Christian?"

One of the Zealots suggested, "We should lock him up. Even though we know he is a crazy man, he might convince some of the citizenry that surrender is an option. People are desperate to stay alive. Who knows how nonsense like that could spread?"

"Well said," Simon bar Giora responded. "Take him to the prison. When we emerge victorious, I will demand an apology for trying to mislead us."

Simon was bound and led away. When the door to the prison swung open, Simon made eye contact with Yosef. His friend was on guard duty that day. Neither acknowledged they knew the other. It would be important to hide their relationship going forward.

From that day on, Yosef made sure that Simon was cared for. Although food was scarce, Yosef was able to provide Simon with enough to stay healthy. He made sure that Simon had enough clean water to drink. Simon communicated with the remaining Christians using Yosef as the middleman.

Titus had waited long enough. It was now eighteen weeks since he arrived at Jerusalem, and he was ready to finish off the rebels and take over the city. His new strategy centered on occupying the Temple. He hoped that occupying the dwelling place of the Jewish God would completely shatter their will to continue fighting.

He chose to reach the Temple through the Antonia Fortress. This imposing structure was originally built by Herod the Great to house the garrison of Roman troops stationed in Jerusalem. It was erected as a stand-alone edifice fifteen years before Herod the Great expanded the Temple Mount. When the Temple Mount's perimeter walls were completed, its northwest wall abutted the south wall of the Antonia Fortress.

Rectangular in shape, the Fortress' footprint measured 500 feet east to west and 200 feet north to south. Built on an elevated rock ledge, the interior space of the Fortress covered about three acres. Massive towers were situated at each of the four corners.

Because the Antonia Fortress was built on a raised rock

platform, its towers and the tops of its walls were higher than the Temple mount wall next to it. From their vantage points in the Fortress' south towers, Roman soldiers could observe any disturbance and quickly send troops from the Fortress to the Temple Mount.

Although the walls of the Temple Mount and Antonia Fortress were virtually touching each other, no passageway existed between the two structures. Over the objections of Jewish religious leaders, the Romans built a twenty-foot-wide wooden gate in the south wall of the Fortress for quick access to the Temple in the event of civil disorder. The gate opened onto a footbridge which led down to the roof of the Temple Mount's north portico. A stairway led from the portico roof to the ground floor below. From there it was a relatively short distance across an open area to the Temple itself.

Titus began his assault on the northern wall of the Antonia Fortress using catapults to weaken the structure. Protected by nearby siege towers, the Romans built two siege ramps. Battering rams were moved up the ramps next to the wall and began pounding the limestone blocks. Zealot fighters who occupied the Fortress fired arrows and dropped rocks and burning oil from the battlements onto the Roman soldiers below. During the first day, no significant damage was done to the wall.

Unbeknown to Titus, while the Romans were building the siege ramps, the Jews were working on a construction project of their own. They built a tunnel that extended under the north wall of the Fortress and ended under the siege ramps on the other side.

One evening after the tunnel was completed, the Jews set fire to the wooden beams supporting the tunnel causing it to collapse. The ground above the tunnel imploded, destroying the siege ramps and damaging the battering rams and siege towers. Roman soldiers, hearing the noise, rushed to the wall and found the work they had done in ruins.

Titus was frustrated but not discouraged. He knew time was still on his side. For the next two days Titus and his officers debated how to proceed. Some officers supported abandoning the Fortress and concentrating on the interior wall adjacent to the Temple Mount. Others suggested focusing on both. At the end of the second day, a consensus had not been reached.

As Titus and his officers returned to their tents, rain began to fall. The rain continued to pour down heavily throughout the evening. The foundation of the Fortress' north wall became unstable due to the collapse of the tunnel beneath it. Suddenly, with a loud crash, a large section of the north wall crumbled to the ground leaving a wide opening leading directly into the middle of the Antonia Fortress. Rain had accomplished what the battering rams had not yet done. The Roman soldiers did not respond to the sound, thinking the crashing noise was thunder from the storm.

By daylight the next morning, the weather had improved. The Roman army awoke to discover the huge gash in the wall. Titus, acting cautiously, sent a scouting expedition ahead to investigate the damage. To their dismay, the scouts saw that the Jews had already built a secondary wall of dirt and rock to patch the breach. One of the scouts was sent back to camp to notify Titus.

The remaining men decided to investigate further. They managed to climb over the secondary barrier and found the

Fortress deserted. The scouts began exploring the interior of the Fortress when hundreds of Jewish fighters emerged from the garrison's barracks and surrounded them. During a brief but bloody skirmish, the entire scouting expedition was slaughtered. Cries of agony could be heard all the way to Titus' camp.

Titus decided to delay an attack on the Fortress until reinforcements from outside the city could join him. After they arrived he ordered an assault through the collapsed north wall. In the middle of the night, a group of 200 soldiers surprised the Jewish sentries guarding the Fortress and killed them before they could sound an alarm. A Roman trumpeter blew several loud blasts as they entered the walls of the Fortress,.

Jewish fighters stationed in the Fortress' barracks were startled out of their sleep. They assumed the entire Roman army was attacking and rushed to their assigned posts. The two military forces reached the middle of the Fortress at the same time. A pitched battle ensued in the darkness of a moonless night. In the close quarters of the Fortress, confusion reigned. Both sides mistakenly killed or wounded a number of their own troops in the closely fought battle.

Motivated to keep the Romans out of the Temple Mount, Jewish fighters gained the initiative during additional hours of intense fighting. Willing to resume the battle at another time, Titus ordered the trumpeter to sound a retreat. His men pulled out through the collapsed north wall of the Fortress and marched back to their nearby camp. The Jews briefly celebrated their victory knowing that more fighting would soon break out.

Titus determined that the limited space within the Antonia Fortress provided an advantage to the Jewish rebels. The Roman infantry was much more effective on large areas of open ground where they could advance in orderly rows and overwhelm the enemy with sheer numbers. Hand to hand combat in close quarters did not favor troops weighed down with shields and armor.

The next day, Titus tore down the remaining north wall of the Fortress. With more space to maneuver, the Roman soldiers were able to drive the occupying Jewish fighters out of the Fortress and into the Temple Mount courtyard. He now had complete control of the Antonia Fortress.

Titus' next objective was occupation of the Temple Mount and the Temple itself. Herod the Great's massive renovation of the Second Temple and its surrounding structures took nearly fifty years to complete. The result was a thirty-six-acre religious complex with the Temple as its centerpiece. Thick high walls of the Temple Mount stretched nearly 1,500 feet from north to south and 1,000 feet from east to west. Porticos supported by forty-foot columns ran inside the length of each of the walls.

Once Titus had control of the Antonia Fortress, he also had control of the footbridge that led down to the roof of the north portico of the Temple Mount. To prevent the Jews from sabotaging the footbridge, he stationed infantrymen under the portico and placed archers on its roof. If the Jews attempted to destroy the footbridge, the infantry and archers could hold them off until reinforcements arrived. An all-out attack on the Temple Mount was now achievable whenever he wished to proceed.

Inside the Fortress, the Romans leveled barracks and administrative buildings and cleared away the debris allowing Titus to amass hundreds of troops within the confines of the remaining three Fortress walls. The increased space also gave the Roman soldiers room to fight effectively in case the Jews were able to fight their way back in.

Phannias ben Samuel sighed deeply. Tears ran down his cheeks. It was time for the morning sacrifice, but in his role as High Priest he had no lamb to offer. The last lamb in the Temple paddock had been slaughtered and sacrificed the night before. Vendors who sold animals for sacrifice in the Court of the Gentiles were no longer in business. Any lambs outside the Temple had been eaten long ago.

"My heart is broken," Phannias ben Samuel muttered to himself. "During my entire lifetime Jewish priests have never failed to make daily sacrifices required by the Torah, one lamb in the morning and one in the evening. Even when Herod was rebuilding the Temple, the sacrifices never stopped. Now we are disobeying God even though it is no fault of our own."

Phannias became the High Priest inadvertently. Tradition dictated that the High Priest must be the direct descendant of a prior High Priest all the way back to Aaron, Moses' brother. Disregarding tradition, the Zealots appointed Phannias, a Levite who was not a descendant of Aaron and had never been a priest, to the position. Phannias' primary qualification was that he was willing to take orders from the Zealots.

In spite of his shortcomings, Phannias took his new position seriously. Based on his synagogue school education and later service in the Temple as a Levite, he knew that God had commanded Moses and the Israelites to sacrifice a year-old lamb every morning and every evening along with offerings of flour, oil, and wine. These sacrifices ensured God's presence in the Temple and His blessings upon those who worshipped there. If sacrifices weren't made, the implication was clear.

Word spread quickly throughout Jerusalem that the required sacrifices could no longer be made. Some Jews believed that without sacrifices, God would abandon them. For the rebels fighting to save the Temple, the news increased their resolve to drive the Romans away. Victory would allow the Jews to resume the sacrifices in obedience to God's command.

The presence of Roman infantry didn't hinder the Jews from making plans to destroy the footbridge. Unless something miraculous happened soon, it was only a matter of time before thousands of Roman soldiers would descend from the Antonia Fortress into the Temple Mount.

Even if the Jews couldn't stop the Romans from amassing troops, they hoped to slow them down. If the Jews could demolish several columns of the north portico, its roof would collapse along with the footbridge. Without the footbridge, the Romans would be forced to breach a section of Temple Mount wall using siege ramps and battering rams. It would take the Romans weeks to punch a hole in the interior wall assuming they could do it at all.

A plan was developed and implemented the following evening. John of Gischala, one of the three Zealot leaders, assembled several hundred fighters behind the south side of the Temple out of view of Roman sentries in the Antonia Fortress towers. At John's signal, half of the men ran along the portico on the east side of the Temple Mount, and the other half ran along the west side. The Jewish fighters then converged on the section of the north portico under which the footbridge rested.

The night was moonless and cloudy, and the Jewish fighters were not spotted until they were near their destination. Roman infantrymen caught sight of approaching forms, and the trumpeter sounded the alarm. Soldiers camped within the Fortress sprang into action. In a matter of minutes, hundreds reached the Temple Mount courtyard where they joined their fellow soldiers in hand-to-hand combat with the Jewish fighters.

Several Zealots were able to reach a set of columns that supported the portico roof. Armed with sledgehammers and iron bars, they pounded away at the marble surfaces. Their efforts caused some damage, but the Zealots were killed before they could complete their mission.

Even though their plan had failed, the Zealots continued to fight. As in previous battles, darkness made it difficult for either side to distinguish friend from foe. Initially, the Jews held the advantage by virtue of surprise. But as more Roman soldiers emerged from the Fortress, they gained the upper hand.

Outnumbered two-to-one, the remaining Zealots fought valiantly. From his vantage point on the north wall of the Temple, John of Gischala saw that his men were in danger of being annihilated. He signaled for them to fall back to the Temple.

Titus did not pursue the retreating Jews. He remembered previous instances when the Jews ambushed his troops after pretending to be defeated. The Roman army was on the verge of complete victory, and Titus didn't want to jeopardize it with a costly error in judgement.

Chapter 23

LIFE

Two days after the Zealots failed to destroy the footbridge, the Roman army began to amass troops on the north side of the Temple Mount. Row after row of infantrymen descended from the Fortress, down the footbridge to the portico roof, and down a set of stairs to the courtyard. Jewish defenders, most of whom were Zealots, moved to positions outside the north side of the Temple. The two opposing forces faced each other separated by only 500 feet of marble tile.

Word of the Roman incursion onto the Temple Mount spread through the entire city. The entire population of Jerusalem responded, believing that this would be the final effort to drive back the Romans. All men and boys who could hold a weapon, whether trained in warfare or not, reported to the section of the Temple Mount south of the Temple, hoping to help the experienced fighters fend off the Roman army.

Yosef was off duty when he heard the news. He rushed to the prison and saw that the front door was open. Upon entering he discovered that the guards were gone, and the prisoners were still in their cells. He unlocked every cell door allowing the prisoners to escape. After they were alone, Yosef turned to Simon. "I have a feeling that you already know what is happening today," he said.

"I have an idea what is going on, "replied Simon. "I overheard someone tell the guards to hurry to the Temple Mount because the Romans were about to attack the Temple."

"That is correct," confirmed Yosef. "The other Christian men and I are going there to help the Zealots. Would you like to come with us?"

"Yes, I would," answered Simon. "Even at my age I feel strong enough to handle a sword or spear."

Simon and Yosef hurried to the Temple Mount and joined the other Christians who had not fled Jerusalem. As Christians they no longer considered Temple worship a requirement. However, they realized that if the Temple Mount were lost, the Roman army would have direct access to the rest of Jerusalem. If that happened, bloodthirsty Roman soldiers would not differentiate between killing Jews versus Christians.

Within an hour the northern courtyard of the Temple Mount was filled with hundreds of Roman soldiers. They were lined up in a wedge formation that the Romans called "pig's head." In the front row of the wedge were the bravest and best trained legionnaires carrying a shield with one hand and a sword with the other. Each row of soldiers was followed by another. The result was a nearly impregnable wall of fighters that could break through the middle of almost any enemy line.

A trumpet sounded and the wedge formation began marching in cadence toward the Temple. Jews on the Temple wall battlements rained arrows down on the Romans. Most arrows either bounced off or stuck in the soldier's shields. Rectangular and slightly curved, the shields were made of three layers of wood glued together and rimmed with metal. They were long enough to cover the area between a soldier's shoulder and knee.

When the wedge formation reached a point four hundred feet from the Temple, the Jewish defenders advanced. Although weak from lack of food, they pressed forward fueled by their passion to save the home of their God. The fighters realized this might be their last chance to drive back the Romans.

Zealots leading the charge threw themselves into the Roman wedge with a ferocity that surprised even the battle-hardened legionnaires. The Roman soldiers were forced to halt their advance to counter the aggressiveness of the Jews, but they remained disciplined. Many of them had defeated barbarians in Britain and Gaul and were confident they would do the same against starving Jewish fighters.

The initial confrontation was a stalemate, neither side gaining ground in either direction. Blood saturated the ground as spears, swords, and arrows found their marks. The relatively close quarters gave the Jews a temporary advantage, but superior armor and weapons provided Romans with the upper hand against the ill-equipped Jews.

As more and more legionnaires entered the battle, the

situation became more dire by the hour. From the Jewish perspective, there seemed to be an unending supply of enemy infantrymen. When a Roman soldier fell, another behind him took his place. The pig's head moved forward slowly but relentlessly as the day progressed.

Simon and most of the untrained volunteers were at the rear of the Jewish forces. Yosef and the other Christian men were nowhere to be seen, presumably closer to the front lines. Suddenly, a sharp searing pain shot through Simon's lower left leg. He dropped to the ground clutching the impacted area. Looking down, Simon saw that an arrow had pierced his clothing and remained lodged in his calf. It entered from the back indicating that he was likely shot by a Jewish archer on the Temple wall.

"I've been hit," Simon shouted to an elderly man standing beside him. "Please help me get this arrow out of my leg." The man knelt next to Simon and tore away the section of robe through which the arrow had penetrated. The wound was bleeding badly but had not severed a major vein or artery.

Simon rolled over on his side to allow the man to break off the back portion of the arrow. The pain was excruciating. Simon then rolled over on his back and the man pulled the other half of the arrow through the front of his calf. Using the piece of Simon's robe that he had torn off, the man fashioned a bandage and tied it on his wound.

"Thank you for your help," Simon remarked. "I dropped my spear over there. If you could get it for me and help me up, I will hobble home."

As the man went to retrieve the spear, Simon saw Yosef approaching. "What are you doing back here? Why aren't you on the front lines fighting?" Simon asked.

"You are the reason," Yosef replied. "Several of our fellow Christians died in the battle. I was fortunate enough to emerge unscathed. It was evident that the Romans would soon overwhelm us and that the battle was lost. The Zealots will fight to the death to defend the Temple, but I wanted to make sure that you were safe. I see that you were wounded."

"I am injured, but God was with me. The man over there removed an arrow from my calf. Now you are here to help me. God is good."

"I certainly am here for you. Let's get you back to my house where I can tend to your wound."

"What about the other Christians? Shouldn't they be told that we are leaving the battlefield? Otherwise, they might endanger themselves trying to find us."

"They can take care of themselves. Some of them left the battle when I did. What's important right now is getting you out of here safely and taking care of your leg."

Yosef bent down and lifted Simon to his feet. Simon swung his arm over Yosef's shoulder and limped away on one foot. The two men exited the south side of the Temple Mount through the Huldah Gate and down the stairs leading to the Lower City. The streets were deserted. Jewish women were hiding in their homes with their children as the fighting continued. Sounds of battle could be heard throughout the city.

By the time they arrived at Yosef's house, Simon was exhausted. He lost a substantial amount of blood and was feeling weak and dizzy. Yosef helped Simon into bed, filled a basin with water, and cleaned the wound.

"You were fortunate that the archer didn't shoot a little

higher," joked Yosef.

"I wasn't expecting Zealots to aim at me," replied Simon. "This might have been God's way of keeping me from being killed in the battle. I hope and pray that most of our Christian friends survived."

Exhausted, his calf throbbing with pain, Simon closed his eyes and fell into a deep sleep.

Despite a valiant effort, the Zealots were forced to fall back into the Temple. Jewish archers shooting volleys of arrows from the Temple battlements gave the fighters some cover. Once the gates to the Temple were closed, Roman soldiers surrounded its entire perimeter.

Titus was now within reach of his target. Before arriving at Jerusalem, he made it clear to his officers that he wanted to keep the Temple intact. His reluctance to destroy it had nothing to do with its religious history. Rather, he felt it was a magnificent structure that would highlight the power of Rome for years to come.

By the time his men surrounded the Temple, Titus' mindset had changed. He recalled the soldiers he lost and the number of times the Jews had made him look foolish. Leaving the Temple intact would perpetuate these unfavorable memories. After consulting with his senior officers who unanimously agreed with his plan, Titus gave orders to turn the Temple into an inferno. The Jews could decide either to die within its walls or attempt to escape and be killed.

Roman archers who had been stationed on the Antonia

Fortress towers relocated to within range of the Temple. Strips of cloth doused with oil were tied to the tips of their arrows. One of the infantrymen lit a torch and carried it from one archer to the next. Once the cloths were lit, flaming arrows were launched onto the Temple roof and through its windows.

Jewish archers stationed on the Temple battlements had to choose between remaining in their defensive positions or putting out fires. The already difficult situation morphed into disaster when one of the flaming arrows flew into the Temple's inner sanctuary. It landed on the ornate marble floor and skipped through the room until it landed at the base of the veil leading into the Holy of Holies.

This was the veil through which the High Priest passed once a year on Yom Kippur, the Day of Atonement, to offer incense and sprinkle blood of a sacrificial lamb on the altar to atone for the sins of the Jewish people. The veil split apart when Jesus died on the cross but was repaired and rehung soon afterward.

The arrow burned long enough to ignite the bottom of the veil. The thick curtain began to smolder and soon was fully engulfed in flames. Hot ashes floated throughout the sanctuary setting the elaborate furnishings and jars of oil on fire.

Jews trapped inside the Temple cried aloud as the Holy of Holies, where God Himself dwelled, went up in flames. Weeping and screaming, they carried water from purification basins in an attempt to put out the fire, but it was too late to save the inner sanctuary.

Thick smoke filled the entire Temple complex from the Holy of Holies to the Court of the Priests to the Court of the Jews to the Court of Women. Those fighting the flames could see only a few feet in front of them, and many were overcome by smoke inhalation. The heat from the fire was becoming unbearable.

Two options were available to the entrapped Jews. One was to remain inside the Temple and suffocate or burn to death. The other was to exit the Temple and risk being killed by the Romans. The decision was easy for the Zealots who were determined to die rather than surrender. However, those who had volunteered at the last minute to help save the Temple were more likely to take their chances outside the burning structure.

Zealots posted men inside the Temple gates to keep anyone from exiting, fearing that opening the gates would allow the Roman soldiers to enter. As the fire spread and the heat and smoke became increasingly intolerable, a group of volunteer Jews conspired to escape. They chose a gate on the south side of the Court of Women as their exit point. One of the men approached the Zealots guarding the gate. A confrontation ensued, creating enough of a diversion for the others to rush the guards and immobilize them. The volunteers opened the gate and ran outside.

As soon as they saw Jews running from the Temple, Roman soldiers stationed outside rushed toward them with swords drawn. The Jews threw up their hands in surrender, but the Romans cut them all down. Seeing that the gate was open and unguarded, nearby troops rushed into the Court of Women and engaged in hand-to-hand combat with Zealot defenders.

After several additional gates were opened, the remainder of the Roman force streamed into the Temple. The ensuing battle was chaotic. Smoke filled the air making it difficult to see the opponent. The Roman forces were too strong and too numerous for the Zealots to overcome. The entire floor of the Temple was covered with blood, bodies, and charred debris.

By late afternoon, the battle was over. The Temple's interior and most of its contents were destroyed. Flames were so hot that gold veneer covering the walls of the inner sanctuary melted. The once magnificent structure was reduced to a skeleton of scorched walls. All of the Zealots who defended the Temple were dead except for John of Gischala. Titus had given orders to capture him alive. He had special plans for the rebel leader.

After occupying the Temple Mount, the Roman soldiers sensed that the entire city would soon be theirs. After removing treasures that he wanted to take back to Rome, Titus allowed the legionnaires to carry off remaining items of value as their reward for a hard-fought victory.

Later that evening, Titus addressed his men from inside the Temple. He praised them for their valiant efforts and promised them an extra week's wages. He then brought an ox, a sheep, and a pig into the Court of Priests and sacrificed them to the Roman gods on the sacred altar. By offering a pig, considered unclean by Jews, Titus showed his contempt for the Jewish God.

That same evening, Christian men who survived the battle met for worship. Only seven, including Simon, remained alive. They met at Yosef's house where Simon was still resting. His lower leg throbbed with pain, but he wanted to be with his fellow believers. The worship service that night was shorter and more somber than usual consisting of a few prayers and songs. After the service concluded, Simon asked for everyone's attention.

"I understand that the Romans captured the Temple. It has

been quiet so far this evening, but I wouldn't be surprised if the Roman army moves into the city tomorrow to eliminate any remaining rebels. I propose that we all meet back here tomorrow morning for prayer. Perhaps we can convince the Romans that we Christians are not a threat to them. I pray that God's peace and protection will be with all of us in the coming days."

Early the next morning Titus ordered his men to bring John of Gischala to his tent. Even though the Temple had been destroyed and its defenders annihilated, Titus was aware that pockets of rebel resistance still existed in Jerusalem. He made a proposal to John of Gischala that could avoid further bloodshed on both sides.

"Your men put up a mighty struggle. It is sad that so many of them had to die. All of this could have been avoided if you had surrendered months ago when you had the chance. Looking ahead, I know there are still Zealots in the city who are willing to fight to the death even though your cause is lost. It will take a week or two for my men to find and kill them, which I am more than willing to do. However, that will take more time than I want to spend and probably lead to loss of some of my soldiers. That said, what would it take for you to convince the rest of your fighters to surrender?"

John was speechless. Titus appeared to be offering him an alternative to torture and execution. After thinking for a few moments, he replied, "There is one thing that would persuade my men to give themselves up. I need your personal guarantee that we and our families will be allowed to leave Jerusalem without harm. If you agree, I will present your proposal to my men. Even so, it will be difficult to convince them that you will keep your word."

"I'm not surprised that you would request your freedom. However, that will not happen. What I can offer is your lives. As a condition of your surrender, I will guarantee that you and your men and your families will not be killed. Instead, you will be sold as slaves to whichever neighboring country pays the highest price. It is a fair trade off. Rome will receive some compensation for your rebellion, and you will avoid death by the sword. What do you say to that?"

"I will not be able to persuade any of my men to surrender under those terms. I know for a fact that all my men will continue to fight to the death rather than be sold into slavery. Slavery is what the Jews have experienced under Roman rule and why we rebelled in the first place."

"Then I believe we have reached an impasse that can't be bridged. I wish that you had agreed to my proposal. It would have saved lives on both sides. Now I will have to unleash my soldiers on the city to find and kill your men. It will be difficult if not impossible to control what happens next. Many innocent lives will be lost. It is a pity."

Titus ordered his men to return John of Gischala to confinement. He planned to bring John to Rome as a prisoner to be included as part of a huge victory celebration. John's public torture and death would be a warning to those who might consider rebelling against Roman rule in the future.

After John of Gischala was led away, Titus made it clear to his officers that all Jews of fighting age were to be killed, reasoning that any of them could have been part of the rebel force.

The elderly, infirm, or those incapable of working would also be put to death. Healthy women, adolescents, and children would be spared and sold as slaves.

The search for insurrectionists would start later that morning, beginning with the Lower City where the working-class people lived. After that section of the city was cleaned up, the army would move against the Upper City where the wealthier population resided.

The operation began shortly before noon. Hundreds of Roman legionnaires streamed out of the south gates of the Temple Mount. When they reached the narrow streets of the Lower City, the soldiers split up into smaller groups to conduct a house-to-house search.

What they found shocked even the battle-hardened Romans. Nearly every home contained the corpse of at least one person who had died of hunger. Often an entire family was found starved to death. The deceased had not been given a proper burial because cemeteries were located outside the city gates and inaccessible after the siege began. As a result, corpses were anointed with spices and wrapped in cloths to preserve them as long as possible in hopes of burying them later.

Word soon spread throughout the Lower City that Romans soldiers were coming to murder the men and take away the women and children. Panic ensued and the streets were filled with Jews fleeing as far ahead of the Romans as they could. The few men who did not run and attempted to defend their families and homes were quickly killed.

Many of the Roman soldiers went beyond the scope of Titus' directive. They were angry that the rebels had killed so many of their comrades. As a show of contempt for Jews, soldiers threw burning torches into the buildings they raided. Flames spread quickly and thick smoke which smelled of burning corpses filled the air.

Earlier that morning before the Roman soldiers began their rampage, Simon and the rest of the Christian men gathered in Yosef's house where Simon had spent the night. Despite the uncertainty facing them, they expressed trust in God's mercy. Even if they were killed, they knew that Jesus had gone to prepare a place in Heaven for them. Throughout the morning, they read from Scripture and sang hymns of praise to God for the gift of His Son.

Shortly after noon, the worshippers realized that something dreadful was happening near their location. Screams of women and shouts of angry men were heard through the windows and became louder and more frequent. Clouds of pungent smoke began wafting into the house.

Sitting upright in his chair, Simon spoke words of encouragement to the others. "Brothers in Christ," he said calmly, "we don't need to be afraid even though the power of Rome is closing in on us. We are not alone. Our Lord Jesus is with us to guard and protect us. If he takes us from this world today, he has promised that we will be with him forever in his kingdom. Be joyful and bold, not sad and afraid. All praise and glory be to God."

After Simon finished speaking, the men sang a psalm of praise and thanks. Meanwhile, the clamor outside the house became louder and closer. Panic stricken men and women ran past the window. With a loud crash, the front door flew open, startling the worshippers and interrupting their song. Two soldiers strode into the room. Brandishing drawn swords, they commanded everyone to stand facing the wall opposite the door.

Simon was unable to comply and remained stationary. Yosef stood in front of Simon to shield him. One of the soldiers grabbed Yosef's shoulder, turned him around, and plunged his sword into Yosef's abdomen. Simon watched in horror, unable to help his friend.

The room was silent until one of the Christians facing the wall resumed singing the song that had been cut short. The rest joined him. The soldiers looked at each other in surprise.

"How can you sing when you are about to die?" asked one of them.

Simon boldly answered on behalf of the others. "We are believers in Jesus, the Son of God. We call ourselves Christians. Jesus died on a cross to make those who believe in him blameless in God's sight. Because our sins are forgiven, we will live with him eternally in Heaven. That is why we aren't afraid of dying."

"So, you aren't Jews?" the other soldier asked. "If not, what are you doing in Jerusalem?"

"I was attempting to convince the Jews to settle their differences with Rome peaceably," answered Simon. "It was evident that Judaea could not prevail against a vastly superior army like yours. However, to be honest, once we found ourselves trapped here with no way out, we did what we could to defend our homes and property."

"In other words, you supported the rebels."

"The only time we took any action was yesterday on the Temple Mount. Several of our group were killed in the fighting. However, we pose no ongoing threat to you or your men. Jesus taught us to love one another, even our enemies."

"What you are saying is confusing. It sounds like something that you invented in order to convince us to spare your lives. Unfortunately for you, we are not in the mood to show mercy."

The front door flew open again. Three more Roman soldiers entered the room. "I was just going to send for reinforcements," said one of the original two. "We were outnumbered and might have had a difficult time subduing these men if they turned on us."

After the Christians who lined the wall were executed, one of the soldiers approached the chair on which Simon was sitting. He braced his feet and pointed his sword at Simon's chest. As the swordsman prepared to complete his task, Simon looked at up him and prayed aloud, "Lord, forgive these men who harm us. All glory to you." The soldier lowered his sword, stunned by the unexpected words uttered by someone about to die.

"Old man," the soldier snarled, "I hope that I can face death as calmly as you and your friends have done." He raised the sword again and thrust it into his helpless victim. Simon's body shuddered as the blade penetrated his chest and embedded itself in the chair behind him.

Simon, as if detached from his body, watched what was happening in slow motion. The soldier pulled out his sword and wiped the blood on Simon's robe. Surprisingly, Simon experienced no fear and felt no pain. He was enveloped in a peaceful calm that exceeded anything he had ever felt before.

As his eyes slowly closed and his lungs expelled the remains of his last breath, Simon's soul arrived in Heaven to be reunited with Jesus and join the souls of loved ones who had gone before. There he awaits the Day of Judgement when God will pronounce Simon and all believers in Christ innocent because Jesus shouldered the blame for their sinfulness. On that day, Simon's soul will be united with a resurrected, glorified, and imperishable body. The result will be a life of unending joy with God in Heaven—free from pain, hunger, and sadness.

Afterword

The destruction of Jerusalem took five months, from April to September of 70 CE. The Jewish loss of life, including women and children, was in the hundreds of thousands. The number of casualties from the Roman force of 60,000 men is not known. The Temple Mount was leveled; only a portion of the west retaining wall remained standing. The rest of Jerusalem was plundered and left in ruins.

Titus returned to Rome a victorious conqueror. Nine years later he became emperor after the death of his father, Vespasian. Titus' reign lasted only two years and featured a cataclysmic volcanic eruption, a fire that burned much of the city of Rome, and a deadly plague that killed thousands of Rome's residents. Titus was poisoned by his brother Domitian who was named the next emperor and ruled for fifteen years until he was assassinated. This concluded the reign of the Flavian Dynasty, which lasted twenty-seven years from 69 CE to 96 CE.

The dynasty that began with Vespasian ended as all earthly dynasties do. There is, however, a dynasty that will never end. In the Gospel of John chapter 14, Jesus told his disciples he would leave them to establish an eternal kingdom where all believers will live in glory forever. On the Last Day he will return to take them there.

No one but God, not even the angels in Heaven, knows when Jesus will return. However, Jesus gave us some indication of what will precede that day. Many of these signs have already happened and continue to happen including wars, famines, earthquakes, lawlessness, and false prophets.

In Matthew chapter 24, Jesus said that when the Gospel is preached throughout the whole world to all nations, then the end will come. That statement, along with advances in worldwide communication, indicates that we are getting closer to the day when Jesus comes again. Radio, television, and the internet have taken the Gospel to almost every corner of the earth. Jesus' command to teach all nations continues to be fulfilled today in ways that his disciples could never have imagined.

Christians have no reason to worry about death. As mentioned throughout this book, if we die before Jesus returns, our souls will leave our physical bodies and enter Heaven. On the Last Day, when Jesus returns to earth, our resurrected and glorified bodies will join our souls. God will judge us and declare us blameless because Jesus endured the punishment we deserve for our sins. We will be welcomed into God's presence to live with Him forever in glory.

God's Word, the Bible, documents the plan of salvation that our merciful God has carried out for us through Christ. It is well worth reading. Readers of the Word will be led by the Holy Spirit to believe that they are saved by grace through faith in Jesus as their Lord and Savior. Out of gratitude for being saved, readers who become believers will be moved to share this message with those who have not yet received it. Every time this cycle is repeated, Jesus' return will be hastened. As children of God who believe in His power to save us through the sacrifice of His Son, we can say with confidence, "Come, Lord Jesus!"

DAVID G. FISCHER

 DAVID G. FISCHER is a second-time book author and life-long Christian. Thanks to parents who understood the value of Christian education, he attended a Lutheran school from grades K–8 forming the foundation for a relationship with God that continues to grow to this day. Whatever success he has achieved in life is due to the grace and love that God has shown to him.

After receiving a BA in Psychology from the University of Arizona, David served in the U.S. Air Force during the final years of the Vietnam War. He returned to the UofA to earn a Master of Accounting degree after which he obtained a CPA certification and began a career in banking which lasted over forty years. He is now retired, living in Las Vegas where he enjoys life with his wife and plays golf several days a week.

www.ingramcontent.com/pod-product-compliance
Lightning Source LLC
Chambersburg PA
CBHW031029310726
48969CB00007B/1921